I0772325

BRIDES FOR A KING

Fathers, Daughters and the National Interest:
England & France 1660-1

A LUKE TREMAYNE ADVENTURE

BRIDES FOR A KING

Fathers, Daughters and the National Interest:
England & France 1660-1

GEOFF QUAIFE

ARPress
45 Dan Road Suite 5
Canton MA 02021

Hotline: 1(888) 821-0229
Fax: 1(508) 545-7580

Ordering Information:

Quantity sales. Special discounts are available on quantity purchases by corporations,associations, and others. For details, contact the publisher at the address above.

Printed in the United States of America.

ISBN-13:   Softcover   979-8-89389-322-9
                eBook   979-8-89389-321-2
                Hardback   979-8-89389-967-2

Library of Congress Control Number: 2024916231

The Luke Tremayne Adventures

(In chronological order of the events portrayed)

Major Characters

Luke's Unit

Sir Luke Tremayne (Colonel)	Magistrate and special agent for Charles II
Sir Mark Cowper (Lt. Colonel)	Royalist courtier and Luke's deputy, newly elected member of Parliament
Miles Oxenbridge (Captain)	Former associate of Luke, captain of foot
Matthew Hatch (Captain)	A leading government spy under the Protectorate, Luke's brother-in-law

Brides for the King?

Lady Agatha Craven	Daughter of Guy, Viscount Craven
Lady Margaret Dash	Daughter of Randolph, Earl of Greenham
Lady Elizabeth Rhodes	Daughter of William, Earl of Maldon

Foreign Embassy Staff

Sir Henry Hunt	Lobbyist for the Venetian government
Marco Conti	Venetian official seconded to Luke

Local Criminals

Jenny "Longlegs" Judd	Leader of a criminal gang, fence
Austyn Bulstrode	Another gang boss, former lieutenant in Parliamentary army

Aristocrats, Gentry, Officials and Their Servants

Lady Dinah Langley	King's former mistress
Lady Martha Langley	Dinah's sister
William Rhodes	Earl of Maldon, pro-Spanish peer, father of Elizabeth
Guy, Viscount Craven	Agatha's father, pro-Spanish peer, former privateer and current smuggler
The Turk	Alias Gilbert Anthony, Craven's captain of *The Lady Agatha* , *former* privateer, smuggler
Randolph Dash,	Earl of Greenham, Margaret's father, pro-Spanish peer
Peter, Baron Coleridge	Nephew of Randolph, cousin to Margaret and Henry

Others

Abraham Lombroso	Silk and linen importer and tailor
John Cope	His assistant
Lorenzo Adamo	A Spanish agent?

Real Historical Characters

English

Charles II	King of England, Scotland and Ireland

James, Duke of York	His brother and heir, Lord High Admiral
Sir Edward Hyde	Lord Chancellor, later Earl of Clarendon
George Monk	Duke of Albemarle, former Cromwellian governor of Scotland, and now Charles II military commander- in- chief

Venetian

| Francesco Giavarina | Venetian Resident (ambassador) to England |
| Alvise Grimani | Venetian ambassador to France |

French

Antoine de Bordeaux	French ambassador to England 1652-60
Louis XIV	King of France
Cardinal Mazarin	His Chief Minister 1643-1661
Henrietta Maria	The English Queen Mother, aunt to Louis XIV

Portuguese

Catherine de Braganza	Infanta of Portugal, bride for Charles II?
Francesco di Melo	Portuguese Resident (ambassador)
Francesco de Sa	Acting Portuguese Resident, nephew of di Melo

L uke Tremayne met regularly with the King in a small room adjacent to the monarch's bedchamber. Luke headed a small group of intelligence officers that were independent, equally from the vast network of civilian agents set up by the Lord Chancellor, and those of military intelligence under the commander-in-chief of all British forces, the Duke of Albemarle. Luke's unit answered to the King alone and had authority to act outside the traditionally accepted parameters of government.

At their most recent meeting the King outlined Luke's latest mission. "Your main role in the past has been to act for me behind the scenes. This latest assignment puts you in the middle of current potential intrigues, which I need to better understand."

"And what is the central issue of these intrigues?" asked Luke.

"My marriage."

"I am not well equipped to help Your Majesty in affairs of the heart. Dozens of your courtiers would be better placed than I," quipped Luke.

"My marriage is not an affair of the heart. Local politicians, foreign governments, and my mother are all harassing me with advice, which is more in their interests than mine, or the country's. A lot of money is flowing into the pockets of even my most trusted advisers to persuade them to influence me to choose a particular candidate."

"And how am I to be introduced into this apparent hotbed of marital politics?"

"I will let it be known to the greatest gossips around the Court that regarding the question of my marriage, I am now taking the advice of Sir Luke Tremayne. You will overnight become the target of all those vested interests pushing particular candidates."

"What are the issues and competing candidates that have surfaced so far?"

"The House of Commons is currently debating a motion that I must not marry a Catholic. Conversely my mother wants me to marry into her Catholic Bourbon family, although France's chief minister Cardinal Mazarin has suggested his own niece, who is indeed a very beautiful woman. The Portuguese have advanced the claims of their King's sister. The Spaniards initially suggested the widow of the Austrian emperor who judging by a portrait I have seen is short on beauty and long in years—the same applies to the Bourbon princess pushed by my mother. The Spaniards now advocate one of two beautiful Italian princesses from Parma, whom I do find quite interesting. I owe the Spaniards a lot—or more pertinently, they expect a lot. There are many local aristocratic women, who now that my brother has announced his marriage to an English commoner, consider they have a chance. Some of my mistresses see a possibility of changing their status, and the Danes, Dutch and many of the German states are scrambling to find a bride for me to further their own political and religious interests."

"Who of the interested parties would you expect to approach me first?"

"The Spaniards! Spain protected and financed me during the last five years of my exile in Spanish Flanders—and they expect me to return that singular favor a hundred times over. My marriage to one of their clients would be accepted as repayment for the fortune they claim they spent on me."

"Sire, a Spanish Catholic marriage would not be a popular choice."

"Unfortunately, most of the leading candidates are Catholic," admitted the King.

"The English people are not too obsessed about English, German, Italian or Portuguese Catholics, but the Spanish or Irish variety are traditional enemies of our country. On the other hand, a residual enmity towards France cannot be ignored."

"Enough Tremayne! you are now revealing your old Cromwellian prejudices."

Luke quickly deflected the comment.

"Surely Your Majesty's renowned ability to select beautiful and intelligent women as your mistresses can be transferred to your personal selection of a wife, without the interference of family, politicians or foreign powers?"

"Come Tremayne, you are not that naïve! Half the world is using this marriage as a lever to obtain some concession from me, and they will utilize any means to prevent others doing likewise."

"Perhaps you can stop such developments by declaring, like your illustrious predecessor, Good Queen Bess, that you will never marry."

The King laughed.

"That would seriously endanger my possession of the throne. This is why I need your assistance. My marriage has to be in my personal interests and that of the country to stabilize my position. There are too many powerful republicans and Cromwellians, who unlike you, have not accepted my return. They will take advantage of any disputes over this issue to undermine my government"

"How do I start this mission?"

"By chatting with one of your former comrades, Sir Henry Hunt."

"I don't recall the name."

"The most effective foreign embassy in London is that of the Venetian Republic. Its English liaison officer and lobbyist is Sir Henry, whom the head of Cromwell's intelligence, John Thurloe, turned into a double agent. All material that went through the Venetian embassy was immediately made known to the previous government. I have kept Sir Henry in his position to serve me in like fashion. While Henry, who is of aristocratic descent served the previous regime, his extended family were all loyal to me, and his uncle is one of my advisers pushing strongly for a particular candidate."

"If you have Sir Henry in such a key position, why do you need me?"

"Henry might uncover some of the information I need, but he is in no position to act on it—that is a role for you and your unit."

"Essentially you want me to uncover the real motives behind your leading advisers in their support for particular candidates for your hand in marriage? —a game of marital musical chairs."

"This is not a game, Tremayne. Already there have been reports of violence between competing parties, and you may need to protect the innocents who get caught up in this deadly display of power politics. One of my former mistresses, and longtime friends, Dinah Langley, who falsely claimed she would soon be my wife, was cruelly disfigured by an assailant throwing acid in her face, an attack from which she subsequently died."

Luke diplomatically refrained from expressing his immediate thoughts that given the King's taste in women and his well-known previous position of keeping his mistresses separate from potential wives, few would give any credence to the marital claims by any of the former.

Instead, he expressed concern. "Sire, since your brother has just announced his marriage to a commoner, do you think that the foreign marriage brokers will embark on a campaign against Your Majesty's English female friends?"

"Most of them are already married, which will protect the matrons in this environment, but the spinsters may be vulnerable. Look into the Langley assault! There may be more to it."

"The sooner you marry, the quicker this unfortunate situation will dissolve," mused the quietly philosophical Luke.

"That may be sooner than I would like. Already the politicians are trying to limit my options. The House of Lords plans to pass a bill annexing Dunkirk. So far, the Spanish marriage proposals require me to return Dunkirk to Spain. The French would like to buy it from me, and in the process provide an immense dowry which my government desperately needs, while the Dutch want it disabled to the extent that it cannot be used as a privateering base against their merchant shipping. I cannot please everybody at home or abroad." Two days later, Luke met Henry in St James's Park. The diplomat was effusive. "I am delighted to meet at last. You dominated my nightmares some years ago."

"How did I manage that?" asked an embarrassed Luke.

"When you were Cromwell's ambassador to the Islamic states of North Africa, Venice believed you were instructed to negotiate a treaty with its most virulent enemy, the Ottoman Empire. You would provide the hated Turk with the most modern of English ships that would destroy the Venetian navy. I had to discover all I could about you for the Venetian ambassador, which was quickly transmitted back to Venice. For a while that Republic saw you as its number one enemy."

"I was certainly instructed to assist the Turk, but not against Venice. The enemy was Spain and the Catholic knights of Malta. But times are very different now. The King as you have been informed has appointed me to investigate the proposals made by various groups for a bride for His Majesty, and in what way the various proponents are acting to achieve their ends."

"It is indeed strange that a man who is idolized by women and has countless mistresses cannot choose a wife without great political pressure and intrigue. If the politicians have their way national or personal interests rather than the King's pleasure will be decisive but put bluntly the candidates that they support will largely be determined by which foreign embassy contributes the most to their personal coffers. Your task in one sense is easy. Find out who is bribing which politician in favor of which candidate, and whether these venal transactions can be reconciled with the national interest."

"Where do I start?"

"Obtain from the King the name of the candidates that each member of his council and senior aristocrats are pushing, and then check on the motives of those advisers. Also trace the flow of money from the various embassies to particular royal officials. A clear picture has emerged already."

"And what is that?"

"There are two dominant players. The Portuguese are pouring a fortune into valuable sweeteners for most of the Royal Council to support the cause of the Portuguese Infanta, Catherine of Braganza, sister of their King. The Chancellor, Sir Edward Hyde, and the army chief, the Duke of Albemarle, have been soaking up a lion's share of that largesse. Their hated enemy the Spaniards are also mounting a major campaign, but largely of moral pressure. The Spaniards claim that they alone supported Charles over the last few years, and now expect to be rewarded—or as they see it, call in their debts. At the last minute they have changed their candidate from the widowed Austrian empress to the Italian princesses of Parma. I suspect Charles is deceiving his pro-Portuguese councilors at this very moment, as his friend the Earl of Bristol is in Italy to negotiate this Spanish nomination."

"How do you know this, if it is a secret?" asked a skeptical Luke.

"The Venetian state monitors all important travelers into Italy."

"Is there no French activity of importance?"

"Too much, but I believe of little consequence. There are at least three rival pro-French claims advanced by different elements associated with the French government. Cardinal Mazarin is pushing the claims of his niece, Hortense Mancini, but as the Cardinal never supported the Stuarts in exile, I cannot conceive that Charles would even consider that suggestion, despite the renowned beauty of the woman. He has virtually expelled the French ambassador by refusing to see him. The Queen Mother has her people trying to arrange a Stuart-Bourbon marriage, while the activities of the young King Louis XIV are currently shrouded in mystery."

"Is the possibility that now that the King's brother and heir has married an Englishwoman, that he will do the same, been taken seriously by the foreign protagonists?"

"Very perceptive Tremayne, or is this where our discussion has been heading all along?"

"What do you mean Henry?"

"A servant at the Portuguese embassy was found murdered last week. One of my men found the body in a lane off Whitehall and recovered certain papers from it which my ambassador sent on to the Chancellor a week or more ago. It was a list of three names—all aristocratic women, all known to the King, although none of them as far as I can ascertain had ever been his mistress. Although, given his gallivanting while in exile, no one can be sure."

2

Luke was intrigued, "Why would a minor servant of a foreign embassy have a list of such names?" probed Luke.

"That is obviously a question for you to answer but it could relate to the King's marriage. It may be a short list of local candidates for the King's hand—women that the Portuguese believe they may have to discredit to enhance the chances of their own candidate. When the King sent a message that you would be questioning me regarding his marriage, I thought it was specifically about that list."

"And given the assault on one of the King's mistresses, who falsely claimed she would marry the King, they may suffer more than discredit. Their lives may be in danger. Who were they?"

Luke listened intently as Henry carefully enunciated the names of three aristocratic women.

Henry immediately suggested, "It would be valuable to know who compiled the list and why. Given it was found on an employee of the Portuguese ambassador, he is most likely its source. Does the current government have agents within that embassy?"

"The Cromwellian administration certainly did. Thurloe had men everywhere, but the current government has not advanced very far in creating an intelligence service," admitted Luke.

"Try a little bribery among the English born servants in all the locally based embassies! They are no less ready to receive sweeteners as their masters," suggested the cynical Henry.

"Clearly you have done this for the Venetian ambassador. Is there any one person among the host of English employees of the Portuguese who is more approachable than the rest in this group?"

"Try Ezekial Poole! He and his fellow servants of the Portuguese drink at The Black Falcon. But I would not go there without an armed escort. Although Westminster is full of the palatial town houses of the aristocracy, there are still strong pockets of poverty and criminality. Most of the alehouses and brothels in the area are controlled by a powerful, charismatic woman, Jenny Longlegs. Never call her that to her face. Her birth name was Jenny Judd, and although she appears to have been married several times, she has retained her maiden name. Her brother, Jared, is the publican of The Black Falcon. They do not look kindly on strangers, except as victims of their well-organized gang of robbers and pickpockets."

On leaving Hunt Luke had two immediate tasks—question the King regarding the aristocratic women on the list, and then visit The Black Falcon and interrogate Poole.

Charles was furious on receiving Luke's information concerning a list of aristocratic women, and the circumstances of its discovery.

"This news justifies the need of a unit such as yours. My own chancellor receives a document, possibly critical to my immediate and personal future, and does not bother to inform me."

"Perhaps he is, as rumor suggests, determined that the Portuguese candidate should succeed, and this list found on a servant of that embassy could be embarrassing to his cause."

"Are you suggesting that my Chancellor is compiling a list of possible English born wives for me should the Portuguese campaign fail?"

"That is a very generous assessment of the situation, sire, but are these women a list of potential wives for Your Majesty, or are they potential rivals to the Chancellor's Portuguese candidate, whom he must in some way disable? How well do you know the three women on the list? Are any of them potential brides, should you decide to take an English wife?"

"I know all three, and with one of them I had a close, but not a sexual relationship. None of them have been my mistress, although I did try very hard to win one of them over. Two of them were probably closer to my brother, James. Who put this list together? What do these women have in common? Why was the list found on the murdered body of a lowly servant of the Portuguese embassy?"

"And why has the Chancellor not passed on this information to you?"

"I will follow up that point. You will probe the rest."

"Which woman on that list were you the closest to?" asked Luke.

"Do you need to know?"

"This list could be a piece of meaningless trivia, or at the worst a killer's list of potential victims. Eventually, I will need to question all of them, but the woman that was close to you, must take priority."

"Lady Elizabeth Rhodes, the only child of William, Earl of Maldon," answered the King.

Luke obtained the details he needed to locate Elizabeth and made plans to travel west to one of her family's estates on the Cornish-Devon border. The King had last seen her eighteen months previously, when his court was in Bruges in the Spanish Netherlands.

Luke discussed the situation with the rest of his clandestine intelligence group—Sir Mark Cowper, Luke's deputy, courtier and now a member of parliament; Matthew Hatch, a leading agent of the Cromwellian government and Luke's brother-in-law; and Miles Oxenbridge who at one time commanded the troops aboard the warship *The Cromwell,* which Luke had commanded in the Mediterranean.

Mark was shocked as he heard the names of the three women. "I know all three very well. We were close friends for some years while on the continent. As usual the King has not told you everything. When Lady Elizabeth arrived at court, Charles was immediately smitten. She did not stay long and moved to the Dutch Republic. Rumor had it that she tried to emulate a former ill-fated Queen of England, Ann Boleyn. She refused to sleep with the King unless they were married. However, I visited her regularly in the Dutch Republic over the subsequent months, up to the time of her return to England. She denied she had ever made such a demand of the King."

"Did she have sufficient status to warrant taking such a position?"

"Yes, she not only has illegitimate Plantagenet blood flowing in her veins, but her grandmother was a Danish princess. She certainly has a better claim to marry a Royal brother than the Chancellor's daughter has in marrying the heir apparent, James, Duke of York."

"Given her status, and your acquaintance with her, Mark, would you travel west and find out her current situation. Miles and I will investigate the murder of the Portuguese servant on whom the list was found and question the clientele of The Black Falcon. Matthew, you find out as much as you can regarding the other two women on the list, Agatha Craven and Margaret Dash, and also which of the foreign candidates particular members of the Royal Council are advocating. Obtain a list from the King's private secretary, but it will not be complete!"

Late that afternoon Luke and Miles, dressed as well-to-do servants, entered The Black Falcon. It was crowded with customers congregated around buckets of freshly brewed ale from which the usual buxom wenches were filling dozens of mugs. At the other end of the bench was a much larger barrel from which a more sober woman, who wore a permanent scowl, drew heavily hops-imbued beer.

Those customers who were not standing around the bench on which their sources of drink stood, sat on long benches around the edge of the room or those around three or four smaller tables. Luke and Miles purchased their beer and moved towards a short bench in the far corner of the room from where they intended to survey the scene.

They never reached the corner. Both men sensed a feeling of resentment and potential danger. They were obviously newcomers unknown to the regular clientele.

Luke whispered, "Separate, deny you are with me!"

While most of the drinkers were in groups, and a few women were alone with a partner or would-be client, Luke espied one man sitting by himself at the far end of the room. Luke pushed his way through a growingly critical crowd and addressed the lone drinker. "My man, may I join you? I seek information."

Luke pushed a silver coin at the man, who eagerly snatched it. "Most strangers here come seeking information on behalf of various important people, and in this alehouse in particular, from rival foreign embassies. My fellow drinkers are always in two minds whether to take the money, and tell a pack of lies, or wait until the person leaves, and attack him for his well filled purse," was a surprisingly honest response.

Luke playing the innocent asked, "Are most of the people here employed by foreign embassies?"

"Not all, but most of the English born employees of the Portuguese and a range of Italian representatives drink here. Deals have been done with Moll Jenn whose gang controls the area. The embassies attract wealthy clients whom the gang robs, but Moll for a share of their takings, protects the servants of the embassies in their dubious activities."

"Not always successfully! I heard a Portuguese servant was murdered in the area a short while ago?"

The man suddenly tensed, "The victim had foolishly manhandled Ezekial Poole's sweetheart."

"Is Poole here at the moment?" asked Luke.

"I am right behind you," came a response as Luke felt the blade of a dagger pressed against the nape of his neck.

Luke turned to find three men had gathered behind his bench, obscuring him and his informant from the rest of the drinkers.

"Why are you here? Spying for the French or the Spaniards, or even worse the Germans, the Dutch, the Swedes or the Danes?" asked Poole.

"Not at all, I am here to buy information. My contact suggested I seek you out for any assistance that I might need."

Poole beamed and asked, "What do you wish to know, and how much are your masters willing to pay?"

"My master is anxious to discover why a fellow servant from the Portuguese embassy was murdered, and even more importantly, and much better paid, information as to the origin of a list naming three female aristocrats that the victim carried on him."

Poole appeared surprised at the latter request. He whispered, "This alehouse is full of my fellow servants. It is not the best place to discuss such matters, and if word got back to the embassy that I was discussing its business with a stranger, I would be sacked. Come with me. There is a brothel around the corner. I am expected there about now."

Luke and Ezekial entered the brothel and were met by a large curvaceous woman who wore nothing but a see-through chemise and identified herself as Mary. "Which of you is first?" she asked.

Ezekial replied "Just wait! My friend and I have important business to discuss in private. Is the other room empty?"

The prostitute giggled, "I did not know Ezekial that you preferred men to women."

"Don't be cheeky wench, or I will not pay you your excessive demands when I do come to you."

"Whatever you are up to, pay me for the use of the room— or I could spread rumors," she threatened.

Luke and Ezekial sat on a bed that had only recently been used. Ezekial was frank. "I do not want to know your name, or for whom you work. Pay me four times what you offered on our way here, and I might have some useful information, but I will not risk my position for a pittance. It is up to you."

Luke ignored his purse stuffed with small silver coins and thrust his hand deep inside his doublet and produced a gold coin. "This should satisfy your needs," he commented.

3

Ezekial immediately confessed. "I do not know who killed Harry Foster. Unless your master is a relative of the deceased, his fate should be of little importance to anybody. Harry was a brutal womanizer who attempted the chastity of almost every woman who frequented The Black Falcon. He was murdered by any one of a dozen men avenging an assault on their wives, daughters or sweethearts."

"Did Foster have any special role within the embassy?"

"We English-born servants only play a minor role, and none at all in terms of political activity. Harry was a slight exception as he had served as a soldier in the English embassy in Lisbon for some years and knew the language—and some of the Portuguese born staff who now serve here."

"The sort of person to be entrusted with a sensitive list?"

"No! Harry would sell his soul, if the price was right."

"Was he carrying that list on behalf of the Portuguese ambassador to a third party, or had he stolen the list, and was about to sell it to the highest bidder?"

"I do not know. What I do know is that the Portuguese claim ignorance of any three-person list, and few outsiders are aware of it. The embassy believes it is a fabrication of the Spaniards to discredit them in the eyes of the King. To me it is more likely a fiction created by Harry to sell for profit."

"Where did he get the names?"

"Before ambassador di Melo, left for Lisbon a week or so ago, the English-born staff at the embassy were quizzed as to what they knew about the aristocratic English Catholic women who attended mass at the embassy. More than twenty such women have done so over the last three months. Why he only chose three from that range of women I have no idea. Who were they?"

Luke revealed the three names and asked, "Are any of these familiar to you?"

"No! I doubt if any of them have attended mass at the embassy."

"I am not surprised. They have only just returned to England from Flanders," commented Luke. "Where then did Harry get those names?"

"Not a problem. Given the strong feeling that the King should marry an Englishwoman, and that his brother has done that, most foreign embassies would be anxious to discover which English bride would best serve their country's interests. If the women on that list are Catholic it could be the Spanish, French or a host of Italian embassies that compiled the list. The most efficient in this type of operation would be the Venetian. If the list is made up of Calvinist women, it could be the Dutch Republic or one of the Swiss cantons. The names may be given to the embassies by people close to the King—often for a price"

"And your Portuguese embassy did not compile it?"

"No need! The Portuguese ambassador has returned to Lisbon on a promise. The King will marry the Portuguese Infanta. That is the rumor circulating through our embassy. Why is your master, whoever he may be, so concerned for the women on the list?"

"He believes it is a death list—that each of the women may be in danger," exaggerated Luke.

"Not so, if it had been created by my masters. The Portuguese never kill anybody. They are convinced that money solves everything. As long as their sugar fleet makes it home each year, Portuguese money will play a major role in determining the future Queen of England."

"If that list was created by or becomes known to other groups the threat might remain. Anti-Portuguese groups such as the Spaniards might see the list as pro-Portuguese, and try to eliminate them one by one," replied Luke.

Mary interrupted them by knocking on the door and declaring that if they did not want her services, she would depart to The Black Falcon for something to eat—and more eager customers.

Ezekial turned to Luke, "I have told you all I can. Take advantage of Mary's availability before you leave!"

Luke was about to refuse the offer, when he suddenly realized that Mary might be an additional source of information.

He nodded to Ezekial and went into the adjoining room. Mary was delighted to see him. Luke put his finger to his mouth and whispered, "Double your normal fee for information! Make a few appropriate noises to let Ezekial believe we are enjoying each other's company."

"What do I know that is worth paying for?" she teased.

"Harry Foster, tell me about him—and his murder!"

"An animal. He raped me many a time. I'm glad he is dead, and no one will give you any information as to who may have done it."

"Ezekial—I have just paid him a fortune. Can he be trusted?"

"Are you stupid? Your silver and gold will buy you information, but whether it is true or false is anyone's guess. Ezekial is loyal to his employers, and he will not sell you any information detrimental to his masters. The Portuguese are not idiots. They use him to feed information, true or false, into other quarters. Everything he told you could be a pack of lies to serve the interests of the Portuguese. He hasn't the brains to assess any situation. He repeats what he has been told. He probably does not understand what most of it is all about."

"Have any of your customers commented on a list of three English women that seems to have been circulating within the Portuguese embassy, and possibly in the area generally?"

"I don't know who was on this list, so I do not know."

Luke named the women.

Mary's face lit up.

"A week ago, one of our lords who visits that embassy regularly, dropped in here on his way home. He asked me whether I had heard any gossip about several women, one of the women you named Elizabeth Rhodes. My answer was no."

"Do you know the identity of this peer?"

"No. He told me he was a high-ranking soldier, but that could have been a lie."

The conversation was interrupted by a slightly irritated Ezekial from the adjacent room suggesting Luke and Mary hurry up.

Luke gave Mary a hug and left the building.

While Luke was questioning Ezekial and Mary, Miles, still in The Black Falcon, struck up a conversation with another customer who was sitting alone.

The loner asked Miles directly, "Are you here to buy information, or be paid for services you have rendered to one of these foreign embassies?"

"Neither I am enquiring about the murder of a menial servant of the Portuguese embassy a week or so ago."

"You won't get very far. The victim, Harry Foster, was a monster—a rapist and pedophile. Everybody is delighted with his demise. Whoever did it will be protected by all of us."

Miles accepted the knockback and changed the subject. "Why did you think I was here to buy information or receive a sweetener?"

"The Black Falcon is the place where the Portuguese and several of the Italian embassies dispense their bribes to our betters. More aristocrats or their servants find their way through these doors than any alehouse in this part of London."

"Surely our leaders do not personally come to this part of London to collect bribes, that might endanger their political position or social standing?"

"Those at the very top send a representative, but Ezekial Poole who handles the Portuguese largesse is well aware of who they represent and does not hesitate to let the rest of us know. The Portuguese government keeps a tighter control over the lesser lights who are required to collect their regular gift in person."

"Who are these lesser lights?"

"Members of Parliament, clerks in various government agencies especially those in the various naval offices."

"Why the naval bodies?"

"Portugal's ability to finance its systematic bribery of English officials depends on its wealth, which in turn depends on the continued arrival of its sugar fleet from Brazil. This needs the assistance of the English navy to prevent it from being attacked by the Dutch or the Spaniards. Venice is equally concerned to monitor what the English fleet might do in the Mediterranean."

Miles asked his informer, "Most customers here work for one of the foreign embassies, do you?"

"Yes, but my government currently has no ambassador nor embassy. I have a room within the Venetian complex. The Grand Duke of Tuscany based in Florence has yet to respond to the return of the English monarchy. I am Clement White, who are you?"

"I am Captain Miles Oxenbridge, a soldier who saw service in the Mediterranean, and during that period learnt to speak Italian. I will be demobilized in a few weeks and am seeking a position. Perhaps when your ambassador finally arrives, he may be in need of additional staff. Could you put in a good word for me?"

"I am not naïve, captain. You did not drop into The Black Falcon on the off chance of finding a position in one of the Italian embassies. You are obsessed with Foster's murder."

"Very perceptive Clement! I am currently assisting a local magistrate. Harry Foster had on his body a document which greatly concerns the English government."

"What is so worrying to the government about this document?"

"It contains the names of three aristocratic women. It is feared that it may be a hit list. Some maniac may kill them one after another. These women are well known to the King, so it raises questions of national security. Has there been any talk of aristocratic women in this alehouse over recent months?"

"Aristocratic women are not the usual subject of talk in this alehouse. I could not name one. It is not a world that we locals inhabit, or are interested in. On the other hand, the question of the King's mistresses is the butt of many a bawdy joke. None of the current batch are English aristocrats—they are common Londoners or foreigners."

"So, none of the gentlemen who come here to pick up a sweetener have been heard talking about their women folk?"

Suddenly Miles felt a tug on his sleeve and turned to be confronted by a small seedy looking drinker whose bleary eyes and slurred speech suggested he had already consumed far too much alcohol.

"Mister, for a tankard I can tell you more than Clemmie White has. He sits here in the corner away from the throng and doesn't overhear conversations."

"Away with you, Davy Windsor! This gentleman has no desire to pay for a pack of lies," said Clement. He turned to Miles and added, "Davy makes his living trying to blackmail other customers over what he claims to have overheard. He will eventually suffer the same fate as Harry Foster."

"No, I won't. I am still here because of what I know. Gents are too frightened to cross me. The truth about them will come out if anything happens to me," slurred a swaying Davy.

"How could your truth come out, if you were killed. You cannot read or write so any information you have, would die with you. Now stop bothering us!" shouted an annoyed Clement.

Miles whispered to Clement, "Let me humor him!"

"I will send for a tankard while we talk Davy, and if you tell me anything useful there will be another—and a few coins. How do you think you can help me?"

"I overheard you ask about any talk of foppish women. A few weeks back I overheard that minion of the Portuguese, that pest Poole, talking with one of his upper-class cronies. Poole asked would the King really marry the lady they were talking about."

An excited Miles asked, "And who was this lady?"

"How would I know?"

Miles felt inclined to strike Davy but expressed his anger in a stream of expletives. When a wench brought the promised tankard, Miles considered pouring it over Davy's head. Sensing that his information had been useless and his imminent tankard in jeopardy, Davy scrambled to reveal further snippets of information. "A few weeks later Poole was talking to the same gent and observed that the lady they had previously discussed would not be marrying the King."

"Had she died?"

"No, but both Poole and his companion agreed that it would have been better for her if she had."

"Anything else that you overheard from these two that might be useful?" said Miles somewhat sarcastically.

"Only that Poole expressed concern that she may be the first of many, who might suffer because of their closeness to the King."

L ater that evening Luke and Miles briefed Mark and Matthew on their day's findings. The group concluded that the Portuguese did not compile the list of three English aristocratic women but which, in its extended unknown original form, possibly included one of Charles's mistresses who claimed the King was about to marry her. Whether this was a list of suitable Catholic Englishwomen that the Portuguese could substitute for their own Infanta, should she be rejected; or conversely a list of rivals to the Portuguese princess or other foreign claimants who had to be eliminated, remained the urgent unanswered question.

Due to the pressure of Parliamentary business, Mark delayed his trip west to clarify the situation of his friend Lady Elizabeth Rhodes, but Luke investigated the attack on Lady Dinah Langley. He questioned a fellow Middlesex magistrate who had investigated the case.

The details were clear. Lady Dinah had alighted from her coach in the vicinity of Whitehall when four men knocked her to the ground, and one of their number poured acid on her face, shouting that she would never destroy another innocent, while the others chanted in unison that she would never marry the King. Her screams alerted the local militia who were on duty in the area.

The soldiers opened fire on the fleeing quartet, killing all four.

"Did you discover anything about these four men?" asked Luke.

"Hardly anything. Witnesses claimed they were locals who congregated regularly in the alehouse around the corner, The Black Falcon," answered the magistrate.

"Did you follow this up?"

"No point. There had been a serious assault, the motive appeared clear, and the perpetrators were all dead. I did question the lady's household who claimed that she had never been indiscreet enough to tell her friends that with the return of the King, he would marry her. This was a lie put about by her enemies."

Luke thanked the magistrate and proceeded to The Black Falcon. He entered with a swagger and immediately engaged in a loud conversation with the nearest group of drinkers. "It's a wonder you still drink here!"

"And why would that be?" retorted the most belligerent of the group.

"I hear one of your fellow drinkers was murdered just around the corner, and four more of your number were shot dead by the local militia."

"The murder victim deserved his fate, but three of the lads shot by the militia were engaged in a harmless prank that got out of hand."

"Throwing acid in the face of a gentlewoman is not a harmless prank," observed Luke with a degree of pomposity.

"That was not the plan. A visitor offered a considerable sum to any group of lads who would frighten a woman who was due to alight a carriage at a particular place and time. Apparently a fourth man unknown to our friends appeared from nowhere, and as the woman lay on the ground, unharmed except for her muddied clothes, this stranger poured acid over her. Knowing our friends, they obviously decided to exit the scene as fast as possible, but the militia shot first, before asking questions."

"Did you see the bodies of your friends?"

"Yes, we collected them from a doctor's room where they had been taken and brought them back for a decent burial."

"Did you see the fourth man?"

"In the doctor's room."

"Did you recognize him?"

"No, he was a complete stranger."

"Was there anything about the body that might help identify it?"

One of the group who had not spoken before asked, "What is it to you? Why all these questions? We have done nothing wrong."

Luke lied, "I am a relative of the lady concerned, and am investigating her death on behalf of the family."

The group relaxed, and the original spokesman replied, "The man was dark skinned, and wore a golden crucifix."

"How dark? Was he an African?"

"Hard to tell. He could have been Spanish, Portuguese or Italian, but his skin color certainly suggests that he was not English."

"You mention a golden crucifix. That is not listed in the magistrate's report."

"I removed it when we collected the bodies of our friends. It paid for their funeral and wake," answered one of the men, with no sign of guilt in stealing from a dead body.

An elated Luke returned to his apartment. Dinah Langley had been killed by a Catholic Mediterranean or African man. This suggested someone associated with the embassies of Spain, Portugal, or a variety of Italian states. It did not exclude someone from the North African coast. It certainly smacked of foreign intrigue.

With this latest information Luke was determined to investigate more thoroughly the circumstances surrounding the attack on, and subsequent death of Lady Dinah Langley.

Two days later he and Miles were at Langley Court, a substantial manor in the Thames valley. They were received by the estate's steward, Lawrence Beecham.

"We are here on the King's business. He was distressed at the death of Lady Dinah and is not happy with the resultant investigation. We had hoped to question the family and servants into the events that preceded her ladyship's trip to London on that fateful day," announced Luke.

"Sir George and Lady Langley have lived in Barbados for the last two years. Sir George inherited a large sugar plantation. Lady Dinah's sister, Martha is at present at the family's town house in London, but she was here with Dinah from the time Dinah returned from Europe until her death," commented the clearly disapproving senior servant.

"I am sure that the household can tell us all we need to know. My first question—did Sir George employ any colored servants or slaves in England?"

"On his last visit home six months ago, he brought with him a couple of African slaves. One of these stayed on at Langley for some time, but eventually we had to let him go. Why do you ask?"

"The person responsible for Lady Dinah's mutilation was a dark-skinned man."

"Are you suggesting a link between Lady Dinah and a colored servant?" asked an appalled steward.

"It is a question I had to ask," apologized Luke.

"If any such unfortunate liaison occurred, it took place on the continent rather than in the environs of Langley Court. Apart from that servant, Seth, I have never seen a colored man. Were there colored people at the King's court in exile?"

Luke expressed his lack of knowledge, but he knew Mark would enlighten him. He continued his questioning.

"How did Lady Dinah spend her time since her return from the continent? Did she stay here, travel, or go up to London?"

"She and her sister went up to London on numerous occasions, but most of the time was spent here. Her maids can give you greater detail of her activities. As steward I run the estate, not the lives of their ladyships."

"Why did your staff think Dinah was attacked in such a brutal manner?"

"The fact that the initial aim of the assailant was disfigurement, rather than death suggests the perpetrator wanted to negate Lady Dinah's major asset in the marriage stakes, her extreme beauty. It was probably a woman who was competing for the hand of a gentlemen with whom Lady Dinah had shown an interest."

This comment surprised Luke. He had simply assumed her death was a result of her alleged frolics with the King. Beacham's information widened the field of possible suspects alarmingly.

"You do not think it was because she told the world that she was to marry the King, and that someone who feared this, was forced to act?"

"Come Colonel, you are a man of the world, and better versed in Royal affairs than I. Of all the women in Charles's Stuart's life, why would he tell our Lady Dinah that he would marry her, when it is widely known that he has made it clear throughout his adult life, that the women he consorts with, cannot expect marriage. Let's be blunt, her ladyship had few virtues other than sublime beauty. And Lady Dinah never claimed she was about to marry the King. I heard it was a rumor put about by her rivals to cause trouble—perhaps to cause the King to lose interest. Her maids, Leah and Rose will tell you more. I will summon them."

The two girls were overawed in the presence of two army officers, resplendent in their red uniforms. Luke tried to put them at their ease, although Miles thought the former's opening words had the opposite effect.

"We have been sent by the King to discover all we can about your late ladyship's activities in the months leading up to her death, in the hope that we can discover who was behind the vicious assault upon her."

Leah was a tall mature brunette whose clothing suggested she was closer to being a lady's companion than a menial maid. This latter description more appropriately suited Rose who was a plump mousy haired young girl with a perpetual grin.

"So, it was true. Her ladyship was a great friend of the King's," uttered an easily impressed Rose.

"Didn't she constantly try to enhance her standing by telling everybody she was to marry the King?" asked Miles, seeking confirmation of the steward's comment.

Leah answered, "Quite the opposite, sir. Her ladyship was sad. We would often find her gently sobbing. She told me that the love of her life had been lost forever. And when I suggested the situation might improve, she said it never could—he was lost forever."

"Was this in reference to the King?" asked Luke.

"Not necessarily! She never mentioned the King at all, although we all knew largely from her spiteful sister, that Lady Dinah had been one of the King's many mistresses—but also that she had affairs with many other gentlemen, any one of whom may have been the cause of her distress," Leah confided.

"Further complications!" muttered Miles half aloud.

Luke assumed he was referring to a possibly jealous sister, and asked the women, "What can you tell me about Lady Martha? Could she have played a part in the attack on her sister, and the false stories that emanated about her?"

"She probably was the source of the many lies told about Lady Dinah, but she would have no part in an attack on her own sister," muttered Leah.

She suddenly paled and whispered to the soldiers, "Yet again the location of the attack may be significant. Lady Dinah was alighting from the family carriage to enter the Langley town house where Lady Martha normally stayed."

"Lady Dinah was visiting her nasty sister when attacked!" reiterated Luke. "I thought they were both residing here in reasonable harmony?"

"Yes, but both took regular visits up to London."

"What caused the tension between the sisters?" asked Miles changing the subject.

"Simple jealousy! Have you seen Lady Martha? She is the ugliest woman I have ever seen. How two sisters could look so different. All the perks that Dinah's beauty brought her, simply increased Martha's bitterness," answered Rose, somewhat cattily.

"Surely Martha did not try to compete with her sister for the affections of the same men?" asked Miles, not expecting an informative answer.

"Martha was stupid, as well as grotesque. Since her return to England Lady Dinah was seeing a lot of a diplomat whose embassy was almost next to the Langley town house. The same diplomat had previously been very kind to Martha, when Dinah was on the continent, and her parents in Barbados. He took pity on the lonely and isolated woman, but she thought it was more."

"Was Lady Dinah having an affair with this man?" asked Miles.

"I don't know, but Lady Martha thought so," answered Leah.

"How do you know?" continued Miles.

"We both heard the sisters in an acrimonious shouting match in which Martha savaged the morals of her sister, who responded by claiming that Martha's almost deformed appearance would be an eternal curse destroying all hopes of a relationship with any man," said Rose who delighted in denigrating Martha at every opportunity.

Luke asked, "Do you know who this man was?"

"Yes, when we looked after her ladyship during an extended stay in the town house, he was a daily visitor—an Englishman attached to the Venetian embassy, Sir Henry Hunt."

5

Luke let out an involuntary whistle which startled the women. "I am sorry for that whistle, but I know Sir Henry."

Miles's mind was racing ahead. One foreign embassy that had many dark colored servants, and probably some Africans was that of Venice. Could Henry have acted in concert with the ugly sister, or did the ugly sister somehow find an agent to disfigure her rival for Henry's affections?

"Have you seen either Lady Martha or Sir Henry since Dinah's death?" he asked.

"No," the women responded in unison.

"Apart from dallying with Sir Henry when at the town house, how did Lady Dinah fill in her time here?" continued Luke.

"She was not without numerous male friends," giggled Rose.

"Were any of these men advancing a serious matrimonial proposition that might have gone sour? asked Miles.

"Her ladyship never confided in us on such matters. Some were lovers, some just friends, and a few she claimed were simply using her closeness to the King to further their own political ambitions," answered the more serious Leah.

"You two have made our task even more difficult. Lady Dinah may have been killed by an ambitious would-be politician or an office holder whom Lady Dinah refused to positively recommend to the King when she next slept with him," commented Luke.

"Not likely!" disagreed Miles. "A disappointed office seeker would not have resorted to disfigurement—the more direct method of murder would have been more likely."

"And it was, captain!" was Leah's surprising intervention. "The doctor who examined the body told Mr. Beacham that he thought the intention from the start was murder. The acid had been deliberately dripped not only onto the face but onto the throat. It was Lady Dinah's inability to breathe that killed her. The murderer knew exactly what he was doing. The disfigurement may have been a deliberate attempt to shift the blame onto Lady Dinah's rivals for the hands of various gentlemen and divert it away from the real culprit."

"Especially to incriminate her sister," noted Luke. "Was there anything else other than men, that helped Dinah fill in time during her period here?"

"She entertained a large number of aristocratic and gentry women, many of whom she knew from her time at the King's court in exile."

"Can you name any of these women visitors? Did Lady Dinah's mood change significantly after any of the visits?"

"No, we were not usually present, and the visitors were announced to Lady Dinah by one of the male servants. Her mood did change considerably after some visits—sometimes it improved, other times it got worse. I can't remember which visitor caused what reaction," was Leah's considered reply.

"It's a pity you never knew or can't recall the names of any of these visitors," remarked Luke.

"Don't cry, sir! You can still find out who these people were. The steward maintains a list of all visitors," said Rose very cheekily.

Before the soldiers left Langley Court, they obtained from Beacham the list of visitors in the months leading up to Dinah's death.

Once back in the unit's apartment in Whitehall, Luke and Miles perused it, evoking cries of astonishment from both men. Two of the three women, who were on the fateful list found on the body of Harry Foster, had visited Dinah more than once—Elizabeth Rhodes and Agatha Craven. A third entry intrigued them even more. The father of the third woman on the potential hit list had also visited Dinah—Randolph Dash, Earl of Greenham.

Their next step was obvious—question Henry, Martha, and Randolph. Luke would report to the King and seek further information on aspects of the court in exile involving Dinah and Randolph, and in a change of plan, would now accompany Mark west to interview Elizabeth.

Next day Luke was in the Venetian embassy sitting in a comfortable leather chair opposite Henry. Unlike the rest of London, the Venetians did not appear to be short of coal as this autumn morning was a freezing harbinger of the approaching winter. As the two men drank mulled red wine and swallowed freshly shucked oysters in front of a blazing fire, Henry asked rather nervously, "What brings you back here. I told you all I knew about the list my men found on the body of that delinquent Harry Foster."

"It turns out that you have become central to a related part of the investigation, the assault and death of Lady Dinah Langley."

"A nasty affair."

"Who do you think was responsible and why?"

"As I understand it the motive appears to be have been disfigurement. I assume it was at the instigation of a rival female, or a rejected lover."

"Were you one of the latter?"

"*Lover*, too strong a word, *rejected* no. Dinah and I were long-time friends who had an intermittent, casual relationship. The Langley town house is just two doors from here. I've known the family for years. Dinah had many lovers, one of whom once was the King, but she was never the marrying type."

"With further evidence, it now appears that the attempt on Dinah was murder, not disfigurement. Her throat, and ultimate ability to breathe and eat were specifically targeted," announced Luke eagerly anticipating Henry's reaction.

"That must change your focus a little, colonel?" commented a perceptive Henry.

"Perhaps more than a little. Did she ever express any concern for her safety?"

"Never! She enjoyed life and was delighted to back in England after years at the royal court in exile, and a month or more touring Italy. With her parents in the Indies, and her sister more often in London, she was mistress of Langley Court, and enjoyed playing hostess to a range of important people—including a long list of lovers, former and current."

"Did she suggest that any of her partners in these affairs had misinterpreted the fleeting nature of the relationship, and was becoming a nuisance?"

"There were two reasons why Dinah was so popular, and until her murder had incited little angst—her extreme beauty, and her discretion. Even to a close friend like myself, Dinah never revealed any information about other liaisons. Although she did say once that some of her friends had done foolish things and were anxious that their indiscretions should be hidden. She gave no names and outlined no indiscretions."

"Did she mention the Earl of Maldon?"

"William! Not in the context of a lover. Dinah's childhood friend was his daughter Elizabeth, and during Dinah's time on the continent the Earl who was on the periphery of the court, became her surrogate father as the two schoolgirl friends remained inseparable."

Luke changed the direction of his questioning. "Many men inadvertently reveal deep secrets to their lovers. Did she know too much about someone? Could she have been a blackmailer?"

"Someone may have thought Dinah knew too much about them, but I doubt that she was a blackmailer. The Langleys are very wealthy, and Dinah was enjoying life. She had no financial need to blackmail. What would be her motive?"

"Revenge for wrongs committed against her," suggested Luke.

"Unlikely, Dinah did not bear grudges. She had a cheery disposition that never faded."

"Earlier you mentioned rival females—could her sister Martha be behind the murder?"

Henry showed the first sign of emotion. His face reddened, his eyes flashed, and he declared, "Absolutely not! Timid, gentle Martha loved her sister, and on Dinah's return from the continent, Martha left the town house to move in with her sibling in Langley Court. What could possibly be her motive?"

"Jealousy!"

"Of what could she have been jealous?"

Luke was beginning to be annoyed with Henry's bland responses. He was giving little away.

"Dinah was a most beautiful woman with dozens of interested males, Martha was one of the ugliest of women, spurned by most men."

"What utter rubbish! Where did you hear such lies? Martha was not the most beautiful woman in the world, and clearly could not compete with her exceptionally beautiful sister, but she was not ugly, nor was she deprived of interested males."

"Including yourself?"

"Not in the sense you are implying. Martha is very young, and I treated her as the daughter I never had. I had many a discussion with her about the men who flocked to the Langley town house, but my contact and influence waned when she returned to Langley Court. It has only been resurrected since Dinah's death, and Martha's return to London."

"Martha never expressed jealousy regarding her sister?"

"Never."

"What was her basic feeling towards her sister?"

"That is a difficult question to answer. Since Dinah's return from the continent, it has been a combination of admiration and concern. Martha moved back to Langley Court because she was concerned for Dinah's safety. Martha had a streak of Puritanism in her regarding the life that Dinah led, as likely to have dangerous outcomes. Whether she ever lectured her older sister on the evils of a promiscuous life, I don't know, but I know that was her opinion."

"If Martha is neither ugly, nor was intensely jealous of her sister, why is such a picture being promulgated across the social elite? And why is it strongest amongst those who were the closest to Dinah?"

"Martha's moralistic convictions were expressed too openly in the presence of these people who would protect Dinah to the end. The hedonistic atmosphere that surrounds the King and his friends, including the late Dinah, remain alien to Martha."

Luke rose to his feet. "Perhaps I am looking at this in the wrong way. Maybe Dinah and her friends knew something detrimental about Martha. Maybe the younger sister had to stop Dinah revealing it."

"Good God Luke, you have developed a completely bizarre interpretation of events, but in one aspect you could be right. There could be a quite different interpretation which involves Martha."

"What do you mean?"

"The intended victim of the murder may not have been the popular Dinah, but the annoying Martha."

"How could that be, given the striking difference in their appearance?"

"Very easily. Both women came up to the Langley town house on a regular basis. Martha had begun to copy her sister by wearing similar clothes. In fact, Dinah allowed her little sister to wear some of her clothes—and both women wore veils when they travelled. Ask Martha when you question her had it been her intention to travel up to London on that fateful day? That, Luke, might give you an entirely different set of possibilities."

"It certainly does—and I will call on Martha immediately I leave here. On a different issue, why did you stay with the Venetian embassy after the collapse of Cromwell's government?"

"Unlike yourself, I was never a devoted Cromwellian nor Royalist. I spent the first decade of the civil war in Italy fighting for the Venetian state with my friend James, who only last year succeeded to the Earldom of Hastings. We opted out of our civil war. I returned to England in the mid-fifties and was appointed by the Venetian embassy to act on its behalf with the Cromwellian administration. James stayed on and was killed only a few months ago fighting the Turk somewhere in the Balkans. His death has left his estate without an occupant and his title vacant. I am trying to sort it out."

"I am sorry to hear that James Hastings is dead. His reputation in the Mediterranean was unsurpassed. When I was ambassador to the Islamic states of North Africa, Cromwell asked me to sound Hastings out for a senior military appointment in his administration."

"It is a personal tragedy. The last letter I received informed me that James had married an English aristocrat in Venice, just before he embarked on his last mission into Albania."

"She would at least temporarily be a very wealthy widow. Who is she?"

"I don't know."

"She will have to reveal herself to claim her rights," concluded Luke prosaically.

Luke thanked Henry and being so close decided to question Martha.

6

He was received into a small room, in which no blazing fire combatted the continuing chill. The valet who had admitted him remained behind the chair of his seated mistress, who made no attempt to dismiss him, despite the intimate information that Luke's questioning might evoke.

The vastly different views concerning Martha's appearance had intrigued Luke—an appearance that could be critical in the relationship between the siblings. He was surprised. Martha was no beauty—but plain, rather than ugly. She was a petite, raven haired, pale skinned woman with a round moonlike face.

Luke explained to her that he was investigating the death of her sister on behalf of the King and had a few questions he would like to ask. He started brutally, "Lady Martha, who do you think murdered your sister and why?"

"She was not killed as rumor claimed because she proclaimed that she would soon marry the King. She never made such a claim, and her intimate relationship with the King was long over—although they remained friends. She had been succeeded by countless other women since her days as his closest confidante at the court in France, and then later in Flanders."

"If her relationship with the King was not a factor in her death, what was?"

"Her life style!"

35

"Her generosity towards men?" asked Luke diplomatically.

"Yes, I expressed my concern to her from the day she arrived back in England. Don't misinterpret me, colonel, I am no puritan. Her behavior towards men was completely amoral, and most of these affairs were pleasant interludes for Dinah. Unfortunately, not all men treated the relationship in the same casual way as Dinah. Some ex-lovers created trouble, and I believe one of these men arranged for her death—probably revenge for being humiliated, when Dinah moved on to the next lover."

"Was there anyone that Dinah particularly feared during the last few months?"

"I was never privy to her relationships. Her companion and leading maid servant, Leah, deliberately kept me away from my sister for much of the period we were at Langley Court together."

"Yes, I experienced a very antagonistic attitude towards you from that person. What did she have against you?"

"Her role was to select would be lovers and encourage Dinah to accept them. She was paid by these men to obtain an introduction to Dinah. Conversely, I was determined that certain males whom the servants were promoting should come nowhere near my sister. I possibly cost Leah a fortune."

"If there is such antagonism between Leah and yourself, why have you retained them?"

"I tried to dismiss them, but Mr. Beacham told me they were employed by father under a very favorable contract, and only father can remove them. Growing up I always thought Leah was a little too close to father."

She grimaced.

Luke decided not to follow up on that piece of information. He changed the subject. "Forgive me Lady Martha, but you appear to have led a sheltered life, especially when compared with your sister. How did you know which men should be discouraged?"

"My near neighbor and a member of the Venetian embassy, Sir Henry Hunt who is a friend and mentor, and one of my sister's long-time admirers advises me."

"I know Henry. Some witnesses have suggested that you were your sister's rival for Henry's affections. Is there any truth in that assessment?"

"Not as a lover. Look at me! What man would want a sexual adventure with me, if my sister was available? Henry and I were nevertheless close friends. Given father's absence overseas for much of my life, Henry was a mix of surrogate father and brother to me."

"Although your sister's murder must be solved and its perpetrator identified, I must also ascertain whether anything about that murder reflects on the security of the state. Did Dinah engage in any political intrigue since her return to England? Could she have been murdered for something she knew that possibly threatened the King?"

"I never thought much about it. Dinah was not a political animal but looking back some of her visitors who struck me as most unlikely lovers, may have been seeking some political gain from her. As a friend of the King, it was widely known she could help promote their interests with His Majesty."

"Conversely she could report any anti-Royalist activity to the King thus threatening the position of some of her lovers and acquaintances," commented Luke. "Did you overhear any political conversations between Dinah and her visitors?"

"Strange you should mention that. I now remember two which appeared to contradict each other—one with the Earl of Maldon, and one with Agatha Craven"

"What did they concern?"

"The King's marriage to a Catholic."

"How did the conversations differ?"

"The Earl of Maldon seemed determined that should Parliament reject any marriage to a foreign Papist, it was imperative that the King marry an English Catholic noblewoman—preferably his daughter, Elizabeth. Dinah suggested he be realistic. The King's marriage would be determined by the politicians in terms of foreign policy, and the King in terms of a sustainable dowry—and given the amount of money being thrown around by the Portuguese they were clearly the front runner. Dinah absolutely refused to assist Maldon in furthering his cause for an English Catholic wife for Charles."

"How did the Earl react to such a forthright refusal of assistance?"

"Absolute fury! He claimed such behavior by Dinah was an insult to his daughter, who had seen Dinah as one of her closest friends, and he would not be deterred by any negative interference from a royal discard. He stormed out of Langley Court, uttering the longest string of expletives I have ever heard."

"What was the issue with Lady Agatha?"

"It appeared to be the reverse issue. Could Dinah advise the King against marriage to any English woman, Catholic or Protestant. His brother the Duke of York had set a bad example."

"How did Dinah react?"

"She repeated what she had said to Maldon. The King would not choose his bride, so anything she said to the King would be useless. After Agatha had left, she commented that the woman had at one stage held high hopes of an affair, if not marriage with the King, but had been usurped in the King's affections by Lady Elizabeth Rhodes."

Luke changed the line of his questioning once more. "I hear your father left one of his African servants at Langley Court after his last visit home?"

"Yes, and it was a mixed blessing."

"In what sense?"

"Seth had a face as black and shiny as Newcastle coal and proved a devoted servant to Dinah, but otherwise was dishonest, lazy and a born troublemaker. He was surly and intimidating, and Mr. Beacham got rid of him."

"Got rid of him! In what sense?"

"He was dismissed."

"Where do these colored people go, if they are not employed?"

"I don't have any idea. I have never thought about it. He would have been hanged if I had had my way. I am sure he stole some of the family silver."

"You may have solved your sister's murder. The man who poured acid on her throat was a colored man—possibly Seth, taking his revenge."

"Not likely! Dinah was the one person at Langley Court that Seth admired, and she protested against his dismissal."

"You played a major part in his sacking?"

"Yes, it was I who gathered the evidence, and persuaded Mr. Beacham to act."

"I have no wish to upset you, but you may have been the intended victim of the attack and not your sister. I gather you wore a similar dress to her, that both of you travelled heavily veiled, and she arrived here at the town house on that fatal day about the same time that you regularly arrived."

Martha inhaled heavily and sighed, "My God, I caused my sister's death. Dinah did arrive here by the family coach at the exact time I regularly came up from Langley Court."

Tears welled up, and Martha began to sob gently. "How horrible! Seth murdered my sister in revenge for his dismissal, believing the veiled woman was me," mumbled a now distraught Martha.

Luke left the Langley town house and moved further down the street to the Portuguese embassy. He would ask the Portuguese resident himself about the compilation of the list of three aristocratic women found on one of their employees.

He was disappointed.

The resident, Francesco di Melo had left for Lisbon the week before to seek updated instructions in his campaign to obtain a marriage treaty with England.

A servant informed Luke that in his absence the ambassador's nephew, Count Francesco de Sa was in charge of Portuguese affairs, and he would speak to Luke.

An effusive and bubbling diplomat entered the room, and embraced Luke. "You are great friend of Portugal. You don't remember me, but two years ago when you assisted our Queen regent against her enemies, I was one of her courtiers. What can I do for you? My servant said you were on a mission for your King."

"It concerns the murder of Harry Foster."

"You surprise me. Why would a former head of military intelligence, an ambassador to the Islamic states, and now part of a secret unit responsible only to the English King, concern himself with the murder of that despicable animal? I was about to dismiss him from our service. The murderer did us a favor."

"No, the murder is not my concern. It is what he carried that has the King concerned."

"I have no idea what he carried. There have been no reports that he carried anything other than a considerable amount of money which was stolen, probably by the murderer. The doctor's report indicated no possessions left on the corpse."

"What was taken from the body by servants of another embassy and passed on to the English government was a list simply containing the names of three English aristocratic women. The King fears it may be a hit list of women that someone needs to be removed, or conversely a reserve list of eligible English Catholic women that some foreign governments would be happy to see as Queen of England if their own candidates are rejected. I am here because the list was found on one of your servants. These are the names."

The count appeared appalled as he perused the note that Luke had handed to him.

"I know of no such list. I have seen all correspondence sent by my uncle to Lisbon. There was nothing that referred to any English aristocratic women."

"Although your uncle did discuss such women with the embassy household?"

"True, but that discussion was not limited to these three names, none of whom I recognize. Many Catholic noblemen and their families take mass in our embassy when they are in London. My uncle was interested in knowing as much as he could about those families to which he had showed hospitality, and who might be useful political links in the future. Somebody could have extracted from that discussion any three names, but not those you mention. They are unknown to us, although the fathers of at least two of them are viewed as our most dangerous enemies among the English nobility—lackies of Spain."

"Could someone in the embassy, other than you and the ambassador, have discovered the names of aristocratic daughters and compiled this three person list?"

"Anything underhand could emanate from an undesirable underling, Ezekial Poole."

"I have met Poole, why suspect him?"

"Poole acts for my uncle in matters that may not be appropriate for a foreign diplomat. Poole fulfills a role for uncle, similar to that which you fill for your King. In particular he is used to feed false information to our rivals."

"So, everything he does is at the behest of your uncle, the ambassador?"

"Uncle might believe it, but we know that Poole also acts on his own behalf and sells information. He probably put three names on a list and told potential customers a pack of lies concerning it. The late Harry Foster was Poole's messenger, no doubt for a cut of the profits in this information peddling."

"It's a wonder that your uncle keeps Poole employed?"

"Uncle is convinced that Poole has done nothing to undermine Portuguese interests, and that he plays a minor, but important role in the embassy's activities. I will call him in, and you can question him freely."

7

oole entered the room. He was obviously alarmed by Luke's presence.

The acting ambassador was direct, "You have already met Colonel Tremayne who is investigating the death of Foster, and the origins and significance of a list of three names apparently found on his body. I have already explained that the list did not originate in any official sense from within this embassy. He has his own explanation which suggests that you are its source, Poole."

Luke intervened, stretching the truth, "The acting ambassador and I are old friends, and he has just asked me if he should immediately dismiss you. As your behavior may not be a security risk after all to Portugal or England, I hesitate to make such a recommendation—until I hear your side of the story."

"And what story would that be, sir?" asked Poole, trying to defend whatever position Luke may have cast for him.

"You make money selling information at The Black Falcon to a clientele of gentry and aristocrats, who gather there to be paid the sweeteners provided by the Portuguese government. You put abroad that you can provide the names of women who will have influence at court, or marry the King, or who are desirable heiresses, or any other grouping that enters your head."

"It is not illegal. I have never stolen documents from the embassy or revealed any material that would harm Portugal or England. All I have done these last six months is to remember the names of wealthy people I have heard mentioned at the embassy, and pretend they are wealthy women desperate for a husband, and recently, given the marriage of the Duke of York to a commoner, possible wives for the King. If people are foolish enough to pay me for unsubstantiated rumor, it is not my fault. But I did not create that list of three names. My lists always include at least half a dozen names. Customers pay more for longer lists."

"What surprises me Poole is that such a capable operator as yourself actually commit names to writing," commented Luke.

"I never do. I often used Harry to pass on the names to clients who had already paid me for the information. Harry probably could not remember the names and had them written down."

"Impossible!" interjected de Sa. "Harry could neither read nor write."

"Not a problem, sir. There is a man who drinks at the Black Falcon who for a fee will commit to writing whatever you want."

"Deceiving the wealthy is not necessarily a crime but putting the life of innocent women in danger might be. Do you regularly change the names on your various non-existent lists?"

"Over time. My current batch will be used for some time, usually until their circumstances change, and they no longer reflect the reasons they were named in the first place."

"Take this as a warning Poole, should anything happen to the listed women, even though you deny involvement, I shall come after you. If we reach that situation the acting ambassador will dismiss you."

"Why punish me? I have never named the women that concern you in any way, and any lists circulating were created by Foster."

"Is that why you had him killed?" asked Luke unexpectedly.

"No, but if Foster was helping himself to some of the takings from my enterprises, he would certainly have been dealt with," admitted Poole.

Before Luke responded there was the sound of many angry voices and then of shattering glass. A servant ran into the room and uttered a couple of clearly distraught sentences in Portuguese. The count turned to Luke and explained.

"The embassy is under attack. There is a mob outside shouting abuse and hurling rocks."

"Do you know who they are, and why they are up in arms?"

"No, but my servant says they are shouting 'No Catholic Queen'."

"Can they break in, and destroy the building?"

"No, this is a fortified manor house. Its walls and doors will withstand serious assault. As we speak the household is being issued with muskets in case the assault escalates."

As if this last comment provoked such an escalation, there was a loud explosion followed by several more. Either bombs had exploded under the building, or a series of grenades had been lobbed through the shattered windows.

Flying debris hit Luke and de Sa, and for some time both men lay unconscious on the floor. Flames began to take hold.

Poole who had not been hit, dragged the bodies of the two injured men out of the room. The embassy's military attaché quickly took command and organized the defense of the premises and created a line of bucket carrying firefighters.

By the time the London militia arrived, the external attackers had disappeared.

Luke recovered consciousness after about ten minutes, and immediately claimed that apart from a cut on the back of his head, and nagging headache, he was alright. The Count de Sa was also conscious, and already assessing the situation.

"Anything significant happen while I was out to it?" asked Luke.

"Yes, while we were under attack, two grenades were also thrown into The Black Falcon, but both failed to explode," said Poole.

"Who is responsible?" asked Luke, of himself as much as de Sa.

"Simple! It is someone who wants to disrupt Portugal's successful mission to influence leading politicians to support our Infanta as the wife of your King. They tried to destroy the source of the largesse that flowed into the pockets of many leading politicians, and then to disrupt the smoothly running network of distribution, operated through The Black Falcon."

"Any details regarding the attackers?"

"Our people recognized many of them as regulars at alehouses in the area. During the attack several of the perpetrators were shot and two of them were dragged into the embassy. I have not had time to question them, join me for the interrogation!"

Luke was led into an adjoining bedroom where two men lay shackled, and also cuffed by their wrists to respective bedheads.

Luke took the lead, "I represent the King. Your attack on a foreign embassy, and the resultant death of some of its inhabitants means you will be hanged as soon as I can negotiate your release from Portuguese jurisdiction. There is a very distant possibility that the Portuguese will not release you, or I will not send you to the gallows, but only if your answers help us understand this attack and bring the ringleaders to justice. Put simply the only hope of saving your life, is to tell us all."

The first invalid whimpered pathetically, "I cannot save myself. I know little. For the last ten years I was on garrison duty in the north and was demobilized only three weeks ago with insufficient recompense, and no job. A group of us former soldiers were approached in The Three Crowns and offered sixpence each to take part in this raid on the Portuguese embassy. Our take was raised to a shilling when one of our number revealed he had purloined a large number of grenades on his demobilization."

"Were you told why you were to attack this embassy, and how you would go about it?" asked de Sa.

"Loot! We were told that this embassy had a fortune on the premises which was being paid regularly to ensure that we had a Catholic queen— an idea anathema to all of us soldiers of the previous regime. My friend shackled to the next bed is a professional burglar. He had tools to break open every trunk or safe we came across. We were to confiscate the gold and silver coin. Others were to raid The Black Falcon and rob those who had just been paid from this hoard. We timed our assault to coincide with the presence of a significant number of gentlemen who were receiving their Portuguese sweeteners. We were to force entry to both premises through the use of the grenades, and then burn both buildings to the ground."

"What went wrong?" asked de Sa.

"The defenders were too well armed. We only had cudgels, daggers and a number of grenades. We had not been forewarned that the defenders would resort to concentrated bursts of musket fire. Many of our men were cut down before they were in a position to throw their grenades. Realizing this many of our comrades fled. Unluckily we were shot and brought here."

"The person who recruited you, was he English or foreign?" asked Luke.

"It was not him. It was a well-dressed gentlewoman who looked completely out of place in The Three Crowns. She may have been foreign or English. She did not speak. Negotiations were carried out with us by two of her male assistants, who were so well dressed they may have been lawyers."

The second patient did not speak. Luke noted that he had been shot in the throat. He was incapable of contributing to any discussion.

Luke and de Sa left the room and settled down in the embassy's library, which was still intact.

"Any further views as to the identity of the attackers?" repeated Luke.

"If it was local then I have nothing to suggest. If it was foreign, I doubt that it was our arch enemy Spain. The Spaniards have an outdated sense of honor. They would have attacked us, not through a group of former soldiers and petty criminals, but by their own staff. The role of a woman, given the intrigues of Cardinal Mazarin over the years might suggest French involvement, but they are our allies, and they have no objection to a Catholic queen."

"Did your prisoners have any possessions on them that might help to identify their female paymaster?"

"Only the silver sixpences and shillings with which they were paid."

"Maybe we can trace the source of this money," suggested Luke.

"Perhaps you can. The coins are not the normal Commonwealth issue, and the King has not yet issued his replacement coinage," replied de Sa.

De Sa had a servant bring the coins to Luke who smiled as he handled the shiny new sixpences. "These are indeed rare. They are not produced by the mint in the Tower of London. They are very recent—since the death of Oliver Cromwell, and as far as I know they were never released to the general public. These were produced by a French innovator who uses various patterns and with machines created a round coin with a milled edge. He is currently trying to convince the King's government that it should use his methods to make the coins bearing His Majesty's head that are about to replace all Commonwealth and Protectorate coinage. He currently has a government approved private mint in Drury House. Maybe he kept records as to whom these sample coins were distributed? Let's go there immediately!"

De Sa and Poole accompanied Luke through the rubble to where the original street entrance to the embassy had been. They headed for Drury House when several shots were heard. Luke turned to see both De Sa and Poole fall to the ground, and a number of armed Portuguese employees running to their assistance.

Luke was relieved when de Sa moved and commented, "I have not been hit. I threw myself to the ground. How is Poole?"

Luke leaned over his body answered, "He is dead, probably through the expertise of a professional marksman—one shot through the heart, fired from a considerable distance. Perhaps Poole knew too much."

8

De Sa returned to the embassy with Poole's body while Luke proceeded to Drury House alone. He was received by a silversmith, Paul Wells, who stated that he was temporarily in charge. As required by law he had kept careful records of all silver and gold obtained, and of all coins that left the premises.

Wells explained that the coins Luke produced should easily be traced.

"How is that?" Luke asked.

"Twelve months ago, it appeared that the Republic would continue for decades, and the government ordered a large number of coins depicting a post Oliver Cromwell design, on both back and front. There were delays in the supply of silver as the mint at the Tower would not transfer any of its reserves to us. We only fulfilled the order a month or so ago, and it was then obvious that the King would return. We retained ninety five percent of the coins and melted them down again in readiness for a Royal contract."

"Of the five per cent of coins that were distributed can you tell me where they went?"

Wells thumbed through his records. "The only batch of those coins put into circulation was to pay off parts of the navy."

"Who in the Navy office received them?" probed Luke.

"It did not go to the Navy Office."

48

"It went directly to the navy's top sailors, the Duke of York or Edward Montague, Earl of Sandwich?"

"No, both officers were at sea, and the Navy Board lacked leadership. The money was approved for dispatch, and received by the same man, the Lord Chancellor himself."

"The Lord Chancellor is too busy to deal with the mechanics of such a transfer. He does not have the time to distribute those funds himself. Do you know who controlled that operation?"

"No, our records end with the Lord Chancellor's signature on receipt of the silver coins."

Later that evening Luke discussed developments with his team. Someone was out to disrupt the flow of Portuguese bribes into the English political environment—someone with sufficient wealth to rent a mob.

Miles was skeptical. "This may have nothing to do with the activities of the Portuguese embassy. The killing of Poole suggests that it was his personal activities that had somebody worried. Why would anybody bother to kill off Poole to disrupt the activities of the Portuguese embassy, when that embassy could simply replace Poole without any disruption to their mission?"

"I agree with Miles," said Mark. "The cause of this attack has more to do with the criminal activities of Poole in selling fraudulent information. Maybe he blackmailed some of his clients as well. It probably has nothing to do with high politics, or the actions of the Lord Chancellor."

"Nevertheless, the King must question the Lord Chancellor on how and to whom the silver from Drury House was distributed," commented Luke defensively.

Matthew, who had sat quietly sipping his Bordeaux wine, interjected, "Gentlemen, you are letting your imaginations run riot. The simplest explanation is usually the right one. Forget Poole's activities, this attack results from the fears of a wealthy man who has been on the Portuguese payroll and given his change of circumstances wants all evidence of it destroyed. Our culprit is a high official who has sold out to the Spaniards or the French, or any other foreign power, and does not want his former links to the Portuguese known by his latest benefactor."

"And the most likely foreign power involved would be the Spaniards. Receiving sweeteners from rival nations is commonplace amongst our politicians and officials. The only situation where being a double agent could be fatal is if you were in receipt of massive Spanish inducements, and they discovered you were also receiving funds from Portugal," added Mark.

"That's a second question, I will ask the King. Who amongst his close advisers is a recipient of Spanish largesse?"

Mark chuckled, "The answer to that is the King himself. For the last five years, he has been funded almost entirely by the Spaniards."

Matt asked, "You are now convinced that the murder of Lady Dinah Langley was also non-political—the result of an aggrieved and mistreated servant?"

"I am not sure. I believe Dinah was killed by mistake. Her sister Martha was a more likely target. If so, was Martha a target because she was seen as responsible for the servant's dismissal, or did she have to be removed because she heard or saw something that others had to keep hidden?" replied Luke.

As arranged Luke met the King very early the next morning. "Tremayne, I imagine you still cannot tell me if the death of Dinah Langley, the list of three aristocratic women and now the attack on the Portuguese embassy are part of a security threat to my government, or completely irrelevant."

"No, but I have two questions which go to the heart of your administration. You need answers from your Lord Chancellor."

"Such a request is very timely. He is due to meet me in about ten minutes. You can ask him yourself. What are the questions?"

"Which of your closest advisors are receiving sweeteners from which foreign embassies? I am mostly concerned with those who are being bribed by more than one foreign power, and anyone specifically committed to Spain.

Secondly to whom did the Chancellor give funds in the form of newly minted, but now withdrawn Commonwealth coinage for the demobilization of part of the navy?"

"You do not need the Chancellor to answer the second part of your first question. I am well aware that the two strongest supporters of Spain among my councilors and aristocrats and recipients of Spanish sweeteners are William Rhodes, Earl of Maldon and Randolph Dash, Earl of Greenham. During the time I spent in the Spanish Netherlands and was reliant on large Spanish subsidies to survive, both aristocrats were responsible for the transfer of funds from the Spaniards to myself. There is no doubt that the Spaniards added considerable sweeteners to both men for keeping me tied to Spain and continue to do so now to thwart any Portuguese marriage."

"Is it not significant that the daughters of these two men appear on the list of three. Could Spain be putting pressure of these two men to ensure that you sign a treaty with Spain, and cease dealing with the Portuguese?"

"Who takes funds from which foreign power or powers is no secret. Foreign ambassadors are well aware that most of my Council take assistance from several competing nations, but I do not think the changing allegiances of my councilors would necessitate murder, or assaults on an embassy. It would most likely simply lead to an increase in the amounts offered by the other parties."

"But surely foreign powers expect a return for their investment. For example, if Spain paid a fortune into the pockets of Maldon and Greenham surely, they would be very unhappy if they realized that both men were also on the Portuguese payroll?"

"It would depend on the situation. Maybe these two aristocrats are double agents, feeding the Portuguese false information about Spain, or the reverse, giving the Spaniards fake news about Portugal. My point is that this acceptance of sweeteners from rival powers is the way of current diplomacy, and not necessarily a matter that involves national security, or requires murders and assaults on embassies."

There was a knock on the door and England's most powerful minister, Edward Hyde, Lord Chancellor entered.

The King was direct. "This is the man who during our time in exile appeared to you as very dangerous, Sir Luke Tremayne. Cromwell's head of military intelligence is now serving me in a similar role. He has put to me a question which you may be able to answer. Some of the money used to pay off the navy were coins minted by that Frenchman at Drury House. In the absence of our leading sailors, you not only authorized the payment of such money, but actually took delivery of it. To whom did you give it for distribution?"

Hyde deliberately ignored Luke and responded to the King. "Several of your aristocrats seek sinecures in the Admiralty and Navy office, and commissions in naval related agencies. With both your brother and Edward Montague at sea, I gave the money to a persistent applicant for a naval sinecure, and somebody we trusted for years on the continent with our money—William Rhodes, Earl of Maldon."

The King and Luke exchanged meaningful glances. Luke bowed and before he left the room the former announced, "You will be without Mark for a few days. He is absent on Court business."

Two hours later after discussing the matter with his depleted unit, Luke was in the lobby of the House of Lords, seeking to question the Earl of Maldon.

After introducing himself, Luke was subjected to a harangue by the earl on the privileges of the restored aristocracy. He advocated the concept that peers should only be tried by their fellow aristocrats, and this extended to any investigation even by royal agencies. Luke considered threatening Maldon with an interrogation led by James, Duke of York, which given the naval aspects of the investigation would have been appropriate. He decided not to irritate the peer. He tried a different approach.

"My lord, I am not here to question you, but as a matter of courtesy to inform you that the King is anxious about your daughter's safety and wants me to ascertain her precise circumstances."

"My daughter's safety! What do you mean?"

"Recently an employee of the Portuguese embassy was murdered. On his body apparently was a list with the names of three aristocratic women, including your daughter Elizabeth. All three women on the list are known to the King. While my prime mission is to ensure that this list is not evidence of a conspiracy against the King, it is His Majesty's wish that I ensure that none of the three women named are in any danger. The recent attack on the Portuguese embassy, the subsequent murder of another of their employees, and the attempted shooting of the acting ambassador has heightened the King's concern. Where is your daughter at the moment?"

"She is staying during the autumn and winter on our West Country estate, which given your accent is in an area you know well, Dartside Hall, on the Devon Cornwall border."

"In case I should find her security at Dartside Hall is not guaranteed, which of your other estates would best provide for her safety?"

"Surprisingly our Northumbrian estate on the Scottish borders would be ideal. Maldon Castle is a fortified manor house, and it has a staff of dozens of able bodied and well-armed defenders. But you will never get Elizabeth to move. She hates the north, and in winter she would be completely snowbound within its wall—which in the circumstances I can see may be a great advantage."

"Do you have any idea why your daughter's name would appear on this list?"

"No, but you must, otherwise the King would not be concerned."

Luke decided to tread carefully.

"All three women are wealthy heiresses, all three are Roman Catholics, all three have had association with the King during his time in exile. In essence if the King decides to marry an Englishwoman as his brother has done, this could be a list of the most likely Papist candidates."

Maldon smiled in potential reflected glory of his daughter's possible future. "If that is the King's view of the matter, why the concern?"

"There are powerful forces within England who would do anything to prevent the King marrying a Catholic. There are several foreign powers who would not want their candidate for the King's wife usurped by local women. The fact that the action has taken place in and around the Portuguese embassy suggests two possibilities—these are the Catholic women Portugal would wish to see married to Charles if their own Infanta is not acceptable, or they are the local candidates that need to be disabled, so that their candidate can succeed. The same argument can be applied to a number of other embassies."

Next day Luke, Miles and five troopers prepared to leave London for the West Country. A clearly upset Matt caught up with Luke just before he entered the stables.

"Luke, delay your trip! I just received a message that my sister, your wife, has had an accident. We must go to her immediately."

"Do you have any details?"

"No, the message was delivered to a servant who took some time in relaying it to me."

9

Given recent rain, it was quicker for Luke and Mathew to sail down the Thames and then into the Medway from which they could ride to Greytowers. It was mid-afternoon when they arrived at this formidable manor house. Luke asked the first servant they encountered, "How is your mistress? What happened?"

The servant appeared perplexed, "This is a surprise visit. Her ladyship will be delighted. She is several fields away, tending to her beehives on a piece of waste land."

"She has not had an accident?" asked Matt.

"She rode out of here an hour or so ago as healthy as you and me," answered the servant

Matt turned to Luke, "This is clearly a case of false news. To what end?"

"Probably to delay our trip to the West Country."

"I agree. Find Matilda and spend the night with her. I will return immediately to Whitehall and have Miles and our troopers on the road west at first light. You can follow later," suggested Matt.

Luke spent the night with his wife, and they agreed that she and the twins would move into Luke's private Whitehall apartment as soon as he returned from the West country.

Making use of the army's network of fast horses, replaced at regular intervals by a fresh steed, Luke easily caught up with the rest of his team. It was late in the afternoon two days later that the seven soldiers arrived at Dartside Hall.

They were met at the main door of the manor by William, Earl of Maldon.

Luke feigned surprise. "My lord, I did not expect to find you here."

"After our conversation, especially when you suggested Elizabeth might be in danger, I decided to put up with the wrath of the King and my fellow peers, desert the House of Lords, and come down here as quickly as possible to protect my only child and heir—but I was too late."

"What do you mean '*too late*'? asked an anxious Luke.

"Elizabeth is not here, and nobody knows where she has gone."

"Did she just wander off, or has she been abducted?" asked Miles, undiplomatically.

"I suspect the worst," replied William.

"Why?" probed Luke.

"She has two personal maids, who never leave her side. They sleep in the same room as their mistress. One has disappeared, presumably with Elizabeth, the other, Mabel, who seems to have been drugged is still unconscious. She may be able to tell us something when she recovers."

"May I question your staff—the steward and housekeeper to start with?" said Luke.

Luke asked both servants to describe the activities of Lady Elizabeth over the past two or three days, and in particular whether she had received visitors during that period.

The steward was direct, "Her ladyship hunted all day, and danced all night. She provided hospitality over three days to the local gentry and aristocracy—and a few visitors from London. She does this every year to highlight her seasonal relocation to the West Country."

"Would any of the gentlemen present be considered a possible husband for her ladyship," probed Luke.

"Not likely!" interrupted William. "As a daughter of an earl, there are very few local families of the appropriate status."

"Is it possible that one of the local Lothario's, knowing your lordship's attitude, has abducted Elizabeth to force her into marriage? The abduction of wealthy heiresses is not uncommon. The act of abduction, and what may or may not have gone on during their captivity, seriously reduces the value of the woman in the marriage stakes and makes marriage to a lowlier suitor kidnapper the only remaining option."

"God forbid!" uttered William, who seemed shocked by Luke's comments.

Luke changed his line of questioning. "Steward, are any of the guests still in residence?"

"No, the last one left last evening."

The housekeeper commented, "But some have not left the area. Half a dozen or so are now staying at the White Lion Inn in the village."

The steward turned to his master, "My Lord, not all the guests were of inferior status. There was at least one earl."

"Courting my daughter?"

"No. He was a gentleman of your age."

"Do you recall his name?" asked Luke.

"Yes, Randolph, Earl of Greenham."

William reacted, as if unhinged, "That scoundrel. We been friends for decades, and he brings dishonor on my family. I will seek him out and demand a duel to settle this affront. Will you be my second colonel?"

"Calm down, my lord! Greenham may have a legitimate reason for being here. Are not your daughters the closest of friends? Was his daughter here as well? Let me talk to the Earl of Greenham before you act rashly!"

Just then a servant entered the room, and informed William that his daughter's maid Mabel, had regained consciousness. The Earl abruptly left the room.

Before following him, Luke produced a handful of shiny silver coins. "Have either of you seen these unusual milled and rounded coins before. They are from a small Commonwealth issue?"

The housekeeper replied, "Yes, Lady Elizabeth gave me several a few days ago to supplement our supplies from the local farmers."

Luke thanked the two senior servants and joined the Earl in the bedroom of the now conscious maid.

William was aggressively questioning the still somewhat bemused maid. "Lady Elizabeth and Dora have disappeared, and you were heavily drugged. What is the last thing you remember?"

"Her ladyship bid goodbye to the last of her guests the night before last. Dora and I prepared her for bed, and all three of us finished off a carafe of wine. That is the last thing I remember. We were all drinking from the same carafe, when I began to feel sleepy. Her ladyship took hold of me and guided me to my bed in the corner of the room. I was not undressed, because as you can see, I am still fully clothed."

Luke intervened, "I was sent here by the King to protect Lady Elizabeth from possible harm. Clearly, I arrived too late. Did any of the guests upset or frighten her ladyship over the past two or three days?"

"Or more bluntly wench, did any men attempt to take liberties with my daughter?" demanded William.

"Several young men showed interest but were immediately repelled by her ladyship's withering stare. She was never alone with any of these over optimistic young men, my lord."

"Does that imply she was alone with other men?" asked a suspicious William.

"Yes, she spent a lot of time with your lordship's friend, the Earl of Greenham, the day before yesterday."

"Alone?" probed William.

"Yes, both Dora and I were asked to leave the room."

"Do you know what they discussed?" asked Miles who had just joined Luke.

"Yes, her ladyship told us that her name and that of her friend, the Earl of Greenham's daughter, were on a list found on the body of a murdered man. The Earl thought that his daughter would have been here over the last week and had come down to see that she was alright. He became very agitated that although invited, Lady Margaret never arrived."

"Did her ladyship know why the three particular women were on that list?" added Miles.

"Yes, she was quite chuffed. In her eyes the three women were the best candidates should Charles decide to marry an English Catholic. She believed the list originated within the Portuguese embassy as women which that government could support if their Infanta missed out, although she did say that all three might fail giving the political views of their fathers—all strong supporters of Spain, and enemies of the Portuguese revolution."

Luke could not miss the opportunity. He addressed William, "Is that true, my lord. For example, were Greenham and yourself the conduit through which Spanish money flowed to the Royal court in exile?"

"From whom did you get such a stupid idea?"

"Don't play games, my lord. Don't forget that I represent the King and act on information he provides. If you are still an agent of the Spaniards, I would seriously reconsider my position as rumors suggest the Portuguese will supply the King with a wife."

Luke did not expect a response and addressed Mabel. "Did Lady Elizabeth receive any other visitors that may have provoked her disappearance?"

Mabel thought for some time. "No, she did not receive any visitors as such, other than those invited to her hunting and dancing festivities. The only unusual event was the arrival of a courier from Whitehall two days ago. Her ladyship did not discuss the contents of whatever message he brought, but she was in a very good mood after his visit."

"Do you know if the message was from the King? Unfortunately, there are hundreds of other possible sources that can use the Royal courier service," explained Miles.

William dismissed Mabel without reference to Luke and declared, "Let's track down that scoundrel Greenham!"

"Hardly a scoundrel, my lord. He, like you, is simply anxious to find his missing daughter, but I will track him down to ascertain if he has any knowledge of where your daughter may have gone."

Luke and Miles's task proved easier than expected. Randolph was still at The White Lion. Luke explained the situation and asked, "Do you have any information regarding the disappearance of Lady Elizabeth?"

Randolph appeared shocked, "Elizabeth has disappeared? I had a long talk with her two days ago, and she was to deliver me an answer yesterday. None came. That is why I am still here."

"Why did you come down to the West country in the first place?" asked Miles.

"Two reasons, the first was to see if my daughter was safe, given the panic that your revelation that three most eligible heiresses and Catholic noblewomen, were on a list found on the body of a murdered man. The dominant rumor was that this was a hit list of an unknown adversary who might set out to kill each of the women. That rumor appears true, Elizabeth has disappeared, and my Margaret is not here. And where is Agatha?"

"And the second reason?" asked Miles.

"My nephew wanted me to test the waters regarding his possible courtship of Lady Elizabeth. I broached the topic yesterday, and after a long discussion she indicated that she was not interested, but she would sleep on it and give me a final answer today. If it was positive, I was to approach William for his permission to formalize the courtship. I heard that William arrived late yesterday for the same reason that I had— protection of our daughters. Your very presence indicates that the King has similar worries."

"You had better come back to Dartside Hall with me. William thinks you may have dishonored his daughter, or at least been involved in her disappearance. You need to repeat what you have said to me, and together plan the recovery of your daughters."

Back at Dartside Hall, Luke persuaded William to embark on a detailed interrogation of all his staff. Luke, Miles and Randolph sat in on the questioning. After several hours and the questioning of thirty or more staff a picture emerged. Late on the evening before last, a coach containing two ladies left the manor. The coachman believed and told the gatekeeper that it was Lady Elizabeth's two personal maids—one had taken ill and was being taken to Plymouth to the family physician. The coachmen waited over night expecting to return with the convalescing maid and her companion in the morning. Neither appeared, and they were eventually told by someone claiming to be the physician's servant to return to Dartside, as the women were too sick to travel.

10

Next morning Luke and Miles were in Plymouth where they established from the physician that no young women visited him during the evening in the previous week. Luke however discovered that a reputable inn a few doors away from the physician's house, did have two young women as guests on the relevant evening. They arrived late and were met by a handsome gentleman. A servant at the inn overheard them discussing their movements for the following day. The women would take a packet to France, and the gentleman would return to London.

The harbor master confirmed that on the day in question four vessels had left for the continent. Luke and Miles interviewed all packet captains, three of whom claimed their passengers on the day in question included a pair of young women.

The King's men had reached a dead end. There was no way to uncover which passengers might have been Elizabeth and her maid.

Matthew was happy with Luke and Miles's return to London. "I have been here on my own since you left. Mark was away on court or parliamentary business. Lady Matilda and your children arrived some days ago and appear well settled. Her ladyship claims they could not wait until your return to relocate."

Luke diplomatically spent a couple of days in marital bliss but was eventually reminded of his continuing mission when he received a message from the Earl of Maldon.

"Dear Colonel, I have just received a letter from Elizabeth. She is in France. She claims she is well, but will remain in hiding, until the whole issue of the three names on that list is settled. Rather naively she argues that if I do not know where she is, then her enemies, if they exist, will have even less chance of finding her."

Luke discussed the situation with Miles and Matt. "We must assume that Lady Elizabeth has of her own free will disappeared to the continent. There are two new lines of enquiry we will follow—trace the whereabouts of the other two women and shed further light on the affairs surrounding the Portuguese embassy. On that second issue, I will question Jenny Longlegs."

"I remember Jenny from my days as an agent for John Thurloe. She is a very powerful woman, and was protected from the full force of the law by elements in the then administration," admitted Matt.

"What were Puritan Cromwellians doing protecting a woman that controls most of the rackets in Westminster and the adjacent boroughs of the city of London?" Miles asked.

"In addition to controlling the brothels, illegal gambling dens and hundreds of pickpockets and thieves, Jenny set up a brokerage organization. She was the super fence. Almost everything that was stolen was sold to Jenny, who then sold the goods back to the rightful owners. This approach from the perspective of the rightful owners was much cheaper than taking the thieves to court."

"Why wasn't she arrested for receiving stolen goods? That would have put a swift end to that enterprise," asked Miles, the simple soldier.

"Information! Jenny knew every robber and thief in London and Westminster. Any of them that stepped out of line or tried to deny Jenny her cut in their thieving was mentioned to the authorities, who could then claim success in their investigations."

"Did Thurloe use her in any political or diplomatic situation?" asked Luke.

"Only to confirm which of Cromwell's ministers were on the take from foreign embassies. In those days it was the French who paid for influence, now under the King, it appears to be the Portuguese."

"Basically, she might have lots of political information that the government could well need?"

"Very likely."

"I will visit her brother at The Black Falcon to arrange a meeting. Matt, you continue trying to locate Margaret Dash and Agatha Craven! Miles find out who is the Earl of Greenham's nephew who wishes to court Lady Elizabeth."

Luke arrived at the Black Falcon alone. The local militia still patrolled the area given the recent attack on the Portuguese embassy. He sought out the landlord who addressed him, "You are the new magistrate investigating what happened here and at the embassy. Rumor has it that you are in fact acting for the King—an interesting position as one of my clients tells me you were a leading agent and general for the late Protector."

"That is correct! My concern now is to protect the lives of the three women whose names appeared on that list."

"Then why are you here?"

"For you to arrange a meeting with your sister. I have no intention of interfering in her activities, as strangely they bring a little law and order to this benighted pocket of our community. We can help each other. I am only interested in those three women, and the behavior of the foreign embassies and English politicians and officials that have truck with them. My focus is on treachery, not criminality."

"I will talk to Jenny and send a servant to Whitehall to inform you if, when, and where she will meet you."

On returning to Whitehall Luke was greeted by a smiling Miles. "Guess, the name of the Earl of Greenham's nephew? You know him well."

"I have no time for guessing games. Who is he?"

"The Earl has no sons. His heiress is his daughter Margaret. Her fortune and his title would go to her husband. Likewise, the Earl of Maldon is in a similar position. Elizabeth is the heiress who would bestow Maldon wealth and title on her husband. Maybe the two earls have a joint plan to marry a relative of the other to their daughters. Greenham's nephew is Sir Henry Hunt."

A servant from The Black Falcon delivered Luke a message within twenty-four hours. Mistress Judd would see him at 10 am at the address listed on the note he was handed.

Luke was surprised. The address was not located in the poorer enclaves of Westminster, but in one of the more desirable streets. The house itself had clearly been a town house of a wealthy gentleman or London merchant. He was shown into a reception room by a servant whose shape suggested that in earlier days he probably had been a wrestler.

After a few minutes a female servant arrived and escorted Luke into an adjacent room where he was effusively greeted by a still attractive woman in her late forties. She could have passed for a gentlewoman who had adopted the French practice of an overuse of cosmetics, and an incredibly low-cut décolletage revealing very ample breasts. As she rose to greet Luke her stature emphasized her nick name. She was extremely tall, a height in her case unusually concentrated from the waist down.

"Welcome Colonel Tremayne, or should I use your former title of General?"

"Thank you for seeing me, Mistress Judd. My days working for the previous regime are a closed book. I am now Colonel Tremayne in the service of His Majesty."

"I know all about you colonel. Several of my men fought in the New Model when you were a colonel of horse, and others remember you as head of Cromwell's military intelligence. I believe you now have a similar role with the King—an allegedly secret unit which already strikes fear into some of my acquaintances."

"Yes, I head a small unit that carries out special missions for the King."

"And he is currently concerned with events surrounding the Portuguese embassy?"

"More specifically he is concerned to protect three English aristocrats whose name appeared on a list recovered from the body of a servant of the Portuguese embassy."

"How can I help? And what do I get in return?"

"You have two assets in this area that the authorities, including the King, lack. You have information, and you have the capability of enforcing any decisions you might make. I want to be able to utilize both your knowledge and power. My concern is the security of the state, not your criminality. Your benefit from any arrangement is that we continue to ignore your illegal activities."

"What exactly do you want to know?"

"Anything that your men pick up that threatens the security of the state, especially details of those close to the King who visit the range of foreign embassies in your area. And anything at all you discover involving the three women on the list."

"Colonel, I think we can work together. As a gesture of my goodwill which forces you to reciprocate in ignoring my crimes, I will clarify what has been happening regarding the Portuguese embassy. Poole was an agent of mine who made us aware of the persons visiting the embassy who received payments. My men then relieved these recipients of Portuguese largesse of their bounty once they left the premises, or more usually while they were at The Black Falcon. I became increasingly amazed at the amount of money the Portuguese distributed, and questioned Poole on where they kept these assets. He described a trunk in a cellar. I planned to assault the building and steal the treasure. Poole was to lead us to the trunk. He had also told us that with the return of the ambassador to Lisbon, there were few servants left in the building, and not enough to resist our onslaught. Poole lied to us. Don't waste your time investigating the recent assault on the Portuguese embassy or the deaths of Harry Foster and Ezekial Poole. They were removed for betraying my organization."

"I never heard what you just admitted, but I will reallocate my resources away from the Portuguese embassy and investigating those two murders. Have your people any information on my major focus regarding the three aristocratic women?"

"I was not aware that the list found by the Venetians had caused the government so much angst. I have not asked my people. I will and get back to you. It is almost time for a midday meal. Would you like to join me for oysters, eggs in aspic and cold roast chicken?"

Over the meal Luke listened to Jenny describe her many faceted and talented careers. She then asked as the meal drew to a close whether he had any further questions.

"Tell me all you know concerning Sir Henry Hunt?"

Luke was surprised at the answer.

"That two-timing double-dealing diplomat. I am amazed that the Venetians who leave the other foreign embassies far behind when it comes to political acumen, continue to employ him. They must know that everything they deal with is immediately reported to the English, and perhaps other governments."

"Perhaps they feed him false news to confuse our people?" suggested Luke.

"All I know is that he comes from an aristocratic background but is always very short of funds. His uncle is an earl, and he hopes to marry a wealthy heiress. He is not being paid directly from any of the other embassies, which makes him a rarity amongst English politicians and officials. I do not trust him, but my people discovered no weaknesses in his character or behavior that we could exploit."

"To blackmail?"

"Now Luke, that is not a nice word," Jenny said and smiled seductively as she filled Luke's glass.

"You found no weaknesses in Henry to attack? I thought he might have two areas you could have exploited. He is short of money, and probably receives financial help from some source that your people have failed to unearth. Secondly, he probably sees his advancement in the world is through marriage, and his attempts to achieve this may not have always been legitimate. Do you know anything about his relationship with another local identity, Lady Martha Langley?"

"Thanks for your advice on how to deal with Henry," was Jenny's sarcastic reply. "I know nothing of his relationship with the ugly duckling, other than they spend a lot of time together."

"Although it is not the main interest of my investigations this area was home to the most radical religious fanatics under the previous regime. Have you seen any signs of them planning another overt attack on the new regime?"

"There are a few Fifth Monarchy fanatics among my people, but they know they have a simple choice. If following their Lord cuts across the interests of Mistress Judd, then they are out. To eventually rule this world in the Lord's name, they must stay alive in the here and now. Working for me saves them from starvation. The biggest danger to law and order here at the moment is the number of demobilized soldiers and sailors flooding the city. The decision to allow them to enter a trade without undergoing the usual apprenticeship may help, but most will be forced into a life of crime. Already a gang of ex-soldiers have tried to take over part of my territory. Perhaps the King's troops can deal with these desperadoes. They are heavily armed and are a serious threat to the authorities."

11

"I am becoming confused. Earlier you admitted this attack was planned and controlled by yourself but the former soldiers I interviewed claimed they were recruited by an aristocratic woman."

Jenny smiled, "Look at me now! I can easily put on the airs and graces of an aristocrat to recruit a group of desperate ex-soldiers. As strangers to the area, they did not know who I was."

"But you paid them with a rare set of coins that only the Earl of Maldon had access to?"

"Probably, that earl has paid me in the past for information. I did notice the latest were very new and got rid of them as fast as possible in case the King declared them worthless."

Luke was convinced.

Jenny Judd had the ability and personality to ape the characteristics of this narrow class of English aristocratic women. She was a multi-talented woman. He thought to himself that if he wanted further information, he must ensure that her enterprises were not undermined by the newcomers.

Luke arrived back at the apartment to find Matt and Miles in deep conversation with the Earl of Greenham. Miles explained, "His lordship has come to give us further information on the disappearance of his daughter, Lady Margaret Dash. She left London where she was staying in the Langley town house with Lady Martha, after she received an invitation from Lady Elizabeth Rhodes for several days of hunting and dancing with large numbers of eligible bachelors. As you know she did not arrive."

"And does my lord have any useful information that we can work on?" asked Luke directly of Randolph.

"Yes, but it is confusing. I visited the Langley town house in search of my daughter and was told that both my daughter and Martha had left for what the servant assumed was a trip west in answer to Elizabeth's invitation. The household was somewhat alarmed to hear that neither woman had arrived. They had not heard from their mistress since her departure."

"That confirms our worst fears—but is hardly confusing," replied Luke. "What is confusing is that they left in a coach and were accompanied by a gentleman who was well known to the Langley household—my own nephew, Sir Henry Hunt. While I am at Dartside putting his case as a suitor to Lady Elizabeth, he disappears with two other women, his cousin Margaret and Martha Langley. Do you know much about this Martha, colonel?"

"Yes, quite a lot. Your nephew has been a long-time friend of Martha and her deceased sister Dinah. Martha is also an extremely wealthy heiress—to a sugar planting fortune—but she is no beauty," answered Luke.

"But why has he disappeared with my daughter without either of them informing me?"

"He could have taken it upon himself to protect one of the women on the list?" suggested Luke.

"What experience has he had. Nothing like that which I, or the King through you can provide?"

"Has he really disappeared? The Venetian embassy should know where he is," suggested Miles.

"They would tell me nothing, except that he was currently out of London on embassy business. You, using Royal authority, may be able to elicit more," Randolph appealed to Luke.

Luke tried. He met the Venetian ambassador the following morning. It was a frosty encounter. "And what does a special agent of the King, who had a record of anti-Venetian activity in the Mediterranean under a previous regime, require of the Serene Republic?" demanded the diplomat undiplomatically.

"Your gesture in passing on to the English government a list found by one of your employees has created a crisis which I have been ordered to solve. Two of the three women on that list have now disappeared, and the King fears for their safety."

"Why come back here? You discussed these matters at length several days ago with Sir Henry," continued the unsympathetic envoy.

"The Earl of Greenham was here seeking to find his daughter, Lady Margaret Dash, as it is believed she disappeared in the company of that very official. The earl indicated that you were far from helpful."

"Quite true, Colonel. Greenham has no standing with your government, and as a Catholic peer, even his membership of the House of Lords was in doubt until the last week or so. He is known to have very close ties to the Spanish government. It was not in Venice's interests to divulge any information regarding its activities to an English peer with pro-Spanish proclivities at this time of international tension and government instability."

"Let me formalize my request. The King, believing that Sir Henry Hunt may have abducted his cousin and another woman, needs to locate the said gentleman in regard to this matter. Where is he?"

"As a member of my staff, Henry has diplomatic immunity and any attempt to detain him would be taken as an insult to the Venetian Republic."

"And any attempt to protect him from English justice should he prove guilty of a major crime, would be a serious breach in our relationship, and may lead to demands for your removal. Note the fate of the French resident—the King simply refuses to meet with him, so the French government has been forced to remove him. As the King is considering the deployment of our Mediterranean fleet, this would be a dangerous time for Venice not to be represented at his Court."

"I can see why the King chose to employ you, rather than have you executed for your activities under Cromwell. All I know is that Henry volunteered two or three days ago to carry urgent documents, which I did not want to entrust to the normal diplomatic courier to my counterpart in Paris. He should have gone alone, but maybe he travelled with the women you mentioned, but I expect him back within the next three days."

As expected, Henry returned to the Venetian embassy where Luke was waiting to interrogate him. "Of the three names on the list, two have disappeared and we have been unable to contact the third. Martha's staff told me that you had visited her ladyship and Margaret Dash, after which all three of you departed for places unknown. Your ambassador told me you had gone to France. Where are the two women?"

"I did not lead them anywhere, and I was not the instigator of their move to France. I visited Martha, and found Margaret there confronting a dilemma. She was about to leave for Dartside Hall to be with her friend Elizabeth Rhodes but had received a late message claiming to be from Elizabeth suggesting they meet instead in France—although she did not reveal the exact location. I offered to accompany them to Paris where I left both of them. Margaret gave no indication of where, or why she was meeting up with Elizabeth."

"Have you told your uncle where his daughter has gone?"

"No, I have just returned."

"Did you pick up anything that might indicate Margaret's motives in fleeing the country? It seems that she left of her own free will and has not been abducted."

"Margaret is alarmed that her name is on the list. She does not believe your investigation would solve the problem, having no faith in the authorities in England to protect her or her friends. In addition, she does not trust her father. Both Elizabeth and Margaret feel safer abroad—perhaps with a family they knew during their period in exile. They were both in France before moving with the court to Flanders."

"Elizabeth disappeared after she received a message from someone at Whitehall, did Margaret hint at the source of her information?"

"No."

"What role does Martha play in all this? Is she just a good friend providing company, or is she a major player in whatever is afoot?"

"I have been a friend of Martha's for years. She now carries a lot of guilt over the death of her sister thanks to yourself, and also appears to have little time for her own father. Maybe she believes that the fathers of the two women are not to be trusted, and having failed her sister, she is determined to save Margaret and Elizabeth from impending disaster."

"With the help of someone in Whitehall?"

"Probably the King himself? He is in an ideal position to arrange a safe retreat somewhere in France, and the French government is desperate to mend bridges with the Royalist regime," suggested Henry.

"The King does have a reputation to set two operations regarding the same issue underway at the same time, without letting either party know of the other. On the one hand he has me investigating the list and its consequences while moving the women involved to a safe house in France. It's a possibility. I will ask him."

Luke reported to the King, whose expression of alarm was explained by his announcement that he had not communicated personally with any of the women—except Elizabeth.

He confessed.

He had sent one of his courtiers west to facilitate her move to Paris, but he knew nothing of Margaret and Martha's movements. He would have his representatives in Paris attempt to track them down.

He cut short Luke's attempt to probe royal intervention regarding Elizabeth by ordering him to locate the third woman, Lady Agatha Craven, as a matter of urgency—and immediately closing the meeting.

Agatha's father was currently attending the House of Lords, where Luke located him, just before he entered the chamber.

Viscount Craven was relaxed—perhaps too much so. Yes, he had heard that his daughter's name was on a list that the government had recovered from a murdered servant. No, he had not heard that the King was very anxious for the safety of the women listed. He had not spoken to his daughter since being made aware of the situation. She was staying with her mother on one of their Suffolk properties. She had not been in the best of health since her return from a holiday in Italy. No, he had no idea why his daughter would be on a list, but his wife might.

Craven Castle was a misnomer. It was not even a fortified manor house. It was a striking Elizabethan mansion located on an excuse for a hill that was just elevated above the surrounding water lands. Luke took his wife Matilda with him, as he had been informed that Arabella Craven was a strange combination of being formidable, and at times away with the fairies—also a woman who was more likely to confide in a female than in a man.

Luke and Matilda were accompanied by five dragoons from a household regiment.

Arabella was immediately on the attack. "Good sir, why has the King sent an envoy into deepest Suffolk to talk to me, accompanied by his wife and armed troopers?"

"The King is concerned about your daughter. Has she raised any serious issues with you over the last few months?"

"Apart from her desire to travel across England to distant Cornwall, unaccompanied except for a few servants, which I stopped—no."

"Why did you stop it? asked Luke bluntly.

12

Arabella replied, "I have seen very little of Agatha in the last six months. She did not return here immediately from Flanders but went on a tour of Italy with a friend before coming home. She regularly joins her father for frequent visits up to London on his ship which he named after her. That girl must settle down. Unfortunately, she is determined to impress her father by trying to be the son we never had."

"Who was the friend who went to Italy with her?" asked Matilda.

"That poor girl who was murdered, Dinah Langley."

Luke noted this connection but was not immediately diverted from his main concern. "We are here because the King is worried about three aristocratic women whose names appeared on a list found on the body of a murder victim."

Luke carefully explained the list, and the reasons for the King's concern. "This list may not indicate any potential harm to the women, but as the two others on the list have fled to France, His Majesty sent us here to check on the wellbeing of Lady Agatha."

"I would not be too concerned about Elizabeth Rhodes and Margaret Dash. They are both strong willed women as is Agatha and they would do anything to escape the control of their domineering fathers, especially now that they are ready to be married. Both are extremely wealthy heiresses whose husbands would become some of the richest and most powerful men in Britain," was Arabella's surprising comment.

"We cannot ignore the list completely," said Matilda. "Why do you think those three particular names were on it. What did the three women have in common? There are rumors circulating that they were the three most eligible English Catholic brides for the King should machinations for a foreign princess fail."

Arabella breathed heavily, "They certainly have relevant assets in common for a Royal marriage—they're aristocratic, they are Catholic, and they are known to the King. But why would they be on a list from the Portuguese embassy? Their fathers all support Spain's determination to destroy Portuguese independence, unless the Portuguese......."

Arabella stopped in mid- sentence overwhelmed by a frightful possible explanation.

Matilda confirmed her thinking, "Yes, they are on the list for one of two opposed reasons. Either they are candidates the Portuguese could support if their Infanta was not successful, or they are potential rivals to the Portuguese Infanta that might gain support from Catholic France and Spain."

Arabella sighed again. "The King worries unnecessarily, unless he does want one of those women as his wife. Their experience in exile convinced them all that life at Court was not for them, and apart from Elizabeth who made it clear to the King that marriage must precede any sexual dalliance, Margaret and Agatha were closer to James, Duke of York than they were to Charles. As his marriage to Lady Anne Hyde has just been revealed, any further link in that quarter is finished—although with those Stuart brothers you can never be sure. All three women had other close male friends during their period in exile. Maybe they have disappeared to renew old acquaintances, as not all of the Royalist exiles have yet returned to England. Many remain in the employ of the French, the Spaniards or the Dutch."

"Are you suggesting that one or more of these women will involve themselves with a particular male to thwart the marriage plans of their fathers? Aristocratic heiresses do not usually successfully obstruct the plans of powerful fathers," was Luke's pompous comment.

"I do not know what the Earls of Maldon and Greenham have in mind for their daughters, but the little I pick up from Agatha suggests these women are not happy with what they anticipate will occur."

"Has Agatha confided in you her own concerns regarding marriage?" asked Matilda.

"No, my husband has not yet taken any steps to find her a suitable spouse. He does not want to lose his righthand 'man'. A clandestine marriage is not the only way Elizabeth and Margaret could thwart their fathers. In the early days of exile the three women concerned, although little more than schoolgirls, made a pact that should life not be going the way they desired, they would escape their domestic situation, and seek sanctuary in a convent—they would become nuns."

"That would be more difficult to achieve than a clandestine marriage," stated Luke. "No convent would accept such women without the large dowry, usually provided by aristocratic fathers, which in these cases would not be forthcoming. None of these peers would endanger their title and estates by permitting such a development unless the women renounced their rights of succession. Running away to join a convent is certainly an explanation I had not considered. Is it possible to speak to Agatha?"

"Certainly!" Lady Arabella spoke to a servant who immediately left the room. She returned a few minutes later in an agitated state.

Arabella explained. "The silly girl has gone off on her own and was last seen punting over the barely inundated water lands."

"Did she give the servants any indication as to why she had done this?"

"Yes, that is why I called her a silly girl. I do not know what the other women have told her about your interventions on behalf of the King, but she was frightened of you, and has disappeared apparently until you have gone. Why she does not want to be questioned by you, now worries me."

"What's the role of punting in this area? I thought the channels around these waterlands were dominated by fast skiffs or multi rowed fishing boats."

"That is correct. The estate has a few small barges that can be punted along the edge of the channels at low tide or across most of the scarcely inundated water lands at high tide. It would be impossible to punt in the main channels and rivers."

"So where would Agatha be heading?"

"Without servants or luggage, I dread to contemplate, especially when warnings of imminent smuggling activity have been evident."

"What do you mean?" asked Luke.

"You would not have been aware of its significance, but ever since you entered the waterlands all of the windmills have ceased working. The sails have all been stopped in a position where they reflect the diagonal cross of St Andrew. This is a warning to the smugglers that the authorities are active in the area and to hold back on any activity until the sails change to a cross of St George. The sight of an officer and several dragoons would have alarmed the smugglers. They would have assumed that you were in the area to deal with them, having been sent by the revenue officers based at Ipswich. These waterlands can be dangerous places with marauding gangs of brutal smugglers on the loose. And your few men would have little chance in any major confrontation."

"And do the authorities ever send troops to control the situation?"

"Yes, only yesterday a dragoon officer and five or six militia men, all in civilian clothes arrived from Ipswich, ready to lie in wait for the imminent smuggling operation. I expect that officer is now complaining that your arrival has alerted the smugglers to a government intervention—red coated royal troops are not often seen hereabouts."

"I will follow Lady Agatha. Is there another barge I can use?" Luke asked.

"No need, the tide is out for some time. Horses can manage most of the shallow channels around here."

"Has her ladyship any favorite haunts that she might escape to?"

"Climb our tower, you can see for miles. There is nothing but flat shallow waterlands lands dissected by deeper channels. You will be able to see Agatha. She only left here a few minutes ago."

Luke climbed the tower, and saw a female figure punting leisurely along the edge of one of the channels. She was not putting much effort into the activity, relying on the receding tide to pull her towards the sea.

He also noticed at the entrance to the channel on which Agatha punted were two relatively large skiffs, vessels more common on the Norfolk Broads. On the slightly elevated peninsula that protected the entrance to the channel, he saw seven or eight carts. Agatha was heading straight into the middle of a smuggling operation.

Luke reentered the reception room and informed Arabella and Matilda that he had sighted Agatha and would immediately ride after her.

He would not alarm the women by mentioning the smugglers.

Luke's unit was about to leave Craven Castle when six or seven horsemen galloped along what amounted to a causeway and their leader announced himself, "Caleb Nicholas, Lieutenant of Dragoons attached to the revenue officers in Ipswich. My group of local militias have had word of a smuggling operation which we believe was scheduled for yesterday but delayed because of your presence in the area. I recognize the uniform of the King's Household cavalry. What brings royal troops into our area? Surely not to assist us lowly revenue officers?"

"Colonel Luke Tremayne, commanding a special Royal detachment. We are here to talk to Lady Agatha Craven whom we are just about to apprehend. From the tower I saw two skiffs unloading goods at the sea entrance to this channel. My quarry is heading straight into the midst of these smugglers. We must join forces and rescue Lady Agatha—and my men can help you deal with the smugglers."

As the joint group of horsemen rode towards the receding Agatha, they and the smugglers had a good view of each other. To Luke's dismay a couple of horsemen left the area of the carts, galloped along the channel's edge, dismounted, and dragged Agatha from her barge.

Caleb was furious, "Damn, they will use that woman as a bargaining chip."

Luke was also alarmed, "That woman is a close friend of the King's. I must get her back."

"Have you done a rough count? There are probably over a hundred men and a few women engaged in this smuggling enterprise. We are fourteen."

"Are they armed with muskets? If not, we may still have the upper hand."

As if directed by an all-knowing power, a volley of musket fire emanated from the tip of the peninsula in the direction of the oncoming troops and militia.

"There is your answer," exclaimed Caleb.

"We are still too far away to be within range, but it is clearly a warning that we should stop advancing. What do you know about this group of smugglers?"

"A lot. It is based here and is popular with all classes. The gentry enjoy their brandy, whisky and French wines, fine laces and spices while the poorer sort have their gin, tobacco and cheap clothes. Its current leader is a wiry Irishman, Gilbert Anthony known to all as The Turk because of the oversized scimitar he always wields."

Luke announced, "Caleb, this is where our joint mission comes to an end. With my men, in addition to yours, you can contain the carts where they are until help arrives. Spread your men across the narrowest part of the peninsula where a few men can hold off ten times their number. Send one of your men for reinforcements, and then you can advance onto their temporary stronghold. Unfortunately, I have few options. My aim is to rescue Lady Agatha and that can only be done by negotiation. Wish me luck! Move the men out of the shallows and prepare a blockade across the peninsula."

"I think the Turk anticipates such a move. One of the skiffs with many armed men has left its anchorage and is sailing towards us. It will provide another angle of fire into our proposed blockade."

13

Caleb led the men ashore to organize their blockade. Luke dismounted, and leading his horse and waving with his free hand, moved towards the smugglers. He was nervous. Any one of dozens of men could kill him with a single shot. As he came closer to the smuggler's embarkation site, a small wiry man emerged from the flurry of activity. He shouted at Luke, "Identify yourself!"

Luke responded, but with caution. He must not reveal anything that might endanger Agatha's position. He lied.

"I am Sir Luke Tremayne, a junior officer attached to the Royal Household delivering an urgent message from the Viscount Craven to his wife. During my visit Lady Agatha wandered off, and her mother asked if I could bring her home. Early in my pursuit of her ladyship, I met the revenue officers determined to curtail your activities."

The Turk smiled, "A pack of lies! The King does not use his Household troops to deliver messages to a Suffolk family that I know are not part of the King's inner circle."

"Believe what you like, but in essence I am not interested in your smuggling activities. All I seek is to return Lady Agatha to her mother."

"Sir Luke, the more you talk the more I disbelieve you. Why would an officer of the Royal Household walk into my area of operation with no defense? Her ladyship for some reason is far more important to the King than you would want me to believe. Some local friends might suggest that I release Lady Agatha, as her father has turned a blind eye to our activities for decades. In fact, one of the carts on the peninsula is already laden with goods for Craven Castle. Perhaps Lady Agatha has simply come to collect it?"

"Then hand her over to me, and I am sure the Viscount's blindness will continue well into the future."

"Don't take me for a fool. Possession of his daughter may gain me further concessions. However, I am willing to forego any such possible advantages, if you have the revenue men withdraw, and allow my carts to distribute the goods across the county."

"I am in no position to direct Lieutenant Nicholas in his mission against you."

"Rubbish, whatever your rank, an officer in the Household cavalry must surely be superior to a regional dragoon seconded to the Treasury. Order him to withdraw!"

"Or else!"

"Don't play games. I have only to brush my forehead and fifty muskets will cut you down. But I am a man of honor. You came to talk; we have achieved nothing. You may safely withdraw."

"That I cannot do. As a man of honor, myself, I must ask to accompany Lady Agatha as your prisoner."

The Turk chuckled. "Your very request suggests that my prisoner is indeed important." He signaled for his men to approach, and Luke handed over his weapons, and was led away onto the peninsula.

"When can I see Lady Agatha? he asked.

"As you can see the two skiffs that were unloading goods have left their anchorage. One has moved upstream to harass the excise officer and his men, the other is putting out to sea to transfer Lady Agatha to my modified fishing trawler moored to the north in a more secluded estuary. You and I will be taken there when the skiff returns."

"How long do you intend to detain her ladyship and myself?"

"Until I discover what is really happening."

"And how will you do that?" asked a cynical Luke.

"I have already sent one of my men to Craven Castle to question his sweetheart, a maid there, as to the reasons for your visit and the flight of Lady Agatha. After he completes his task, he will report directly to me on board the trawler."

"So, you are deserting your men on the peninsula to their fate? Niggled Luke.

"Why do you constantly attribute the foulest of motives to me? I will protect my men to the last—and I will not lose a single man."

"Then why move to your fishing trawler well away from the imminent assault on your men here?"

"I am beginning to think you are not the brightest of officers, Sir Luke. The excise officer has undoubtedly sent to Ipswich for reinforcements. They will not arrive until well after dark, perhaps not until tomorrow morning. As soon as it is dark, local barges will land on the opposite side of the peninsula and most of the goods will be unloaded from the carts and placed on them. The horses will be removed from the carts and loaded with the rest of the goods and they will make their way across the water lands unseen by the revenue officers. By the time revenue mounts its offensive in the morning, there will be no goods and no smugglers to be found. All they will find will be eight or nine empty carts."

A chastened Luke sat between two of the Turk's men awaiting the return of the skiff.

It was late evening when Luke and the Turk boarded the latter's fishing trawler—a trawler that had not seen fish in its hold for years. It was a vessel used to smuggle goods from the continent and ocean-going ships that it met in the Channel.

Luke's asked again to see Lady Agatha. The Turk remained courteous. "Come Sir Luke, none of us have eaten. You and Lady Agatha will join me in my cabin for a late supper in about an hour. Until then I must lock you in part of the hold, that has just recently been emptied of the most expensive French brandy."

Luke had no trouble filling in the hour. He fell asleep. He had to awakened by one of the Turk's men gently kicking him. He was led to the master's cabin where the Turk and a diminutive but attractive young woman were already seated around a circular table.

Luke was aware that Agatha was observing him closely, and that the Turk was watching them both for any give away body language. Luke recognized that the Turk was a formidable opponent.

And he was pedantically formal. "Lady Agatha, this is Sir Luke Tremayne, from the King's Household cavalry who has been sent by your mother to rescue you from my grasp."

Both of Luke's companions smiled, which disconcerted him.

The Turk continued, "He has lied to me consistently, so I am holding both of you as my guests until I discover why a royal official is concerned with your welfare—and why you ran away on his arrival."

Luke was surprised at the spiritous response from Agatha, "I did not run away. Mother and I had had an argument concerning my planned trip to Cornwall, which she stopped for no acceptable reason. Sensing she would be busy talking to this officer who I saw coming across the water lands with a body of troops, I decided to escape for a while. Mother need not have sent this man after me. Punting along the shallows is a regular past time of mine."

"But punting into the middle of a smuggling operation is not," countered Luke. "This is what provoked your mother into sending me after you."

Again, his two companions smiled. What did they know that he didn't?

"Let us not argue. Let's enjoy this meal, enhanced by many of the luxury goods I have imported. If my man who has been visiting Craven Castle returns with no incriminating information, I will release you both in the morning," the Turk quietly announced.

When Luke awoke next morning, he was immediately aware that the trawler had left its anchorage and was battling its way up or down the Channel. He was surprised that the door of the hatch in which he had slept was unlocked. He made his way on deck and spied the Turk at the helm of the laboring vessel.

He explained to Luke, "An unexpected departure! Before first light a warning beacon was sighted indicating that a revenue cutter was making its way from the south, no doubt intent on keeping us contained within the estuary. I was therefore forced to sail north against both the wind and the prevailing tides."

"And where are we heading?"

"I was due to collect cargo at Dunkirk the day after tomorrow. We will arrive there a day early despite this enforced detour."

"Will you release Lady Agatha and myself when we land? It is currently under English military control."

"Not likely—unless you and her ladyship can give me answers that would suggest my continued possession of her ladyship is not to my advantage."

"What do you mean?"

"My man who was sent to Craven Castle returned last night with the most intriguing story. You are Colonel Luke Tremayne of the King's special intelligence unit. This sailor's sweetheart is the Viscountess Arabella's personal maid. She was present all of the time that you talked to her mistress. Lady Agatha's name appeared on a list found on the murdered body of a servant of a foreign embassy, and the King is so alarmed about her safety that you were sent to assess her situation. Has her father been told?"

"Yes, but he gave the impression he felt she was perfectly safe at Craven Castle. That is what I am really investigating."

"Why lie? The real situation is much worse than the rubbish you told me yesterday!"

"I had no intention of putting Agatha into any greater danger than she already may be in."

"Why Colonel is the King so interested? My man's sweetheart believes it is because he wishes to marry the girl. Do I have as my prisoner the future Queen of England?"

Again, the Turk gave the growingly irritating smile.

"If only it was that simple. The King's anxiety, and my mission are based on two simple facts. We do not know why three particular women are on that list, and even more frustrating we do not know whether that list is of no importance, critical only to the future of those women, or so vital that it could undermine the security of the state. In essence, I do not know why the names are on that list, or even if the list is important."

"And what is Lady Agatha's explanation of it?" asked the Turk.

"I do not know. The only time I have seen Lady Agatha or spoken to her was in your presence last night."

"And I gathered she was not over enthusiastic about discussing anything with you. I will get my boatswain to take over the helm and you can question her ladyship in my presence. Both your freedoms may depend on her answers."

Luke explained to Lady Agatha that their freedom depended on her answers satisfying the Turk. "Why do you think that your name is on that list?" Luke asked.

"It has nothing to do with national security, so the King need not have become involved," was her spirited reply.

"I think the King is as much concerned with your safety, as with the interests of the state," Luke responded.

"If that list appeared years ago when all three of us were at the court in exile, it would have been meaningful. Elizabeth was very close to the King, even refusing to respond to his sexual advances unless he married her, and I was in a similar position with his brother James, the Duke of York. Such closeness lasted only a few weeks, and neither of us became a mistress of either royal brother. They both moved on to tempting Margaret, who I believe gave a similar response. We quickly realized that life at court, should the King ever return to England, was not for us. We made a pact."

"Involving what?"

"We would not commit ourselves to any man, without all three of us agreeing that he was suitable."

"Have you kept to that agreement? Elizabeth and Margaret have disappeared with the aid of males who are very close to them."

"I know."

"Who are these males? Why have Elizabeth and Margaret disappeared? Why have they gone to the Continent?" asked Luke, not expecting an answer. "Elizabeth has a long-standing lover, and Margaret may have fallen for a close relative. Both need to escape the tyranny of their fathers, although they both realize that unless they do something extremely stupid, the will of their father's regarding their marriages will probably prevail."

"And your situation, my lady?" asked the Turk with obvious concern.

"Unlike the situation with Elizabeth and Margaret, my father has not begun negotiations over my marriage. Given what is happening to the other two women, and the death of our friend Dinah Langley, I may seek two or three years in a convent on the continent. The life of nun would be better than an unhappy marriage. Father's title and lands would go to a cousin."

Luke seemed to detect a tear running down Agatha's face and a look of overwhelming melancholy suddenly descended.

She then claimed she felt ill and hurriedly left the cabin.

14

hen Agatha later returned Luke resumed his questioning. "Are any of the three women going to abide by the pact against the pressure from fathers and lovers? Or is it just a girlhood fantasy?"

"It is more than a fantasy. If none of their lovers meet the approval of the other two women, they are likely to renounce all men, and enter a convent, as I am about to do for a short time at least."

"Ridiculous!" commented the Turk. "Your ladyship is not the religious type."

"Do you know which men are currently involved with Elizabeth and Margaret?" probed Luke.

Agatha laughed, "Yes, as do you. Elizabeth is besotted by your own deputy Mark Cowper, while Margaret is playing with fire with her older cousin, Henry Hunt."

Luke was surprised. Mark had admitted that he knew the women from his days at the court in exile, but not of any deep relationship with any of them.

"All this may be true my lady, but it does not remove a threat to your own safety. Persons with access to that list may see all three of you as ideal for kidnapping and being held for ransom. The wealth and status of your families would bring a high price."

"Indeed, it would! chuckled the Turk. He turned to Luke and commiserated, "You have an impossible task, colonel. Any enterprising man with a vivid imagination, who heard that there were three names on a list, obtained in strange circumstances, and involving three very wealthy women would see great advantages in getting control of one or more of these women, and negotiating a financial settlement. I am surprised that these women have not already been abducted."

"Perhaps they have," admitted Luke. Is the move of Elizabeth and Margaret to the continent assisted by their lovers to keep them safe, or was it a coordinated covert abduction?"

The Turk and Lady Agatha were stunned into silence.

The Turk eventually changed the subject, "Colonel, I have to bring this discussion to an end. Given the increasingly difficult weather, I have to confine you to the forward hold. I need all hands to man the boat, not to guard you."

As the swell increased, Luke found some solace within the hold as he imagined those on deck would be finding it difficult. He would not have been quite so content if he had known what was transpired in the captain's cabin after he left.

The Turk addressed Agatha in a paternal tone. "How are we going to get rid of your limpet-like Royal appointed protector without arousing suspicion?"

"Mother probably did not ask him to follow me. She had only just given me the latest instructions from father to pass onto you. You have operated with him, and on his land for two decades, and I have just resumed my role as his courier, as I was for years during my teens. Now that I am back in England, I hope to see you more often, and benefit personally from the luxury goods you continue to import. Father's latest list is of the goods that he suggests you obtain, and letters of introduction to several new sources. It should keep you busy for some time. By the time you return to our lands this Royal busy body will be well gone."

"I am not sure. He is senior officer of the King who is clearly alarmed that your name is on a list. Why are you really on that list? There must be a reason, that you may not want to divulge to the King's man."

"I do not know, but a possibility which I will not mention to Colonel Tremayne is one that might endanger father—a situation that you also would not wish to occur."

"And what is that?"

"What is it that the fathers of the three women on that list have in common—a situation increasingly uncommon among the political class, since the King's return to England?"

"Tell me! I know nothing of the other fathers."

"They are the three most overtly pro-Spanish aristocrats in England. During the Protectorate you know full well that father with your help prepared our local area to receive Spanish invasion forces that ultimately went elsewhere with no success. The fathers of the other women, the Earls of Greenham and Maldon were the agents during the King's exile that received Spanish money to be transferred to the King. Father is concerned that the King will turn his back on Spain and favor her new arch enemy Portugal. According to father there are already politicians suggesting anybody who continues to favor Spain should be tried as a traitor."

The Turk decided not to explain to Agatha the real nature of their invasion mission. He returned to the list.

"So, this is list compiled by the Portuguese of the heiresses to the three English families, they can least trust? If your views are correct, then the colonel is right. You are in danger of abduction or worse—by agents of the Portuguese."

"Perhaps that is why my two friends have fled to France?"

"Do you wish to join them? I can put into any port you wish?"

"Yes, but I can't. I have nothing with me, but the clothes I am wearing, and father needs to be kept informed of developments."

The Turk thought for some time. "My lady I will drop you and the Colonel off in Dunkirk, which is currently under English occupation. I will explain to him that I operate in the water lands of eastern England with the connivance of local landlords. Friendly relations with Viscount Craven is more valuable to me than any ransom money, I might be able be obtain."

Luke slept. When he awoke it was morning and the boat had docked. A crewman opened the doors of the forward hatch and escorted him to the captain's cabin for something to eat. Agatha was not there but the Turk's cordial reception disconcerted him.

The Turk immediately put him at ease. "Colonel, I have decided to release both Lady Agatha and yourself. I accept that the return of Agatha to her mother is your prime consideration, and my free trading activities are not your concern. My activities depend very much on the good will of the local aristocrats of which Lady Agatha's father is one. His continued support is more valuable to me than any ransom money. In case you have not recognized where we are, it is Dunkirk. I have already informed the English governor that I rescued one of the King's leading officers, and an English heiress from a sinking vessel. He will send a coach at ten to take you both to his residence."

Within two days Luke and Agatha were back in England. Agatha joined her father in Westminster, and Luke prepared a report for his unit and the King. He remained uneasy but could not clearly articulate the problem.

Luke spent his first two days back in London with his wife. Matilda had been informed by the soldiers who returned from Suffolk that Luke had been captured by smugglers and was missing when they captured the gang's deserted positions. She spent a couple of anxious days, not knowing where Luke was, or even if he was still alive.

On the third day after his return, he met the King with his report on his dealings with the Cravens.

Luke was relieved of one concern with Charles's immediate confession. "I took steps unbeknown to you to rescue Lady Elizabeth from any possible harm. While you visited Dartside to understand what may be going on, I sent Mark, who has a close relationship with Elizabeth in the past, ahead of you to take Elizabeth to Plymouth from whence to embark for a safe house I have retained in Paris. I know where she is, but I will not tell Mark nor yourself."

"Did Elizabeth know where she was going?"

"No."

"And did you also relocate Margaret Dash?"

The King looked alarmed. "No, why do you ask?"

"Lady Margaret, disappeared apparently into France aided by your man in the Venetian embassy, Sir Henry Hunt."

"That is disturbing! Elizabeth and Mark are close, and I was very close to Elizabeth. I felt I had a duty to protect her. Margaret was more my brother's concern. What game is Henry playing? His uncle apparently sounded out Elizabeth and her father regarding a possible marriage between Elizabeth and Henry, but Maldon would not consider a betrothal to anyone of mere gentry status. If either Mark or Henry are to have any hope of success, I will have to elevate them to the aristocracy. What is Henry's precise relationship with his cousin Margaret?"

"According to Lady Agatha, he is besotted with her."

"Find out exactly what Henry is up to, and I will deal with him. If he is a problem here, I will send him to Venice as my ambassador and remove him from the picture."

After Luke and the King discussed the Cravens the former commented, "Sire, you show less concern regarding Lady Agatha, while I believe Viscount Craven may provide the greater security threat to you, than the Earls of Maldon and Greenham."

"Although you have combined the issues raised by the discovery of the list, the security of my person and the state, and the well-being of the three women, they are separate. I feel a degree of declining responsibility from Elizabeth through Margaret to Agatha, yet my concern regarding the threat to my throne is in reverse order. The Earls are less of a threat than Lord Craven. Your report confirms some of my fears."

"And what are they?"

"As you know over the past few years, because you thwarted many of them, Spain had a myriad of plans to invade England on my behalf."

"Yes, we were well prepared for intrusions along the major waterways of Kent, Essex and Suffolk from the Medway to the Stour."

"Exactly, you expected a Spanish fleet to attempt the major waterways of the Medway, the Thames, or the Stour, but the Spanish authorities in the Netherlands had on their payroll a smuggler, the man you know as the Turk. He supposedly acted under orders from Viscount Craven. Craven or the Turk suggested an invasion by smaller boats up lesser-known waterways that the fleet of the English republic could not sail."

"Did you support such a scheme?"

"At the time I was aware of a major incursion proposed for the Medway, but the scheme to use the waterways of the Craven estate was not passed on to me. The Medway plan came from Madrid, whereas the Craven scheme was hatched by the Spanish authorities in the Netherlands. The Brussel authorities and I fell out in the year before my return from exile, and they began to act without reference to me."

"Did the Turk lead a flotilla of smaller Spanish ships into the waterways of Essex and Suffolk?"

"No."

"Why was the plan never executed?"

"I do not know. The Earl of Maldon who retained close relationships with the Brussel as well as the Madrid authorities believes that the latter overruled the former and cancelled the project on the grounds that both the Turk and Craven were unreliable—probably double agents."

"As former head of military intelligence, and at the front of the Cromwellian defense of our Kent and East Anglia waterways at the time, they were not Cromwellian agents."

"Double check with the Cromwell's spymaster general, John Thurloe, who has a tiny office here in Whitehall helping the Lord Chancellor create a similar organization for myself. Maldon says the Spaniards feared that Craven and the Turk were double agents for either France or Portugal."

As Luke bowed and left the room the King called after him. "And probe Henry's behavior more deeply!"

On returning to his headquarters, Luke was immediately accosted by Mark who began to spurt out a confession of his activities on behalf of the King.

Luke stopped him mid-sentence, "Relax Mark, His Majesty has explained what you did."

Mark responded, "The basics of the King's interpretation is true but some of the detail is skewed. He knows my feelings towards Elizabeth and that I would do anything to protect her. He also knows that I would do anything for him, as any hope of Elizabeth and I marrying, depends on me being elevated to the peerage. What he neglected to say is something he revealed to me after a night of heavy drinking before he returned to England."

"Which is?"

"If the intrigues of high politics failed to deliver him a suitable bride, he would take an English wife, and his first choice would be Lady Elizabeth. The recent marriage of his brother to an English gentlewoman may have renewed such an idea in his mind."

"The King has often said his government would be a mixture of the transparent and the devious—and we operate the devious aspect of it. The King's contradictory behavior, and disregard for the truth, is a factor we must become accustomed to," responded Luke.

15

Luke revisited the Venetian embassy and was soon in conversation with the ambassador. "Your excellency, I am here to inform you on behalf of the King that Henry Hunt no longer has the confidence of His Majesty, and therefore is no longer in a position to advance your interests at the English court. He should be replaced immediately. May I speak to him, and if necessary, escort him from the premises?"

"You mean arrest him?" "If necessary."

"Of what crime is he guilty?"

"He is suspected of inappropriate involvement with several women who are under the personal protection of the King."

The Venetian smiled, "Your King is almost an Italian in his attitude and behavior towards women. Henry must have been very foolish."

"Most dangerously of all—more obsessed than foolish."

"I thought you had come to explain Henry's renewed absence. I cannot hand him over to you. He has disappeared again."

"Has he sent you an explanation for this absence?"

"No."

Luke left the embassy frustrated. Where was Henry?

Normally he would visit Henry's long-term friend and near neighbor, Lady Martha Langley, but the last information he had of her was that she had gone with Margaret to the continent. Maybe her servants knew of her current whereabouts?

He was surprised when Martha's servant assumed that he wished to speak to his mistress and led Luke into her reception room.

Luke exclaimed, "I thought you were in France with Lady Margaret Dash. I came here hoping that your servants knew the whereabouts of Sir Henry."

"Henry returned from France, days before me. Is he not at his lodgings beside the Venetian embassy?"

"No, and he has not been seen for a day or to. Did he indicate to you that he would be away?"

"No, I have only just returned from France, and not seen Henry since he left Margaret and I at the Venetian embassy in Paris."

"So, Margaret is not with Lady Elizabeth in Paris?"

"Margaret expected Elizabeth to contact her to achieve this, but she had heard nothing from Elizabeth since the message from Dartside suggesting she move to France rather than visit her there."

"Does Elizabeth know that Margaret is at the Venetian embassy?"

"I assumed that Henry or the King will relay that vital information to one or both of them."

"Not possible. Only the King knows where Elizabeth is located, and he has told no one at court. Neither Mark nor I are privy to that information. The King is totally unaware of Henry's expedition with you and Lady Margaret, and I am sure that the Venetian embassy in London is not aware that Margaret is in their Paris residency."

Luke left Martha and returned to Whitehall where he sought out his old comrade, Cromwell's spymaster general, John Thurloe.

Thurloe occupied a small attic room not far from the Lord Chancellor's apartment. He was pleased to see Luke and commented, "Only this lackadaisical government would allow two leading intelligence officers of a preceding and antagonist government to meet alone within yards of the King's quarters. The King must trust you implicitly."

"No, I think it is recognition of the simple fact that any threat to the King will not come from agents of the previous regime, apart from a few religious fanatics. It tore itself apart after Cromwell's death, and any possible leaders of a resurgent republican or Cromwellian coup have been cleverly incorporated into the new Royalist regime, including both of us."

"To what do I owe this visit?"

"During you time as Cromwell's intelligence chief did Viscount Craven from Suffolk, or a smuggler The Turk ever come to your attention?"

"Come Luke, I do not remember all of the countless issues I had to deal with. I cannot refer back to the documentary evidence because when I was removed as spymaster general by the last republican regime, I was careful to burn most of the documents I had accumulated over several years."

Luke smiled, "I don't believe you John. I know the way your mind worked. You would have retained all the evidence that you could, in case it came in handy in the future. Your life might have depended on what you knew about leading Royalists. The fact that the King saved your life and appointed you as assistant to the Lord Chancellor in developing a royal network of agents is probably related to what you know about leading officers of the new government."

It was Thurloe's turn to smile, "Still able to read your opponents, Luke! Give me a couple of days. I will see what my non-existent documents reveal."

"Thanks John. And how is your creation of a royal network of agents proceeding?"

"Very slowly, but I have put in place a network whereby the entry and exit of leading foreigners can be monitored. The Governors of Dover Castle, Plymouth and Dunkirk are reporting almost daily the movements of foreign diplomats as those nations compete for the King's favor."

Luke saw his opportunity. "Then you may be able to help me on another matter. Do you have any information regarding the movements over the last month of an Englishman working for the Venetian embassy, Sir Henry Hunt?"

"That name is familiar. Let me look at the reports! Give me a few minutes."

Thurloe left the room and returned within minutes. "Yes, I decided to put him in a category to be monitored carefully. He has made two trips to France within ten days of each other."

"When was last?"

"Two days ago, our agents at Dover reported he left there for France, and a week or so earlier our Dunkirk man reported his arrival and two days later his return to England. The Venetian embassy failed to inform the Lord Chancellor of such movements by a member of its staff."

"Regarding the last visit, the embassy did not know that Henry had left the country. You did not have a report from Plymouth a couple of weeks ago of a Lady Elizabeth Rhodes bound for France?"

"Not likely, the system has not been developed to the point that every English citizen can be traced, but you may be in luck in that the Governor of Plymouth reported that his deputy would be absent for some days as the King had ordered him to escort two women to France. One was probably your Elizabeth."

Luke decided to confirm several of his assumptions. What exactly did the King and the Venetian embassy know of the various trips to France. Luke suggested to the King that he should unite Margaret with Elizabeth. He volunteered to escort Margaret from the Venetian embassy in France to the King's safe house in Paris. The King agreed and reluctantly gave Luke the address. He also gave Luke a letter for Henry ordering his immediate return to England.

The Venetian embassy was happy to give Luke a letter giving him authority to remove Margaret from their Parisian embassy, and to consider Henry, if he should visit them, no longer a servant of the Republic. The ambassador added, "The matters that you raise are of serious concern to my government. I know you have only a smattering of Italian but as you will be dealing with our embassy officials, I would suggest that you take with you as interpreter and liaison with our officials in France, my most able officer, Marco Conti. You should have much in common, Marco is our intelligence officer and has authority to override all Venetian officials except the resident himself. He will help you overcome any obstacles our people might unwittingly create."

"I would be very happy to have Marco's assistance, and I will free him from that role immediately Lady Margaret leaves Venetian jurisdiction."

With Marco as a companion Luke did not need to take any of his unit with him. The King was relieved that nobody other than Luke would need to know the address of the Parisian safe house. Luke avoided the monitored passage through Dover or Dunkirk, and the long journey through northern France that it entailed. He and Marco took a package from Portsmouth to Le Havre and voyaged up the Seine directly to Paris. They were within its city walls without having to confront anybody. They took a room in an inn not far from both the English and Venetian embassies.

The following morning, they visited the Venetian embassy where the ambassador, Alvise Grimani was chuffed to receive a visit from a personal representative of the King of England, and a former comrade. His complexion darkened as Marco explained in Italian the nature of their mission.

He indulged in a series of oaths and then to Luke's surprise responded in English. "I have grave fears for Lady Margaret, who was a delightful guest for over a week. Two days ago, Henry returned, and told me he had orders to take her to a safe house in Paris designated by the King of England himself."

"Why did that alarm you?" asked Luke.

"At the time it didn't. That evening one of my staff returning from the south of France had seen Lady Margaret and Sir Henry riding south well beyond the city walls. They were leaving Paris."

"The safe house is within Paris and to the north of us. Henry was not going to the safe house nominated by my King," Luke re-iterated.

"What do you think has happened?" asked Marco.

"At the worst Margaret has been abducted—but for what end?" asked Luke.

"And the most positive explanation? continued Marco. "Two lovers have run away together," Luke replied.

"How can that be? asked Grimani. I understood from what Henry told me when he first arrived that Margaret was his first cousin."

"Lust is more powerful than church law," Marco answered.

He turned to the ambassador and asked, "Can I speak to the official who saw Henry and Margaret?"

Grimani agreed and Marco interrogated the man in Italian. After a long series of questions Marco explained to Luke. "They were seen three hamlets south of the city, along the road to Orleans. It is a village at the end of which coming from the south the highway, is obstructed by a tiny church. As it was approaching nightfall our friend assumes that they would have stayed in the only inn in that village overnight. We may be able to find out more from the innkeeper."

"It's several days ago, but it is better than nothing. I hope you speak French as I do not," admitted Luke.

Marco replied, "I was stationed here for five years, before I moved to England. My French is even better than my English."

Next day Luke and Marco arrived at the inn and the latter immediately asked whether an English couple had stayed there several nights before. The positive reply was immediately passed on to Luke.

"Good news. We have just missed them. The lady concerned had a heavy cold or the flu, and they remained here until this morning."

Marco asked the innkeeper whether they gave any indication where they were heading, and whether they acted a husband and wife, siblings or relative strangers?

The answers were reassuring and useful. They had separate rooms and the innkeeper had been told by the man that they were cousins, and relevant to their relocation, the man had asked directions to the Chateau Vargeau, the ancestral home of Antoine, Comte de Vargeau Luke asked Marco, "Do you know anything about this count?"

"Yes, I do. The count was and probably still is, the right-hand man of France's real ruler for over a decade, Cardinal Mazarin. It was Vargeau that help negotiate the peace treaty with Spain, and the recent marriage of King Louis to its Infanta."

"What is his connection, if any, with England, that might explain Henry taking Lady Margaret to his chateau?"

"I don't know, but my guess is it has something to do with the campaign to persuade Charles to take a French wife. He would be pushing for the acceptance of Hortense Mancini, Mazarin's niece. We must return to Paris and receive an update on these issues from ambassador Grimani, before we visit Chateau Vargeau."

16

The ambassador's briefing was enlightening. The French court was in flux. The young King was beginning to assert himself, while the aging chief minister struggled to keep control of the government. On the question of the English King's marriage there were rival French contenders. Louis agreed with his aunt, the dowager English queen mother, in developing a dual Stuart-Bourbon alliance by marrying Charles's sister to a Bourbon prince and marrying Charles to a Bourbon princess. Mazarin on the other hand pushed the claims of his beautiful niece Hortense, further sweetened by the massive dowry he could provide.

The French claims were struggling to be heard because of traditional English antagonism to France, and the strong support offered by Mazarin for the previous republican and Cromwellian governments. Mazarin's long-term ambassador to England was refused an audience with King Charles, and was in the process of being replaced, while the English queen mother had just arrived in England to advance the cause of a Bourbon princess.

Luke and Marco discussed their tactics for the imminent visit to Chateau Vargeau. Luke as a personal representative of the King would claim he was sent to monitor the wellbeing of Lady Margaret on behalf of the King and her father. Marco would concentrate on Henry. Both were obliged to inform Henry that he was no longer an employee of the Venetian Republic.

Their arrival at the chateau clearly created consternation. The servant that met them was informed that representatives of the King of England and Venetian Republic wished to speak to the count as a matter of urgency.

They waited in the reception hall for over half an hour when the servant finally returned with apologies. The count was at the far end of his estate and would not be with them for some time. They were offered a spread of eats and drinks while they continued their wait.

Luke wondered if the count was really at such a distance from the house, or whether he was using the time to conceal Henry and Margaret, or even giving them time to escape.

Marco was less suspicious. "The count is an experienced diplomat. He is more likely checking on our credentials."

Sometime later a small man dressed from head to toe in clothing of a most luminous blue with gold trimmings entered the room alone. He introduced himself as Antoine, Comte de Vargeau. Unlike most French courtiers he did not wear a wig but displayed shoulder length hair that was still predominantly black, although wisps of grey were noticeable.

Luke's fear that he would deny the presence of their quarry was immediately dispelled.

"Gentlemen, I suspect that you are here regarding my two guests of the last few days, Sir Henry Hunt and Lady Margaret Dash. What is your exact concern?"

Noticing that Marco was translating what he had said to Luke the count commented, "Let us conduct this discussion in English as I gather Sir Luke has little French."

Luke nodded in gratitude and answered. "Lady Margaret is a close friend of the King, and her sudden disappearance without his permission raised fears of abduction. She is an extremely wealthy heiress."

"And I am here on behalf of the Venetian Republic to inform Henry that he is no longer a member of its London embassy having absented himself without their approval," added Marco.

"There were fears that Henry had kidnapped Margaret in the hope of forcing her to marry him," admitted Luke.

"Are they still here? We would like to question both of them?" asked Marco.

"With what intent?" the count replied.

"In my case simply to inform Henry of his dismissal, and that he can no longer claim any diplomatic privileges, which you may have extended to him."

"And if he has kidnapped Margaret, I would seek your assistance in taking him back to England for trial," said Luke. "In any case I must try to persuade Margaret to return willingly to England with me."

"At least you are honest. I do not need to inform you that neither of you have any authority here, and should any action be required against my guests, it will need my support."

"But I am sure as a right-hand man of the Cardinal you would not wish a diplomatic incident to occur especially as my master has just forced your ambassador to leave London, and your young King is beginning to exert himself in the realm of foreign policy," said Luke undiplomatically. "And this raises the obvious question, why are you harboring these two people whom my government may consider fugitives."

"Henry contacted me and asked if I could protect Lady Margaret, until pressures against her in England subsided," Vargeau answered.

"Did he explain what these pressures were?" asked Marco.

"Yes, he said Lady Margaret's name appeared on a list of three English wealthy aristocrats that some may have interpreted as a hit list. The first name on the list had been whisked away on orders of the King, and Margaret desired to join her, but Henry did not know where she was."

"Why did he choose your chateau as her potential haven?" probed Luke.

"I have had many missions to England and got to know Henry quite well. Often when our ambassador was out of the country the Venetian embassy acted for us, and the officer I dealt with was Henry."

"May we now interview Henry and Margaret?" asked an anxious Luke.

"No, not until I have discussed their wishes with them. If they are happy to be questioned, you may do so tomorrow. If not, I will ask my men to escort you from my estate. In the meantime, you will stay here the night, and dine with me later."

Alone in the apartment allotted to them Luke and Marco discussed the situation. "The count is certainly convincing. Everything appears to be as he claims. His version agrees with what we have been led to believe. Henry is simply getting his cousin into a safe location in case her name on that list involves danger for her," summarized Marco.

"The count is one of France's most successful diplomats and his skill in presenting a situation as he wants us to see it is unsurpassed. The weak link in his story is why Henry brought Margaret here? Casual diplomatic encounters with the count in London does not make Chateau Vargeau a safe place. There must be a deeper link between Henry and Vargeau, or Vargeau and Margaret," commented Luke.

A few minutes later the count arrived at their apartment unannounced by any flunkey.

"Forgive my intrusion gentlemen. I have just been called away to Paris and therefore have to withdraw my invitation to dinner. My servants will bring your evening meal to this apartment. I should be back for tomorrow's morning meal at ten o'clock when I should be able to present Henry and Margaret, or at least their answers to your request to interview them."

After the count left Luke expressed delight at developments. "I am sure he is going to Paris either to receive advice concerning the situation, or to ensure that our quarry is hidden somewhere else. If he is seeking advice from the Cardinal or the King, it suggests we may have stumbled on a plot beyond our expectations."

"You are letting your imagination run wild. We have no evidence for anything that you have just said," said the practical Marco.

At ten the next morning, Luke and Marco entered the dining hall. The table was resplendent with a variety of cold and hot poultry—partridges, ducks, chickens and quail. On another tray was a plethora of freshly shucked oysters while servants were ready to serve chicken or fish soup.

When Luke indicated they would wait for the arrival of the count a servant indicated that he had not yet returned from Paris.

They enjoyed the repast in relative silence. Then they observed a liveried horseman trotting up the long driveway to the chateau.

Within minutes a servant ushered the liveried horseman into the refectory. Luke recognized the livery. It was that of the chief minister of France, Cardinal Mazarin.

The messenger delivered to Luke a sealed letter and indicated that he expected an immediate reply.

It was in English, and Luke showed it to Marco It was from the Count of Vargeau who indicated that he was with the cardinal, who wished personally to discuss their mission. Given the cardinal's ill health and advancing years the count requested that they leave Vargeau immediately and move to Versailles to meet him, and if necessary, the King himself.

Marco was astounded. "You were right Luke. This is much more than a good deed by Henry to protect Lady Margaret Dash if Mazarin and the French King are involved."

Noon, on the following day, Luke and Marco waited in a reception room of Cardinal Mazarin's apartment in the Palace of Versailles. They were soon joined by the Count of Vargeau who indicated that France's chief minister wished firstly to speak with Luke alone.

Mazarin wasted no time on formalities. "Tremayne, you and I have never met, but I am well aware of your activities. Seven or eight ago you saved a good friend of mine, Henri de Michel, Marquis des Anges from disgrace and death, and two years ago you acted for both your own Lord Protector and the French government in assisting our mutual ally the Queen Regent of Portugal."

"And on both occasions, Your Eminence intervened to aid my missions. But why has my current minor assignment of tracing the whereabouts of two English fugitives led to in this meeting."

"Forgive me! I am being very opportunistic. On hearing from Vargeau that you were the English officer involved, I decided to seek your help to get a secret message to your King, and hopefully to protect the interests of France, and above all prevent a plot to upset the peaceful international relations I have done much to achieve."

"I am aware that the relationships between King Charles and your government are currently stressed. Your ambassador has in effect been sent home with my King refusing to talk to him."

"Yes, I am essentially to blame for that by being such a strong supporter of the previous Cromwellian regime, and my representative unfortunately failed to adjust to the changing political situation. I am now Chief Minister in name only. King Louis will formally assume direct control of the government in a few weeks, and I will retire with little time left on this world. I would like to put relations between France and England on a better footing before this happens."

"How can I help? Are Margaret and Henry involved?"

"Hopefully Lady Margaret can play a useful role. She has been a French agent for years."

Luke was astounded, "But her father is one of the two most outspoken supporters of Spain in all England."

"That very fact led her to provide information to us from her early days at Charles's court in exile in Paris, and then in Spanish Flanders. When the court was in France, Margaret Dash was very close to your Duke of York who fought in our army. After whatever relationship between Margaret and the Duke ended, she became involved with one of his French officers, Pierre De Bussy."

"So, Margaret was pro-French even before her father fell into the Spanish camp."

"Yes. When the Earl of Greenham became engaged in activity that Margaret believed was not in the interests of England nor France, she informed other French agents, who got the information to us. Remember at the time France and England were allies. We were both at war with Spain."

"I am still surprised. Lady Margaret never appeared to me to be particularly political."

"No, her initial motives in doing what she did had nothing to do with politics, they were deeply personal. Her father forbade her relationship with De Bussy, but they continued to see each other."

"Is it still continuing?"

"I was until just before Charles moved his court back to England. De Bussy was murdered while visiting her in Bruges."

17

"Was it her distress over this that encouraged her decision to come here and perhaps enter a convent?" asked Luke.

"Not exactly. She came to France and was staying at the Venetian embassy awaiting news from her friend Lady Elizabeth Rhodes to join her. I persuaded Henry to take her from there to the Chateau Vargeau, after I received three alarming pieces of information, which you must pass on to your King."

"Which are?"

"The first was that our agents in Flanders discovered that Pierre de Bussy had been murdered on orders of an English aristocrat, The Earl of Greenham, Margaret's own father."

"Does Margaret know of this?"

"She had her suspicions at the time of the outrage, but it was only confirmed to her in the last few days by Henry. This helped persuade her to leave the Venetian embassy and disappear into rural France under the protection of the French state."

"Why is the French state so interested in this minor aristocrat?"

"My second piece of alarming news may explain our overall concern. Our agents within the Spanish administration in Flanders have warned us for some time that rogue elements in the Spanish government there have been planning a major disruption to the re-establishment of Royal government in England. In the last few months of his time on the continent these very officials refused to pay Charles the allowance that the Spanish government in Madrid had provided."

"I am not naïve, your Eminence. You had as little time for King Charles as the Spanish officials you describe. Why are you suddenly concerned about what they might do in England?"

"Initially I wasn't. If the Spaniards disrupted the Royal administration in England it would probably assist the interests of other powers such as the Dutch, Portuguese and ourselves. That was until the third piece of information with which you are vitally concerned—the list of aristocratic Catholic women—was brought to my attention."

"How does a list of the daughters of the three most pro- Spanish peers in England affect French interests?"

"Think Tremayne! What if one or more of these women were abducted, or worse, murdered, who would be blamed? Spain would deliberately point the finger at her two enemies—Portugal and ourselves. If the English believed the story that enemies of Spain had embarked on whatever heinous crime is committed, the chances of a Portuguese Infanta as your queen, or even a Bourbon princess are dead in the water, and the English French relationship will sink even lower. When I heard that the King's top agent, investigating this list had followed Margaret Dash to France, I felt it imperative to tell you what I know, not only in the interests of the women, but in the interests of France."

"Do you think Agatha Craven is also in danger of a Spanish inspired abduction or murder? Her father supported the Spaniards during the Cromwellian regime, and actually encouraged a Spanish fleet to land in Suffolk."

Mazarin laughed, "I am glad that Cromwell's head of military intelligence does not know everything. Guy Craven before he became viscount, and his offsider, the Turk, were privateers operating out of Dunkirk, overtly on behalf of the Spanish government. From the beginning Craven was one of my best agents and we asked him to encourage the Spaniards to attack the Suffolk coast. Your ships were engaged to the north and south, preparing to repel the expected invasion at Harwich or the Medway. The French fleet was waiting in ambush.

Should the Spaniards have attempted to land forces in Suffolk we would have wiped them out. If the Spaniards become aware of Guy's double dealing, his daughter would certainly be in danger."

"So, your assessment is that this is a hit list that Spanish agents from the Netherlands will try to effect?" probed an increasingly alarmed Luke.

"Yes, but I do not know how a Spanish list finished up in the Portuguese embassy and was then sold off to several buyers."

"Is Sir Henry Hunt also one of your agents?" asked Luke.

Mazarin smiled, "Yes and no. That is why I wanted to speak to you alone. France has paid Henry for years. He receives income from Venice, England and ourselves but from reports, he never has enough. The fact that he has attempted to be close to two of the three women on the list worries me. His attempt to court Lady Elizabeth, and his association with Lady Margaret is to what end? His status is such that neither father would contemplate his marriage to them. I suspect he may be on the Spanish pay roll as well. He is not a man to be trusted. There is something about his role in this list affair that worries me. My intuition tells me he is more personally involved than appears, but I have no evidence."

"I see where you are heading. He could be a Spanish agent preparing to use the women for his own advancement, or to set them up for others to kidnap or kill. His known French associations would add weight to any claim that any incident that occurs has been the work of the French, or their bitterly anti-Spanish allies, the Portuguese. What is to be done with Henry? Perhaps he should just disappear?" suggested Luke.

Mazarin smiled again, "I had a similar thought, but it may be better to leave him where he can be monitored. He could lead us to other enemy agents.

I will speak to Conti and suggest that France would appreciate it if Sir Henry was re-employed by the Venetian embassy in England, and that he should accompany you home to England immediately. Keep a careful watch on him! We do not want him to become a loose cannon."

Back at Whitehall Luke passed onto the King what the Chief Minister of France had divulged to him. Charles was astonished.

After some time, he spoke. "I have little time for either party in this alleged plot. Mazarin sided with the Cromwellian regime, and expelled me from France, while the Spanish officials in the Netherlands over the last year refused to pay me my subsidy. This Italian born French minister has a reputation for convoluted plots, and continuing intrigue. Is this another plot by him to destabilize my government, while relations with my cousin are momentarily fraught, or should we give substance to his allegations?"

"I don't think this is a Mazarin plot. He has been made aware that the Spaniards are planning some outrage here in England for which we will all blame the French or the Portuguese. This is a given which we must investigate. Whether the assumption that this Spanish plot involves harm befalling the daughters of pro-Spanish aristocrats may simply be the Cardinal's opinion, but given the existence of the list, it is a plausible assumption."

"Why did you not take Margaret to be with her friend Elizabeth? That is why I sent you to France," asked the King.

"Margaret was already in the hands of the French, and I was never permitted to see her. With due respect, it will make the work of any plotters more difficult if the women remain separate, and I am sure the security which Mazarin will impose will be watertight. I hope your safe house is as secure. I got the impression that Mazarin knew exactly where it was."

"What do we do about Hunt?"

"Keep him where we can see him! Mazarin will influence the Venetians to reappoint him, if you indicate that he has regained your confidence."

"This whole business has sown seeds of doubt concerning previously impeccable men. Henry may be involved in this Spanish plot, but so might your deputy and my friend Mark Cowper, as well as the fathers of the girls."

"Mazarin had little to say about The Earl of Maldon, but he did accuse the Earl of Greenham of murder. The Spaniards probably know of this and may be blackmailing him into following their orders."

"What about the Cravens?"

"Surprisingly, despite outward appearances for over a decade, they are firmly in the French camp. Given the Viscount's double dealing during the last decade he and his daughter might be the next victims if the Spaniards discover the truth. We must offer them increased protection immediately."

"What will you do?" asked the King.

"I have absolute confidence in Mark. I believe we should have a man on the ground in France monitoring the two women, liaising with the Cardinal, and representing Your Majesty at a personal level with your cousin, King Louis."

"Are you seeking such a diplomatic appointment, Tremayne?"

"No, sire, but Mark would be an ideal choice."

"Cousin Louis is not as anti-Spanish as his chief minister. He has just married the Infanta of Spain to cement eternal peace between the two countries. I will appoint Mark as a special representative in France, but as far as Louis is concerned, Mark is only there to keep an eye on two favorite women of mine. He will readily accept that as my motive," commented the King with a wry smile.

"When the Cromwellian regime went to war against Spain in 1656 there was considerable opposition from pro-Spanish elements in this country. I will visit John Thurloe and see if he can name the leaders of that faction which may still be very active. I recall that several London merchants were involved. Another source of information on pro-Spanish activity will be the Portuguese embassy. Spain has not given up its constant attempt to reconquer Portugal despite pressure from other powers to accept its independence." concluded Luke."

"Well, Tremayne, you have a lot to do, but first, brief Sir Mark on the information you received from the Cardinal, and then ask him to join me for breakfast."

Luke informed his whole team and intimated to Mark that not only was he to proceed immediately to the King's chamber for breakfast, but that he was most likely to be sent to France immediately.

After Mark left, Luke addressed his two remaining associates. "Matthew, as one of John Thurloe's top agents I want you to obtain from him a list of the most dangerously pro-Spanish politicians and merchants that opposed the late Protector's war with Spain. Miles, you visit the Portuguese embassy and the surrounding area and to isolate any pro-Spanish activity that our Portuguese friends have detected! I will revisit the Cravens."

Luke discovered Guy, Viscount Craven in an inn in Westminster resting between sessions of the House of Lords. His daughter Agatha was with him. Neither seemed pleased to see him.

"To what do we owe this visit?" asked Agatha coldly. "Increased alarm concerning your safety, my lady."

"If all you have is that list, which could be good news for the three of us, I am not worried."

"I have a lot more. Whoever compiled that list in the first place it now appears that certain elements will use it to cause serious disruption between foreign powers here in England. It now comes under my remit regarding the security of the state."

The Viscount commented, "All this is very general. Are you at liberty to tell us more? Who are these elements, and how does their proposed disruption affect us?"

"The alleged villains in this anticipated disruption are supporters of Spain."

"Then the Cravens should be safe. It is known that I have been a strong supporter of Spain for decades. I once was master of a privateer out of Dunkirk and we attacked ships of the English Republic, the Dutch United Provinces and Portugal. Since I relinquished my privateering commission my trading enterprises have largely been with Spanish territories. And it was well known that a few years ago I encouraged the Spaniards led by our King to invade England through the waterways on my land in Suffolk. I would have expected you were here to see what I knew about such Spanish endeavors, and whether I would be involved in any planned disruption."

"This pro-Spanish reputation is the very reason you might be in danger from Spanish sources. If your daughter, or any of the other women on that list were abducted or murdered, who would get the blame? The enemies of Spain, which currently are clearly the Portuguese and to a lesser extent the French and the Dutch. If Agatha was kidnapped Spanish supporters across the country would point the finger at the Portuguese. Their marriage negotiations with the King would be dead in the water."

18

"You have been busy Tremayne. You are certainly living up to your reputation. Where are the other two women on the list?" asked Guy.

"Both women are hiding in France- one under the protection of King Charles, and the other protected by Cardinal Mazarin. I cannot claim credit for what I have just told you. It was the Cardinal who linked our list with his information regarding a Spanish mission to create a disruption and blame it on Portugal or France. He also suggested that Agatha may be the victim rather than the other two women because of your double dealings. The Cardinal revealed that both of you are his agents and should the Spaniards have become aware of this both of you might be severely punished. How did you fool the Spaniards for so long?"

"When I was a privateer, I had a double commission, an overt one from the King of Spain, and a secret one from the Cardinal. I was never placed in a position where my loyalty to our King, and my deal with the French openly came in conflict with the Spaniards. My main role for the French was not action, but information."

"Do you want to hide me in France with Margaret and Elizabeth?" asked Agatha.

"No need," said her father. "The safest place for you to hide or rather be safe is aboard our trading trawler. The Turk and his men can protect you better than anybody."

Luke changed the focus of his questioning. "My lord have you heard any open pro-Spanish talk at Westminster?"

"No open discussion at all. Most people are aware that the majority of the King's officials and members of Parliament are anti-Spanish, many on the virulently anti-Spanish Portuguese payroll."

"What about secret talks? To the outside world you are still seen as one of the strongest supporters of Spain, have you not been approached by Spanish diplomats or their English supporters?"

"No, Spain has been slow to reestablish its embassy. Officials from the Spanish Netherlands seem about to usurp positions that should have been filled from Spain itself. I cannot see any English aristocrat, no matter how strongly they support Spain, playing any role in the abduction, or murder of their fellow supporters, let alone those with daughters who are close to the King. Over the last five years it has been the pro-Spanish aristocrats that were the closest supporters of King Charles. I cannot believe that the Earls of Greenham and Maldon would condone an attack on each other's daughters or on my Agatha."

"I tend to agree, especially as any such attack would infuriate the King, and at the moment the Spanish faction led by the Earl of Bristol and Sir Henry Bennet are desperate to maintain their current favor."

"The danger comes from Spanish agents infiltrating the country at this time of flux. The Turk who is constantly trading with them has often told me that there are elements within the Spanish administration of the Netherlands that despise Charles, and do not trust him an inch."

"But what is the alternative for these rogue Spaniards? If they removed Charles, his brother James would be King. James is solidly in the French camp having fought in their army during his exile."

"They don't want to remove Charles. They are obsessed with the need to regain Portugal. They would do anything to stop a Portuguese alliance and marriage between England and Portugal. They are also determined to regain Jamaica and Dunkirk. They are convinced that their King, Philip IV, and his chief minister Don Luis de Haro are too trusting. They are convinced that Charles, despite his treaty with Spain in 1656, will never return or vacate English possessions in the

Caribbean, return Dunkirk, provide thousands of Irish troops for Spain to attack Portugal, suspend all penal codes against Catholics, or break off any alliance with Portugal."

"If the Cardinal's intelligence is correct, and it usually is, I need to ferret out a cell of Spanish extremists who will do anything to stop Charles ignoring Spanish interests," said Luke.

"I shall ask the Turk on his next trading venture to discover all he can from his contacts, but I hope you will have destroyed any such group before that."

"And we shall soon know Spain's official position on some of these issues as both their ambassador extraordinary, the Prince of Ligne, and their new resident ambassador ordinary, Charles, Baron de Vatteville have arrived in England," explained Luke.

"And both of them are from the Spanish Netherlands, not from Spain itself," commented Craven gravely.

Miles reported back to Luke that evening. He had questioned the employees of the Portuguese and various Italian embassies as they drank in a number of inns and taverns in the area. The message of fear that he deliberately promulgated was that there was a dangerous cell of Spanish extremists that were about to engage in disruptive and probably murderous activity. As he was leaving one tavern, he was approached by a man who indicated that Jenny Longlegs has information of interest which she would only reveal to her favorite colonel. Luke was expected at her mansion at ten the next morning.

Luke was once more warmly received, and immediately plied with mulled red wine and an array of edibles. Jenny was in no hurry to discuss issues, other than the constant irritation of gangs of demobilized soldiers trying to take over her patch. She knew where they were based and suggested that Luke direct the authorities to their eradication.

Luke was well aware that this was the quid pro quo. He promised to eradicate her opposition, and she would reveal the information that would interest him.

Eventually Jenny broached this subject. "You may recall that that vile animal Harry Foster was removed by one of my men to stop his campaign of rape and violence against innocent women. Let's call this avenger Tall Paul."

"You immediately moved him out of London, just in case the authorities discovered what he had done?"

"Exactly Luke, but not before I asked him to hand over anything of value that Foster had on him. He said the man had nothing. I was therefore surprised that someone else had found a list of names on the body."

"It was a small list that could easily have been missed by a murderer anxious to escape the scene."

"That is precisely what I thought until a day or so ago."

"What changed your mind?"

"Paul returned to London a week ago, and some of his companions jokingly ribbed him that by his carelessness, he may have failed to obtain a valuable list of names, which might have brought him a fortune. Paul was adamant that he had searched the body carefully. There was no list. Then one of his companions confessed that he had seen Paul kill Foster. After Paul had left the scene, this acquaintance also searched the body. He found nothing and assumed that Paul had removed everything of value."

Luke was amazed. He declaimed, "If you are right, Harry Foster had no list!"

"This means that the person who found the list on the body actually inserted it at the time, or a third party planted the list on the body after my two men had searched it, —or more simply that the list was never on the body. at all."

"The Portuguese embassy was telling the truth when it said that it had not composed a list containing the three names indicated. Poole or anyone else associated with the embassy may also have been innocent. It gives a completely new focus to my enquiry and may be related to the new issue that my man Miles was investigating in the area yesterday—a clandestine Spanish cell out to cause trouble."

"In what way?"

"I do not know at the moment, but it will be to embarrass or confuse the Portuguese embassy."

"Maybe this Spanish scare is a red herring. The list was found by the Venetians. Venice is a catholic ally of Spain. I'd start with the Venetian embassy and my old friend Sir Henry Hunt. The Venetians are a clever lot—and Henry is always short of money."

Luke was not willing to admit that Henry was already considered untrustworthy. If Henry had created the list and then claimed to have found it on an employee of the Portuguese embassy, it was indeed a master stroke.

But to what end? To help Spain or himself?

Luke thanked Jenny for this potentially crucial piece of information and moved to another issue. He continued, "I promised to remove the new gangs that are encroaching on your territory, but any enforced removal may be very disruptive to the King's peace. Would you be willing to use the existence of at least one of these gangs to increase your own influence?"

"What exactly are you suggesting?"

"That you incorporate one of these new gangs into your organization, and we persuade them to move into a new area where at the moment you have little or no influence. An influx of veteran soldiers on your side, rather than as your enemy, can only be an advantage."

"You would have made an effective crime boss, Luke. The strongest and potentially the most dangerous rival gang is based at the Royal Lion. You and I could go there to see if your proposal has any chance of success," suggested an agreeable Jenny.

"Won't that be dangerous? I will call for reinforcements."

"A company of Royal troops will not be an effective negotiating tool, neither would just appearing at their favorite haunt without warning. I will send a message to the Royal Lion indicating that I and a representative of the King, will call on their leader at 3 o'clock this afternoon. Nevertheless, my men will shadow us, and be ready to act if these veterans become aggressive."

Luke and Jenny arrived at the Royal Lion—a small seedy alehouse that consisted of one large room with several barrels of freshly brewed ale. There appeared to be no seats, and a dozen well-armed men stood aside as Luke led Jenny to the nearest barrel. He declared, "We have come to discuss matters that may be to your advantage. I am Colonel …."

"Luke Tremayne," added a tall heavily built man. "I served under you in Ireland, and then until we were disbanded, I have been in the garrison at Chester. Most of the people you see around me served in that garrison, but we were dismissed, and replaced by Royalist forces five weeks ago. We have become known locally as the Chester Boys. I was Lieutenant Austyn Bulstrode. I am now simply known as The Bull, and I lead the Chester Boys."

"My companion is Mistress Jenny Judd who controls a lot of activities in Westminster, and parts of London which the Chester Boys have perhaps inadvertently interfered with. Rather than persuade me to call in the troops to destroy you, she wishes you to join her organization," announced Luke.

"I can see why Mistress Judd would want to negotiate with us, but what does one of Cromwell's leading generals, and now an officer of the King have to gain from this meeting?"

"Very simply peace. The authorities have not yet established law and order across parts of London and rely on Mistress Judd's organization to impose it. We would prefer the Chester Boys to add to this discipline, not undermine it. And depending on what you and Mistress Judd decide I would like to have a small element of her organization made up of experienced veterans that the King may call upon from time to time."

Jenny spoke, "With formalities and introductions over is there a quiet area where you and I can discuss my detailed propositions?"

Jenny and Bulstrode disappeared outside the back door while Luke became reacquainted with two more of the veterans that had served under him.

Half an hour later the two gang leaders reappeared.

Bulstrode immediately addressed the gathering, "Gentlemen, meet your new leader, Mistress Judd. I will be her deputy in the vicinity of this alehouse and to the north-east. She has guaranteed us an income greater than we may be able to achieve on our own. I had little choice as failure to accommodate her wishes would have led to an attack led by Colonel Tremayne to remove us from London. I am well aware of his ruthless reputation. We would probably have all been shot and buried without trace. Mistress Judd has agreed that should the need arise, we are free to act independently for the Colonel."

Luke smiled. He had created a private army for the very dark operations that must never involve the King, but which he might need.

19

As they made their way back to her house the perceptive Jenny had not missed the implications of such a deal. She commented enthusiastically, "What a master stroke! You have not only prevented a bloody gang war, and in the process preserved the King's peace, you have created for yourself a hit squad that you can utilize for the King without having to involve any royal officials or troops."

"There are some things which the King does not want to know about," admitted Luke." "My unit was created to deal with such matters."

"Be careful Luke! Some might conclude that you have created a military force, no matter how small, independent of any Royal control. What are you going to do now?"

"I will visit the acting Portuguese resident, De Sa, and update him on developments."

De Sa saw him immediately but indicated that he could not spend much time as the imminent arrival of his enemy's two ambassadors had greatly increased his workload. He had worked tirelessly over the past few days to counter any expected activity of the Spaniards to undermine Portuguese support among the English leadership.

"Why are you here, my friend?" he asked Luke.

"It is related to your current problem—Spanish interference." "In what way?"

"Two pieces of new information throws fresh light on that list of names found on your late employee, Harry Foster. A foreign source picked up from agents in the Spanish Netherlands that Spanish authorities were plotting a major disruption in London, to coincide with the arrival of their top-ranking diplomats."

"Why would they do such a thing? It would only harm their interests."

"Not if they could convince the English government and public that whatever deed they commit is in fact done by Portuguese or even French interests. What if they murdered the daughter of a pro-Spanish aristocrat? It would be plausible to believe it was committed by the Portuguese, and all the money you have expended, would be worth nothing."

"A dastardly plot, but I do not believe it. The Spaniards are our enemy, but they are men of honor. They would never murder an aristocratic woman. They are not like the Italians or the French."

"I agree. It is most unlikely that the Spanish government would contemplate such a scheme, but there are elements in Europe and in this country that would not hesitate to advance Spanish interests at whatever cost, because it is in their own interest. Elements connected to the Spanish administration in the Netherlands, hiring criminals in England, are the most likely perpetrators."

"And what was the second piece of new information that would interest me?"

"It makes the scenario I just outlined more likely. You initially denied that this embassy compiled the list of three women found on your late employee, and I think we both assumed that Poole or Foster had put it together to sell to the highest bidder with whatever story they attached to the names. It now appears that both deceased were innocent."

The Portuguese diplomat gasped, "How do you know?"

"The person who killed Foster and an onlooker who searched the corpse after the murderer left the scene, both claim there was no list on the body."

"Then a third party inserted it, probably to cause us embarrassment if not worse—probably a pro-Spanish agent," commented De Sa.

He was silent for what appeared minutes and whispered to Luke, "Or it was fabricated by the alleged finder, our neighbors here, the Venetians. Venice and Spain have been long term allies in the fight against the Ottoman Turk. If Spain had not been forced to place thousands of troops on our Portuguese border, they would have been available to fight alongside the Venetians against Islam."

"I have had similar thoughts," confessed Luke. "Can the Venetians be trusted?"

"The news of some Spanish activity to highlight the arrival of their diplomats and gain sympathy for their cause is not new. Our agents in the Spanish Netherlands reported similar news a week ago, but it is good to receive confirmation from another source," replied De Sa

"Have you received any inkling of what that might be? Have you detected any Spanish activity on the ground locally?"

"No, I had tried to preempt their success by providing further subsidies for several dozen more politicians, but I am well aware that many of your politicians and officials are taking sweeteners from more than one foreign power."

"In the absence of Spanish envoys who do you think is pushing Spanish interests, especially opposition to a Portuguese marriage?"

"A group of returning English aristocrats who acted for the Spanish authorities in dealing with the King over the last few years of exile in the Netherlands," answered the diplomat.

"The very men whose daughters' names were on our notorious list, the Earl of Maldon, the Earl of Greenham and Viscount Craven. Is any foreign embassy helping them?" probed Luke.

"One of the Italian states may be involved. From what you suggested, Venice would again be the prime suspect."

"I am not too sure. The local Venetian embassy is strongly influenced by the French. Their pressure led to the re-instatement of an official over whom they had some doubts," countered Luke.

Luke returned to his Whitehall apartment. He had no sooner entered the building than servant after servant accosted him with the same refrain, "The King requires your presence immediately."

The King was holding court with one young woman sitting on his knee and another kissing him passionately. On seeing Luke, he discarded the two females, and headed for his private chamber.

Luke had rarely seen the King displaying such a serious visage.

"What is it, Your Majesty?"

"Serious trouble, the impossible has happened. Lady Elizabeth Rhodes has been kidnapped."

"Was she not safely hidden in your Paris safe house, the location of which you revealed to no one?"

"Exactly! Just before he left for the safe house as we decided, Mark received this letter. It was from Elizabeth. She thanked Mark for persuading me to transfer her from the safe house to be with her friend Lady Margaret Dash, and looked forward to the coach and escort that I would send to move her."

"Her letter was genuine?"

"Yes, but the one she received was not. Neither Mark nor I sent any such letter indicating that she would be moved."

"Where is Mark?"

"Hopefully approaching the French coast. Her letter was dated three days ago, and the abduction has probably already occurred, but I decided there was no time to waste. Mark was riding to Plymouth within minutes of my decision, heading for the safe house to stop any move. I want you to join him immediately."

Facing inclement weather, it was three days later that Luke arrived at the safe house. He was met by a distraught Mark who filled him in on the enquiries that he had made.

The English merchant whose house it was, had suspected nothing until Mark's arrival. Elizabeth had been elated that she was joining her friend and clearly accepted the letter as genuine.

Luke summoned the commander of the guard that King Charles had sent to the safe house when Elizabeth came into residence.

"Did you see Lady Elizabeth depart?"

Lieutenant Allen replied, "Yes, a coach arrived three days ago which bore armorial emblems that I did not recognize but assumed were those of the noble French family that was protecting Lady Margaret and now welcoming Lady Elizabeth. It was escorted by a soldier whose uniform was not recognizable. It was neither that of the Kings musketeers, or the Cardinal's guard. One of my men commented that the horse he rode was similar to the cavalry horses ridden by the Spaniards in the Netherlands."

"Didn't this alarm you?"

"Not at all. I am aware that Lady Elizabeth's father, the Earl of Maldon is very pro-Spanish. Moving his daughter under Spanish protection was no cause of alarm."

"Did you know where the coach was heading?"

"A massive piece of luck. A farmer, bringing vegetables to the household, came down the great northern road and was surprised to see such a lavish coach leaving Paris."

"Why surprised?"

"The farmer recognized the armorial designs. The coach belonged to a family who had estates in the vicinity of Spanish held Ostend. Even though Spain and France were now at peace, coaches from Spanish territories other than those associated with new queen, are still rare in Paris."

"That may be a bit of good news. Ostend could be the port from which Lady Elizabeth will be returned to England. If it was intended to keep her in Spanish territory, they would have headed in a different direction."

"We do not know if they did head towards Ostend. We only know that the coach came from that area," commented a disconsolate Mark.

"What's the family name of the owners of the coach owner?" asked Luke.

"Rougemont"

"First thing in the morning we will head for Ostend to see if we can trace the coach. Now that it appears that Lady Elizabeth has been kidnapped are there any other developments that occurred here over the last week that may be relevant," Luke asked Allen.

"One of my men has just told me told me that as from about a week ago several horsemen seemed to dally outside our gates on more than one occasion. The same horsemen were seen outside the far fence of the property. With hindsight they may have been casing the property in preparation for Lady Elizabeth's removal."

While they were talking, one of the guards approached his commanding officer, "Sir, I overheard what you just told the colonel. Those same horsemen I saw not so long ago, following these gentlemen as they approached our main gate."

"We may then expect to be followed tomorrow," concluded Luke.

"But why?" muttered a confused and unhappy Mark.

Next morning as Luke and Mark prepared to leave, they were surprised to find Lieutenant Allen and six troopers ready to accompany them. The commander commented, "Colonel, we were seconded here from the Dunkirk garrison with orders to return to our unit when Lady Elizabeth was no longer present. We can escort you part of the way until the roads to Dunkirk and Ostend diverge. Our presence may discourage anybody who is determined to follow you."

The group headed north and spent the second evening in Lille. Next morning Allen suggested that the whole group now take the northwest road direct to Dunkirk from which Luke and Mark could follow the coastal road on to Ostend.

After some discussion Luke decided that he and Mark would take a more direct route to Ostend as time was an important factor, even though it meant they would spend much longer in Spanish territory.

Several hours later as Mark and Luke approached the border between French and Spanish territory along a largely deserted road, Mark expressed some alarm. "There is a body of horsemen galloping after us."

"By the gait of their horses and the speed they are travelling they are military."

"Do we make a run for it? The border is just ahead."

"It depends on who they are. If they are pro-Spanish troops crossing the border will play into their hands."

"Who else could they be?" asked a nervous Mark.

20

As the group came closer Luke breathed a sigh of relief. "They are allies rather than enemies. They are the Cardinal's guards and the way one of them is waving his hands, he wishes to talk to us. We'll wait here for them to catch up!"

Luke was right. Their leader identified himself as Emile de Bussy of the Cardinal's guard.

"Why are you following us?" asked Mark.

"The Cardinal wanted to ensure that your movement out of France was not obstructed by those that kidnapped Lady Elizabeth Rhodes."

"What does the cardinal know about the abduction?" probed Luke.

"We had the King of England's safe house under surveillance from the moment the woman arrived," admitted De Bussy.

"So, it was your men around the house in recent days, not those of the kidnappers?"

"Yes."

"Your men saw Lady Elizabeth's departure?"

"Yes, that is why I had to speak to you. Half an hour ago I received a courier from the Cardinal with an urgent message for you."

"Which was?"

"Our men followed the coach to Ostend and the lady concerned boarded a ship which immediately left for England, apparently very willingly. The Cardinal suggests that you leave for England also and that we escort you to Calais to catch the fastest packet home."

"Did your men discover the name of the boat?"

"A bit of confusion there. Apparently she was meant to be taken home by *The Lady Agatha*, but the kidnappers could not wait for its arrival. The substitute vessel was not identified."

Luke was confused. Was this good or bad news?

The Lady Agatha was owned by Guy, Viscount Craven and named after his daughter, one of the three women on the list. Had Lady Elizabeth for her own safety been kidnapped by friends?

In addition, Viscount Craven was one of the Cardinal's most trusted agents. Or was he? Double agents were always a risk. Perhaps his loyalty remained with Spain, and he had fooled the French for years—and more recently Luke?

Luke thanked De Bussy and readily accepted their offer of an escort to Calais. De Bussy then added, "The Cardinal reminded you to maintain the secret identity of all French agents in return for this continuing supply of information."

Luke replied, "I envy the Cardinal. He is at the center of this issue, and yet his real role is totally unknown."

Suddenly there was a flash and the sound of what Luke initially thought was a musket shot. His horse reared and nearly threw him. As he struggled to control his steed, he noticed that the other riders were also having trouble controlling their mounts.

The cause of this equine disruption was immediately obvious. A series of lightning strikes and thunderclaps were a prelude to a torrential downpour. The storm continued all that day and their arrival in Calais was seriously delayed by flooded streams and inundated bridges. On arrival at the seaport the storm in the Channel was even more ferocious. No ships would depart that day.

Much to Luke and Mark's frustration these dangerous conditions in the Channel continued throughout the next two days preventing any ships leaving port.

Three days later than they anticipated, the two officers leant over the side of a packet as it crossed a much more subdued Channel. Mark asked, "Did Maldon ask Craven to take his daughter out of the hands of the King, and return her to him?"

"A possibility, and if that is the case, we have little to worry about. I cannot see any of those fathers putting their only daughters, and their valuable heiresses into any danger. What is worrying is if pro-Spanish agents have kidnapped Elizabeth, put her temporally into what they see as the safe custody of their assumed ally, Viscount Craven, to be used later in whatever they have planned. Maybe through some heroic actions of Spanish agents she will be rescued from alleged Portuguese or French captivity. I just cannot see how they will blame anti-Spanish groups. There lies the danger. There must be something we have missed."

"Craven might have the answers," uttered a much more cheerful Mark.

On arriving back at Whitehall, Luke immediately sought an audience with the King. Charles was furious. "Even if the motives are acceptable, to remove someone from my personal protection, without my approval, could be considered treason. You have no idea where Elizabeth is?"

"From the French evidence, she should be safely with Viscount Craven."

"That may be why you have a visitor. She arrived last night and refused to talk to anyone until she had spoken to you."

The visitor was Arabella, Viscountess Craven. She dispensed with formalities and as Luke kissed her hand she announced, "Guy sent me here to report a disturbing development."

"My trip to France made me aware of what this might be— the disappearance of Lady Elizabeth Rhodes from the King's safehouse in Paris and her proposed transport to England in your family's vessel *The Lady Agatha*," commented Luke.

"Yes. On his last visit to Ostend, the Turk was informed by elements in the Spanish administration that they would like him to collect Lady Elizabeth on his next visit, and for her to be held in hiding at Castle Craven until a fortnight after the arrival of the Spanish ambassadors, when she could leave. She was to be told that her father wanted her safely secluded in Craven Castle, rather than in Paris."

"What went wrong?"

"When the Turk arrived in Ostend a few days ago later than expected, because of the storms he was told that because French agents were harassing her ladyship and its escort, and may attempt to kidnap her, it had been wise to dispatch her to England by the first available ship, and not wait for *The Lady Agatha*."

"Do you know the name of the vessel?"

"A Spanish coastal trader, La Sirena Giorda. The Turk was told that they would put Elizabeth ashore in a cove near Craven Castle, and escort her there. She never arrived."

"Probably kidnapped by the Spaniards, and now well on her way to Iberia." commented Luke.

"Far worse! The Turk was further delayed by that ferocious storm and believes that La Sirena Giorda, which set out in the middle of it, was driven further south than intended and could have sunk or run aground anywhere along the English or French coast, or at the extreme, driven out into the Bay of Biscay."

"Yes, it was a ferocious storm. It delayed my return by two days. Ships caught in the middle of it would have little chance, unless they found a safe haven very quickly."

"Can you do anything?" asked Arabella.

"We do not have the resources to search the entire south coast of England, and the opposite French lands. We must wait until the various ports report losses, but I will inform the Earl of Maldon."

"Guy has already had our people search along the Suffolk coast, and will go as far as the Thames estuary."

Luke thanked the viscountess. She left and Luke moved into the adjacent room where the King had been listening. "We may not have the resources to search for Elizabeth, but we do have the agencies to provide us with information. I shall inform all lord lieutenants that Lady Elizabeth Rhodes is feared shipwrecked somewhere along the south coast, and they should enquire from all seaside towns any details of shipwrecks caused by yesterday's storm. I will talk to Maldon myself."

"Try to ascertain whether he knew anything of the movement of his daughter from Paris to Craven Castle."

The Earl denied any part in his daughter's planned move from Paris to Craven Castle. The distraught peer left London immediately for his West Country estates from which he would organize a search of the Devon Cornwall coastline.

The King now became tied up in the extravagant formalities of welcoming the Spanish ambassador extraordinary, the Prince of Ligne. Luke was able to spend several days with his wife and children.

Four days later a heavily disguised man and woman were escorted by the Household Guards to Luke's private apartment. The man removed his outer clothing and headwear. It was Guy, Viscount Craven. The woman remained heavily veiled.

"What brings you here, my lord?"

"Good news, and the need for advice."

"I am the good news," said the woman as she removed her veil and over garments. It was Elizabeth Rhodes."

Luke was delighted. "I never expected to see your ladyship again. I followed you from Paris to the Spanish Netherlands border, but was told that you had embarked for England, not aboard Guy's ship *The Lady Agatha* but on a Spanish freighter."

Luke turned to Guy, "My lord how much does her ladyship know of what is happening around her?"

"Only that her father considered she would be safer with my Agatha in Craven Castle, than alone in a Parisian mansion."

"Which was not true. The letter she received was fake. It did not come from her father or Sir Mark Cowper. My lady, tell me how you got from Ostend to here!"

"The Spanish ship was to land me in the vicinity of Craven Castle but was hit by a terrible storm which drove the ship past the Suffolk coast. The ship was de-masted and driven towards the shore. The sea was too turbulent to launch any boats. We were at the mercy of the gods. Eventually we were lucky. Instead of being crushed against rocks, we were driven on to mud flats or sandbars. I had no idea where I was."

"We stayed stuck on the bar for two days while the captain tried to raise a temporary mast and sail, and the tides slowly loosened our position. Finally, he decided to jettison some of the cargo to completely free us from the bar.

He realized we were in the Thames estuary, and he was prepared to sail up the river for me to disembark in London, not far from the family's town house."

"Before this happened the Turk and I aboard *The Lady Agatha* came across the stricken vessel. I decided in the circumstances to bring her ladyship to London myself," interrupted Craven.

"I am not a fool, Sir Luke. What is going on?" asked Elizabeth.

"I believe that you were in fact kidnapped by agents of a foreign power. Luckily these agents believe that the Viscount is one of their supporters and he was asked to keep you in Craven Castle for a fortnight or more before letting you go your own way or using you to their political advantage."

"Why was I to be kept in isolation for that period, and then released?"

"I don't know exactly. These agents are planning some disaster which they intend to blame on a rival power to increase the support for their policies among the English elite. It is probably focused on the King's future marriage—a Spanish plot to destroy the credibility of the Portuguese and the French."

"How could keeping me in isolation achieve such a result?"

"I don't know that either. And I do not think it is a good idea to speculate"

"What should I do now?" asked a confused Elizabeth.

"The choice is yours. Your rescue from a potential shipwreck could be made known, and you return to your father—or any other safe place. Alternately you can go to Craven Castle with the Viscount. He is thereby seen to carry out his part of the bargain with the foreign agents, and we may be able to capture them, as they implement whatever it is that involves you. But it could put your life in danger. The death of the heiress to the fortune of the most pro-Spanish peer in the land, allegedly at the hands of Portuguese agents would destroy the campaign of our leading politicians to have the King marry the Portuguese Infanta."

"But would Spanish agents risk losing the support of the father and his friends? Murdering the daughter of one of your strongest allies is not a friendly act," asked a pragmatic Elizabeth.

"It would have to be done in a way that does not incriminate any Spanish supporters and be so clearly an act of the Portuguese that your father would never suspect Spanish involvement. It would probably be designed to strengthen his pro-Spanish position."

"What does the King advise?" asked Elizabeth.

"Above all he would want you to be safe."

Elizabeth was silent for some time. She turned to the Viscount, "My lord, when do we leave for Craven Castle?"

Luke had second thoughts. "My lady, the King is in his private chambers at the moment. I am sure he would wish to see you. Discuss the situation with him, while the Viscount and I discuss how to respond to the current situation." Elizabeth was led away by a servant, and Luke addressed Guy. "My lord, if her ladyship moves to your castle, the first stage of our response is in place. You are fulfilling your part of the enterprise, and her ladyship is in a position where the Spanish agents think they can use her in whatever way they see fit."

"What if the King persuades her to change her mind?"

"Then we find someone to impersonate her. My first choice would be the Marchioness of Nith with whom I have worked on previous missions, but she is too old. Any astute Spanish agent would see immediately that it was not Lady Elizabeth, the second choice would be my wife, but she suffers from the same age disability."

"No problems, Sir Luke. Agatha has a maid whose similarity to Lady Elizabeth has been noted in the past. She could play the role if necessary."

"Great! In addition, I shall send a couple of platoons of troops, out of uniform, to strengthen your defenses. Having Agatha and Elizabeth together will make our task easier."

"As it will our enemies," muttered Craven.

Ten minutes later an elated Elizabeth returned. "Charles would prefer I return to a safe house, and not risk any adventure at Craven Castle, but conceded that whatever you recommended Colonel would be acceptable to him."

"And what is your decision, my lady?" asked Luke.

"I will go to Craven Castle. My only condition was that my father be informed that I have been rescued, and am perfectly safe, but for security reasons we cannot meet. The King has already sent a courier to inform him."

"Come my lady, I would like to catch the tide. It will make our trip down the Thames much faster," announced Guy as he guided Elizabeth from the room.

No sooner had they left when the door burst open and Sir Edward Hyde Lord Chancellor of England entered the room, announcing as he came in, "The King said I would catch you here. You are currently engaged in a matter that is very close to my heart—the Portuguese marriage?"

"Yes, evidence has emerged that the Spaniards will create uproar amongst the English political elite, but which they will cleverly blame on the Portuguese, thus undermining support for the Portuguese marriage."

"You are right. Their campaign has already started, but in a very small way. The coach of the newly arrived Spanish ambassador was stoned this morning. He has made an official complaint that it was by a mob of Portuguese inspired hooligans."

"How do we know they were Portuguese inspired?"

"According to the ambassador they were shouting out in Portuguese 'death to the Spanish king', and other pro Portuguese slogans."

"Hardly any Londoners can speak Portuguese, certainly not enough to constitute a London mob. I will investigate and get back to you."

Next day Luke met Jenny Longlegs. Yes, her men had made up the mob that stoned the Spanish coach. They were paid for by a servant of an English peer, who deposited the money with her brother at the Black Falcon.

Luke asked, "Were there any other facts that may help me determine the true significance of the attack?"

"Yes, my men were told not to use large missiles. The aim was to intimidate, not to destroy the man or the coach. Secondly the boys reported their group was infiltrated by a dozen or so men of a darker complexion shouting abuse at the coach. I thought it was in Spanish, but I later learnt that it was Portuguese."

"Thank you, Jenny. This was the first, and almost trivial attempt by pro- Spanish factions to embarrass and humiliate the Portuguese. The men who infiltrated your mob were part of the large entourage the Spanish ambassador brought with him. Every second Spaniard has at least a smattering of Portuguese. Did your brother recognize the servant who brought the money or the identity of his master?"

"I never asked him," was her reply.

After discussing the situation with his unit, it was decided to proceed on three levels—test the loyalty of Henry Hunt by imparting to him a series of half- truths; make a concerted effort to find who paid the mob to attack the Spanish coach; and finally, the need to clarify from the King his position regarding the looming Spanish-Portuguese conflict. It would be counter-productive to foil the Spanish plot, if it was what the King actually wanted.

Next morning Luke presented for their regular pre-breakfast meeting. He outlined the possible scenarios involving the women and possible Spanish disruptions. "Sire, we need some guidance as to your policy regarding this Portuguese-Spanish tension. Some suggest that you are pro-Spanish, but your ministers are pro-Portuguese. Should I allow the Spaniards to play their cards without interruption?"

"Not if it involves harm to any of those women. Yes, I have continued to show pro-Spanish attitudes, until I can rely on French help should the Spaniards become aggressive. The Spanish ambassadors are very poor diplomats. While the Portuguese offer us rewards, the Spaniards demand that we make concessions, which the current Parliament would reject. I am playing for time. Anyhow I cannot believe the Spaniards would harm any of those women. "

"So, we continue to monitor any Spanish activity and control it?"

"Yes."

"You have Elizabeth and Agatha safely in Craven Castle guarded by a mixture of former privateers and units from the regiments guarding me. Are you leaving Margaret in the hands of the devious Cardinal?"

"Whatever Your Majesty pleases."

"Bring her home and place her with the others. They are still my responsibility."

"But you would be placing her in the same potential danger that Agatha and Elizabeth have willingly submitted to."

"You exaggerate the danger. The Spaniards may simply invade Craven Castle and rescue the three women claiming they had been kidnapped by Craven on behalf of the Portuguese friendly French. If they have uncovered that Craven is a double agent, they will not hesitate to execute him. If anybody's life is in danger it is Guy, and his henchman the Turk—not the women."

Luke smiled at the King's chivalric attitude and commented, "I will go to Paris and bring Lady Margaret home."

Later than morning Luke was at the Venetian embassy talking to Henry. "An update on the three women on that fateful list! There was some panic regarding Lady Elizabeth. I thought she had been kidnapped by our enemies.

The situation became dire when she was lost at sea believed drowned. In the end she was found by Viscount Craven who claims she had been removed from France by her friends."

"Where is she now?"

"Craven Castle with her friend Agatha." "And Margaret?"

"Still somewhere in France protected by the Cardinal."

"Is that wise? The Cardinal is about to retire. King Louis may have very different views to his aged minister. She would be safer back in England, perhaps with the others."

"You may soon have your wish. The King has a similar view, but Lady Margaret may not wish to return."

"She would not defy the King."

"On another matter, do you know anything about the attack on the Spanish ambassador?"

"Clearly Portuguese inspired!"

"Or so the Spaniards want you to believe. The mob was paid for by a servant of an English peer, according to my sources. Any ideas?"

"Your sources are wrong. Our embassy has closely monitored the area to see who has visited the Portuguese."

"The Venetians are working for the Spaniards?" asked Luke. "No comment. There have been no characters that meet your description reported to me. There was one stranger to the area who is well known to me, who was in the vicinity that might have been incorrectly identified as the mob's paymaster, my cousin, Lord Peter Coleridge."

"You have not mentioned him before."

"I have not seen him since he was a boy. He was a second son, and as he was not expected to inherit the family estates, took himself to London and worked for the Levant Company, who appointed him to a position within the Ottoman Empire. His older brother was killed at the Battle of Naseby, and with my uncle's death a few months ago Peter has become the new Baron Coleridge. He has just returned to take up his title and estates. His return to England might help persuade Lady Margaret to do the same."

"Why?"

"Peter was always Margaret's favorite cousin when we were little. If Margaret does not marry, Peter inherits the title and lands of the Earl of Greenham, being the nearest male heir."

"He has precedence over you?"

"Yes, our mothers were sisters, but Peter's was the eldest." "Perhaps Margaret may not be happy with Peter's return. It is in his interest to ensure that she does not marry. Is he married himself?"

"I don't know. What is your uncle's view on his daughter's sojourn in France?"

"He has not been asked. All I know is that Margaret sent him a message that she was well, and for him not to worry, and that she felt safer in France, until the King was firmly established in England, and the significance of the list became clear."

Luke left the Venetian embassy perplexed. He did not trust Henry. Was the whole story of his cousin Peter aimed to deflect attention away from himself? Was Henry implying that the outrageously pro-Spanish Earl of Greenham had asked his nephew Peter to pay for a mob? Was Lord Peter also a Spanish agent? If the authorities removed Randolph and Peter for treason, Henry would become heir to a very wealthy earldom, provided Margaret did not marry before her father's death.

It was time to talk once more to the Earl of Greenham. The House of Lords was still in session, although they were not meeting that afternoon. With luck Luke might catch his lordship in his town house, which was within walking distance from the Venetian embassy.

Randolph, Earl of Greenham received Luke warmly in anticipation of hearing the latest regarding his daughter.

"My lord, The King has asked me to go to Paris to bring your daughter back to England."

"Excellent, I have never trusted the French. If she won't come home, I would prefer her to be in the Spanish Netherlands. I cannot understand what the attraction in France might be."

Luke was not going to reveal that his daughter had for years been an agent of Cardinal Mazarin.

The earl continued, "Tremayne, I fear that the only plausible explanation for her stay in France is that she has taken a lover, which could ruin my plans for her marriage and the need to produce a male grandchild, to inherit the family lands and titles."

Luke decided to lie, "I had heard rumors that you were seeking approval from the Pope to enable Margaret to marry one of her first cousins, Lord Peter Coleridge or Sir Henry Hunt."

"Hunt is an impoverished gentleman who has ambitions well above his status. He had me try to persuade Maldon to allow him to court his daughter Elizabeth, and when that failed, he did raise the question of my own Margaret. I made it clear that his status was not sufficient to entertain such an outcome, even if the Pope approved the marriage of first cousins."

"Does that also apply to Lord Coleridge?"

22

"Until two days ago I last saw Peter when he was a schoolboy. He just visited me then on his way home from Constantinople to take up his title and estates. He has never raised the matter of marriage with me. He may already have married while in the Ottoman Empire. I had heard rumors that he had a way with women. Fifteen years ago, Margaret and he were great school friends. They were educated together on my home estate."

"Do you know where he is at the moment?"

Randolph smiled, "He is in the next room. He is staying here until the weather clears, and he can risk the journey north. Would you like to speak to him?"

"Yes, his name has come up in reference to another matter. I would like to clarify his role."

The earl signaled a servant who left the room and returned with a soberly but richly dressed gentlemen, whose appearance temporarily astounded Luke. He immediately apologized, "I am sorry, my lord, but your appearance reminded me of his late Majesty, Charles I."

"Yes, it has been remarked on countless times before, which led to completely false rumors that I am an illegitimate son of that monarch, and half-brother to the current King. That misinformation has been more dangerous than beneficial. Why did you wish to see me?"

"The attack on the Spanish ambassador's coach."

"Uncle and I are very strong supporters of Spain. Why would we attack its ambassador's coach?"

"To blame the Portuguese for what happened, and thereby undermine their influence on our politicians, in regard to the King's marriage to their Infanta."

Peter looked at Randolph who nodded positively.

Peter then confessed, "Yes, I delivered funds on uncle's behalf to a criminal at The Black Falcon, who organized the demonstration."

Randolph intervened, "Tremayne, you know that I believe that the King is making a major mistake if he deserts Spain for France and Portugal. I believe it is my national duty to convince the King that his and the country's future lies in supporting Spain against Portuguese rebellion and French aggression in Flanders. You have the King's ear, try and impress him with our message. We pro-Spanish peers remain the most loyal members of his aristocracy. So many of our kind have sold out to Portuguese money, and French pressure."

"Was this attack on the Spanish coach at the behest of the Spaniards themselves, or a locally devised plot?"

"Totally a local affair. It did not involve anybody from the embassy. Why do you ask?"

"Our agents have uncovered a plot that Spain intends to cause considerable disruption here in England, and like you, blame it on the Portuguese. Unfortunately, we also believe that it could involve your daughter and the other women on that notorious list. That is why the King wants Lady Margaret home."

"Is Lady Margaret in trouble?" asked Peter.

Luke outlined in detail the situation involving the three women, and then accepted an invitation to dinner.

He was not convinced of the truth of what he was being told.

During a lengthy meal and a range of wines and strong spirits all three men mellowed. Randolph, Earl of Greenham became more depressed as the night wore on, and finally revealed to Luke, "Our attempt to build up a strong Spanish alliance and win the King away from any Portuguese, Dutch or French marriage is doomed to failure."

Luke waited for the Earl to explain but he appeared to fall deeper into melancholia. Luke asked, "Why my lord are you so pessimistic?"

"Because our loss will not be caused by Portuguese money or French cunning, but through the arrogance and incompetence of the Spaniards themselves."

Peter intervened, "Uncle is very upset that the Spanish embassy refused to receive any of their local supporters, even senior English aristocrats such as himself. It seems they believe they can accomplish their aims without any local advice or assistance, and rumors already suggest this is further alienating the King."

Luke deliberately added to the concern of both Randolph and Peter.

"Yes, that is certainly true. All other nations are offering the King something, Spain alone wants Charles to give them something—namely Jamaica, Dunkirk and 6000 Irish troops to subdue Portugal."

Luke hesitated about continuing, but nevertheless ploughed straight ahead. "Maybe the Spaniards are avoiding their local supporters because they plan to use you without your knowledge in their anti-Portuguese campaign."

"In what way?" asked Peter.

"The kidnapping of Lady Margaret and others by alleged Portuguese agents, whom they will suddenly and courageously rescue, bringing glory to Spain, and ignominy to the Portuguese cause. Quite correctly they probably believed that no father would put his daughter at such a risk. So much could go wrong."

"Such as?" asked Peter.

"The death of a daughter of a well-known supporter of Spain would be of immense propaganda value."

"No! The Spaniards are too honorable to harm Margaret or her friends?" asked Randolph.

"Perhaps but Margaret is not so sure. This would explain her refusal to come home," explained Luke.

He continued his questioning of the mellow and pliable aristocrats. He was surprised that they revealed so much—but were they laying a web of false information?

Randolph sensed Luke's hesitation in accepting their comments, "Colonel, everything we have told you, except for very recent events is already known to the King. One of his favorites keeps both him and us informed."

"And who would that be?"

"The King's ambassador in Spain, and the person who co-ordinates our endeavors from a distance," answered Randolph.

"That is Sir Henry Bennet," explained Peter "He is about to return home and join the King's ministry—much to the Lord Chancellor's disquiet."

"That explains a lot," Luke replied. "Sir Henry is indeed one of the King's favorites, but a bitter opponent of the pro-Portuguese Lord Chancellor. It would certainly give the pro-Spanish lobby a considerable boost."

"And that explains our current policy—to delay the King's decision in favor of Portugal until Sir Henry arrives and convinces the government of the need to maintain a close alliance with Spain. After all, our only action so far did no harm—a few stones thrown at a coach. And in the Lords, we managed to stop a Bill put forward by the Commons that the former Spanish possessions of Dunkirk and Jamaica be incorporated in the English Crown. We can hold the line until Sir Henry arrives, unless the Spaniards do something silly. I almost hope you can stop them," concluded Randolph.

Luke had said his farewells when the Earl asked, "Luke, could you do me a personal favor that may help your mission to my daughter. Take Peter with you to represent the family interests!"

Three days later Luke and Peter embarked from a vessel that had taken them up the Seine from Le Havre to Paris. The King had readily agreed to Peter's inclusion in the mission, observing that in the end the protection of Lady Margaret should be a family responsibility. He also decided to upgrade the status of the mission by appointing Luke as a special envoy to his cousin King Louis, and the bearer of a sealed letter, the contents of which were not revealed to him.

Luke presented himself at Versailles to be told that King Louis was away, and not expected back for at least two days. This gave Luke and Peter an opportunity to obtain an audience with the Cardinal.

Mazarin immediately revealed that he had been briefed on Luke's mission. "Welcome Tremayne, I hear you have arrived in a semi-diplomatic capacity to see my King. You may reveal the nature of this visit to his most trusted minister?"

"I cannot accede to your request for two simple reasons—I have clear instructions to deliver the sealed letter in person to the King, and no one else, and I have no idea of what it contains. This special envoy role was added to my initial mission at the last minute."

"And what was that mission?"

"To discuss with you or the Count of Vargeau, the return of Lady Margaret Dash to England."

"Has she requested such a move?"

"No, as far as I know she has not contacted anybody in England, certainly not her family. This request is driven by my King who is taking your intelligence of a Spanish plot to discredit the Portuguese and yourself by in some way using one or more of the three women on the list. He wishes that she be under his protection, or that of her family. I have brought with me her cousin, Lord Peter Coleridge to talk to her on behalf of her father."

"That Spanish besotted Randolph, Earl of Greenham!"

"Yes, but I can give you some intelligence on this issue which you may wish to exploit in our mutual interest. There is a major divide between those among the English elite who strongly want an alliance with Spain who seem to be led from a distance by the King's ambassador to Spain, soon to return to a major position on the King's Council; and those Spaniards in England associated with their embassy."

Mazarin was silent for a while. "Not happy with that news, Tremayne! I was hoping that the incompetence of the Spanish diplomats would destroy their position. If respected, but misled English aristocrats can maintain their pro-Spanish view untarnished, we may yet lose the battle for your King's support."

"The Lord Chancellor needs to force the King's hand regarding marriage with the Portuguese Infanta because when Bennet returns the fanatical pro- Spanish faction will certainly have the King's ear. Now may we question Lady Margaret?"

"One of my officers will escort you and the baron to the chateau where she is living. Farewell Tremayne, we will not meet again as I am retiring from my position in a few weeks. King Louis will be his own chief minister."

Luke bowed slightly and withdrew.

The next morning a Captain of the Cardinal's guard arrived to escort them to Margaret's sanctuary. It was led by Luke's earlier acquaintance, Emile de Bussy.

As the three men entered the reception room of the chateau where Margaret awaited them there was an awkward moment.

Margaret eyed Peter up and down, and announced to De Bussy, "Why was I lied to? I heard that Colonel Tremayne was accompanied by my cousin. Where is Henry? And who is this stranger?"

Peter replied gently, "I am no stranger. I was once your favorite cousin. I did not think my appearance had changed so much in fifteen years."

Margaret's face belatedly showed a sign of recognition, and she came forward and gave the baron a prolonged hug. "Peter!" she exclaimed.

Luke allowed them time to question each other and reminisce.

He and De Bussy left the room and discussed their mutual military experiences against the Spaniards. Emile asked Luke directly, "Why has the baron come with you?"

"He is here to represent Margaret's father."

The two soldiers re-entered the room to be confronted by Margaret's direct statement. "I will not return to England, if I must live with my father."

Peter took up his designated role. "Why such a vehement response? Your father only wants the best for you and given your name on a list the Colonel has explained to me, protection by your own family should be your first priority."

23

"Peter, I am only on that list because of the political extremism of my father. Whether it is a hit list of the Spaniards, the Portuguese or father's enemies in England, I simply feel safer here in France."

"Surely your father's pro-Spanish attitudes cannot help you here?"

Margaret looked at Luke for guidance on whether to reveal her role as a French agent.

Luke intervened. "Margaret never espoused the views of her father and the French probably feel that they may use her to persuade him to change his position. That is why the King sent me here. He feels we must protect Margaret, not only from any Spanish activity, but also from friendly French pressure."

De Bussy grimaced, but privately applauded Luke's caution, in not revealing Margaret's strong pro-French opinions.

Margaret breathed more freely not having to reveal to her cousin her political stance. "Another reason I do not want to return home is my father's constant pressure for me to marry. He has a long list of potential suitors. It is one major disadvantage or is it an advantage of being the daughter of an earl—the field is limited to those who father considers of the right status, and there are so few who reach his standards. All this is to your advantage, Peter. If father dies before I marry, you become the Earl of Greenham."

Luke decided to complicate the discussion. "Or you two could marry each other, to make doubly sure of Peter's succession?"

"Don't be ridiculous," remarked Peter. "We are first cousins."

"It did not stop your mutual cousin Sir Henry Hunt from raising the possibility and suggesting that the Earl should seek exemptions to enable first cousins to marry."

Peter seemed surprised—and concerned, "How did uncle react?"

"He rejected Henry not because he was a first cousin, but because of his lowly status."

Peter turned to Margaret, "Did you encourage poor Henry?"

Margaret blushed, "We are close, but I was not stupid enough to do anything that devalued my position as a wealthy heiress."

Luke and Peter gave each other a meaningful glance. De Bussy smiled.

Luke suddenly became very serious. "Lady Margaret I must end our pleasant chat. I am under orders from the King to take you back into England. You do not have to return to your father. The King suggests you join your friends Lady Elizabeth Rhodes and Lady Agatha Craven under the protection of the Viscount at Craven Castle. There you will be protected not only by the viscount's well- armed men, but also a detachment of the King's troops. I have authority to consider any other safe refuge you may prefer."

"I wish to be with my friend Martha Langley," was the surprising response.

"And be close to Cousin Henry!" added Luke almost vindictively. "Not possible my lady. Town houses cannot be adequately protected, and your residence in London makes you very vulnerable. The Langley country estate if I remember it correctly, is not one that has natural defenses, or a staff able to prevent intrusion."

"What if I refuse?"

"I am no lawyer but to disobey a direct order of your King must be serious. And I need to remind you that your great Protector in France the Cardinal, will no longer have any power within weeks. You may not be able to rely on King Louis to the same extent. If the Spaniards are your enemy, remember that King Louis has just married the Spanish Infanta. He may have a different attitude to them, than his retiring chief minister."

Two days later a reluctant Margaret agreed to be escorted to Craven Castle. Their immediate departure was delayed as King Louis had not returned to Versailles, and Luke was reluctant to leave the personal letter between the two Kings to any underling. Peter suggested he take his cousin to her designated sanctuary, while Luke await the return of the French monarch.

Luke agreed. He felt the quicker Lady Margaret was out of France the better. While she remained, she might change her mind. Obviously determined to throw as many obstacles as possible in the way of her would-be rescuers, Margaret asked that they return by way of Calais, rather than Le Havre. She would like to spend a few days there before she left France probably for good. This request involved several extra days moving through France, in addition to time spent in the seaport town—probably an extra week compared with Luke's preferred Le Havre to Portsmouth route.

Luke was suspicious and unhappy but acceded to her request on the condition that they wait for him in Calais.

Peter and Margaret left the next morning. It was two days later that Luke received a summons to present himself at Versailles. Unable to speak French, he was presented to King Louis by England's resident ambassador. Luke approached the throne, bowed and presented the sealed letter to the French King. He was in the process of withdrawing when the King signaled for him to stay put.

Louis read the letter and spoke to the English ambassador who translated for Luke. "His Majesty would like to reply to the message from his cousin Charles. His reply will be delivered to you tomorrow."

Luke withdrew, annoyed that his departure would be further delayed.

He stayed at the English embassy for two nights as the King's reply was not delivered until the third day after his reception.

His trip north to Calais was uneventful and on arriving at the designated inn where he was to meet Peter and Margaret, he found they were no longer there. The innkeeper said they had left two days earlier.

Luke was not greatly concerned. He assumed that his delay at Versailles had persuaded Peter that he should get Margaret out of France and not wait for him.

On his return to Whitehall Luke delivered Louis's reply to Charles; updated his unit on developments; and asked Mark to find out when Lady Margaret had arrived at Craven Castle.

Luke hoped that it could be done easily if Lord Coleridge was still at his uncle's town house before he travelled north to his own estates. Luke's hopes were dashed. Neither the earl nor his nephew were at home. A servant said that Lord Peter had gone to France and had not yet returned.

Luke was slightly alarmed.

Mark was more optimistic. "Peter probably stayed over at Castle Craven for a few days. The Viscount's hospitality is well known. We can't visit the castle personally. Our unknown enemies might suspect the Viscount's loyalty, if either of us were seen visiting his home."

Instead, they sent a heavily disguised Miles to confirm the arrival of Peter and Margaret. Miles wore civilian clothes, and an elaborate wig. Miles's overt objective was to find out for the King, if Craven needed any more assistance to properly protect the three women. If the couple had not arrived, he was not to alarm the Castle Craven community by indicating that there was anything amiss.

Two days later Miles reported back. His news was devastating. "They have not arrived. And the Viscount is unhappy. He had expected to be consulted before any decision was made to transfer Lady Margaret to his care."

Luke reluctantly reported the situation to the King who was furious. "Not good enough Tremayne! You trusted my charge, Margaret, to a former merchant of the Levant company whom neither of us knew. What has happened to them?"

"A range of possibilities, some good, some alarming and some potentially fatal."

"Humor me!" said a decidedly unhappy monarch.

"The possibilities that should worry us least are, that Peter acting on behalf of Randolph has taken her to her father; or that Margaret has persuaded Peter to take her to a destination of her choice to avoid a return to England. The alarming possibilities are that Peter and Margaret have run off together, or that he has kidnapped her ladyship, maybe to force her to marry him, or to ruin her reputation, so that no one else would marry her. He did show a lot of interest when I told him of Henry's hope of obtaining a Papal dispensation to marry his cousin. The potentially fatal possibility is that Peter is an enemy agent and has handed Lady Margaret over to an unknown enemy with unknown consequences."

"I will immediately order the Lord Lieutenants in the relevant counties to have the local militia search the estates of the Earl of Greenham and Baron Coleridge for either of the missing duo. Now, what are you going to do to redeem yourself?"

"I will seek the help from your civil intelligence agency. They have already established a widespread monitoring of who enters England through its leading ports. It would be useful to discover whether Peter and Margaret actually left Calais and arrived in Dover. Will you instruct your ambassador in France to seek any relevant information from the Cardinal? With luck his guards may have followed them to Calais, or wherever they actually went."

A depressed Luke made his way through Whitehall to the office of his old adversary John Thurloe. "I see more of you now than I ever did when we worked for the same master," quipped the former head of Cromwell's effective intelligence network. "You must be in serious trouble."

"I am. I have lost an enigmatic baron and a would-be endangered daughter of an earl."

"Not one of those women on that list! The Lord Chancellor has me looking into it now. He doesn't trust you, or the King. He fears it may be the tip of an iceberg to somehow discredit his favorite Portuguese to the benefit of the hated Spaniards. He has admitted that the King is soft on Spain and that you might be acting in their interests on behalf of the King. So, I cannot release any information that is not in the Lord Chancellor's interest."

"You could justify revealing what I ask for. It could help in the effort to stifle Spanish influence. I want to know if either Peter, Baron Coleridge or Lady Margaret Dash arrived at Dover from Calais in the last week. I am simply trying to establish whether the couple are in England, or still on the continent."

"The sooner you find the missing duo the better. It would be quicker if you went to Dover yourself. I will authorize the Governor of Dover Castle to make available to you the information of entries to England through that port during the relevant period. Save time by sailing down the Thames. If you hurry you can catch this afternoon's tide."

Early next morning Luke was in Dover Castle confronted by several volumes of material containing the names of arrivals of sufficient status to interest the intelligence service. This automatically included all senior aristocrats.

For hours Luke poured over the documents. Servants brought him lighted tapers so that he could continue into the night. It was a fruitless search. The names of Peter and Margaret did not appear as passengers on any Calais to Dover packet. It was at this late stage that he realized the futility of his search for their names. They had probably changed their identity.

He then began looking for couples that might have been his quarry. This time he stopped his search more quickly. There were dozens of such couples and as the documents did not give details of appearance or age, he could not identify them.

This failure ended a disastrous week for Luke.

24

Luke returned to London a frustrated investigator. Christmas was approaching. The Court in mourning for the death of the King's younger brother, the Duke of Gloucester in September, was rocked further by the sudden demise of his eldest sister Mary, the princess of Orange, on Christmas Eve. She was visiting England in anticipation of her brother's coronation.

Luke decided to spend this lapse in court and administrative activity for a week or more with his family. They escaped Whitehall for their Kent retreat.

Luke's plan to continue this break into the New Year was suddenly curtailed. On January 6, London burst into insurrection. A Fifth Monarchy led rebellion of religious fanatics attempted to take over the city, planning to capture the Tower of London and Whitehall. They would then execute the royal family and replace them with the Lord Jesus.

The rebels were confronted by George Monk's yet to be disbanded personal regiment. The initial encounter solved nothing as the rebels dispersed before they were defeated. Two days later they returned in force, and after ferocious street to street fighting, the authorities eventually were victorious. Hundreds of rebels were slain.

The unstable government overreacted, and all government agencies including Luke's were directed to seek out and arrest anybody that may have been sympathetic to the rebel cause. This was a godsend to the extreme Anglican Royalists who took the opportunity to blacken the name and unfairly arrest many of their moderate Presbyterian and Independent members of the Church of England.

This activity threatened to undo the careful policy of reconciliation that Charles had pursued since his arrival in England.

Luke was recalled to London and as both he and Matthew had experience in dealing with Fifth Monarchy extremists, their unit was allocated a series of houses, workshops and warehouses within the city of London, where given the large number of such fanatics at the local parish churches, a concentration of these subversive radicals might be found.

Instructions from the army high command was direct—arrest on the flimsiest of evidence and shoot to kill if the slightest resistance was encountered.

Luke, Matt and a dozen troopers made their way to Copper Lane where a concentration of dyers, tailors, weavers and fabric importers were located. They had specific orders to arrest a John Carson and a Richard Smith. Their home and workshop was reported to be on the ground floor of a two storeyed building on the corner of Copper Lane and Farthing Alley. The upper level was occupied by an importer of fabrics from Flanders.

Luke surveyed the scene and was delighted. He could station some of his men on three sides of the building, as it backed onto an unnamed alley. Anyone attempting to escape through the back of the premises would be apprehended.

With his men in position, Luke hammered on the door demanding entry in the name of the King.

Luke could hear movement and raised voices as the inhabitants reacted to his demand. Luke thought he heard voices in a foreign tongue.

Eventually the door was opened by a small man with a long beard. He looked exactly like the pictures of Jesus Christ Luke had seen. This must be Carson or Smith imitating their leader, in appearance at least.

"Call everybody here into this room while my men search the premises."

The little man asked, "What are you seeking to find?"

"A nest of traitors who supported last week's uprising," answered Luke.

"Sir, you are making…."

"Be quiet, I will ask the questions," interrupted Luke.

Suddenly one of the searching troopers grabbed a man and threw him to the ground. The man quickly rose to his feet pushed past a number of soldiers and scarpered out the front door.

The trooper fired at the fleeing man, as did the soldiers stationed in the street. He was not hit—and escaped.

Luke immediately questioned his trooper. "Why did you attack that man?"

He resisted my attempt to search him, and then he withdrew a paper from his pocket and tried to swallow it. I pulled some of it from his mouth as we tumbled to the floor."

"Where is that paper now?"

"It must be here somewhere," answered the trooper.

He searched the floor and found a half-chewed small piece of paper.

Matt commented jokingly, "Not another list Luke?"

Luke looked at the half-eaten object and whistled, "It's not a list, but it is some sort of code."

He handed the note to Matt who perused it silently for some time and eventually exclaimed, "I know this code. It is a Spanish military cipher. When I worked with Thurloe, we had a whole book of these ciphers. This is known as the vowel cipher. Twenty-five letters in the alphabet are given a two-vowel replacement. The five sequences of vowels for example aa, ae, ai, ao, au, then ea, ee, ei, eo, eu and so on could be used in any order. I and j are treated as one letter. I can probably translate what remains of it."

Luke turned towards the little man, "What is the name of the man who ran? Do you know why he fled?"

"His Christian name is Lorenzo. That is all I know. He only arrived ten minutes ago."

"That is hard to believe," replied Luke.

"It is true. I received a shipment of linen fabrics from Flanders just before you came. The man who fled came with the consignment. The ship from Ostend docked last night on the Thames, and my goods arrived by local carrier ten minutes ago. They are still on the landing. I do not know why Lorenzo fled as I had not paid him for the goods. His employer back in Bruges, my brother, will not be happy."

"So that man has just arrived from Spanish Flanders?" "I assume so."

Luke slowly realized his mistake. They had raided the premises of the fabric importer, and not the workshops and home of the Fifth Monarchy dyers, tailors and weavers. They must be on the upper floor, not the ground floor, as their now clearly faulty intelligence had indicated."

He apologized to the little man and asked, "Do you know if Carson or Smith are upstairs?"

"Not likely. Since the uprising last weekend, I have seen no males climb the stairs. All you will find upstairs are women and children."

"And who are you, sir?"

"I am Abraham Lombroso, silk and linen importer, and tailor to the aristocracy. I am the English representative of my family business centered in Bruges. While you are here sir, have a look at what I have to offer. Very reasonable prices!"

Luke felt that as an effort at reconciliation, he should at least look at the racks of clothing that lined the back of the large workshop. He was particularly struck by the most opulent and rich looking garment he had ever seen—a golden and white silk outfit.

Abraham picked up on his interest.

"A beautiful garment, but unfortunately with respect sir, ten to a hundred times what you could afford. It is an order made some months ago while he was in Bruges, for one of England's richest noblemen."

Abraham was correct concerning the Fifth Monarchy community that shared his building. There was not a single adult male on the upper level. They were met by absolute silence, broken only by the crying of numerous babies.

Two hours after they returned to their headquarters Matt explained to the group his translation of the paper that the man had tried to swallow

(gap) Iiie uiieiieeoooiee aooeeeoi uaiouauueieiae
eouaioieauua (gap) uaiuuuioua ouuuii (gap)

"It is a relatively easy cipher. The vowels were in sequence but started at Z instead of A—a was represented by uu and z by aa. Unfortunately, the name of the recipient and sender, and most unfortunate of all, that of the intended victim were all missing, probably eaten by the bearer."

"And what did it say?" asked an eager Luke.

Matt handed Luke a sheet which contained his translation. It read .

(gap) no contact with embassy
Remove(gap) blame fan(gap)

"And how do you interpret it?" asked Mark.

"An instruction from a Spanish source independent of the embassy to assassinate someone and to put the blame for it on the religious fanatics."

"In other words, in seeking the predicted Spanish outrage, we now have three possible sources—the pro-Spanish aristocrats, agents from the Spanish embassy and now minions of a possible rogue element in the Spanish administration of the Netherlands who are openly aiming at assassination."

Given the government's obsession with further radical Puritan uprisings, Luke was surprised to be summoned to a pre breakfast meeting with the King in which he raised an issue closer to Luke's heart.

"Despite my personal grief, and this dangerous uprising, I have not forgotten my responsibilities toward Margaret Dash."

"Unfortunately sire my investigations did not get very far, although yesterday by sheer luck we did uncover another source of Spanish intrigue."

Luke explained what had happened.

The King smiled. "I also have better news, Tremayne! Remember I sent a direction to my Lord Lieutenants to report anyone in their areas that could possibly be Lord Coleridge and her ladyship. Yesterday I had a reply from my man in Cumbria. A week or so ago a couple who could be our duo were reported arriving at Coleridge Court."

"Did your men check them out?"

"No, they were under strict orders to observe and report, not to act. I want you to take a platoon of men and force your way into Coleridge Court if necessary. I believe it is a large Elizabethan manor house on the shores of one of those beautiful lakes. Peter's father held out there for my father for several months before a barge-led assault by Cromwell himself, captured the by then half destroyed edifice."

Ten days later Luke and Miles with six troopers and a dozen local militia descended into a valley at the bottom of which the gleaming white building, Coleridge Court, could be seen. Luke had reported to the local Lord Lieutenant who offered to augment his group as the Coleridges for decades had had a reputation of rarely obeying local or central authority.

The manor on the landward side was surrounded by tall dry constructed stone walls. The sole entrance was large and consisted of massive iron gates. As Luke's unit approached these, a man emerged from a small gate beside the entrance. "I am Francis Bent, steward of Coleridge Court. Who are you and why do you approach us with so many armed men?"

"We are agents of the King, with instructions to search the premises by force if necessary."

The steward appeared shocked, and almost in disbelief asked, "What are you looking for?"

Luke played hard ball. "I am not at liberty to say. Now will you open the gate to let my troopers through."

The steward did not answer and did not move.

Luke did not hesitate

"Arrest this man Captain Oxenbridge!"

As Miles complied, Luke went through the gate from which the steward had emerged, and within minutes had opened the heavy gates to allow his troopers to ride through. They then followed a long winding path that brought them to the front of house, which faced the lake.

Luke knocked on the main door which was opened by a valet who asked, "What is the meaning of this? Where is Mr. Bent?"

25

"**M**r. Bent has been arrested for disobeying the orders of the King. We are here to search the premises for a missing couple. Take me to your master or mistress so that I can explain this intrusion."

"They are in the garden at the back of the house. Follow me."

Luke was pleased. Peter had obviously brought Margaret home to his estate. She was relatively safe. "I will find my own way to the garden, you can assist my men, as they search the house."

Luke left the backdoor of the house, and found the couple sitting under a large oak. He quietly approached them and was about to address them when the man turned around.

Both Luke and the man and were surprised. It was not Peter.

It was Henry.

Then the woman turned. This was even more surprising. It was Martha.

"What are you doing here so far from London?" asked Henry.

"I might ask you the same question. I was sent here by the King to bring Lord Peter and Lady Margaret back to London—her ladyship for her own protection, and Lord Peter under arrest for suspected kidnapping. How do you and Lady Martha come to be here?"

"My uncle, the Earl of Greenham approached me some weeks ago. He told me that my cousin Peter had been delayed on the continent and was not in a position to take possession of his family estates for some time. He believed that it was essential for a family member to step in and sort things out pending Peter's return."

"Seems reasonable, but why are you here, Lady Martha?" She looked at Henry for guidance as to what she should say. "Tell Luke all. We have nothing to hide," he replied.

"Peter felt that you would have people scouring France and England looking for them. To lay a false trail that his lordship had taken Margaret under his protection and had moved her to his northern estate might allay your fears—and you would call off any search. Henry asked me to accompany him north to create this false impression."

"This was to be confirmed by the Earl who was to inform the King that his daughter was safe, and under of the protection of his nephew," added Henry.

"This is sheer stupidity. Peter and Margaret are in great danger. To mislead us is simply playing into the hands of our enemies."

Henry remained silent.

"The Earl has not informed the King, probably because the court routine has been completely disrupted by a Fifth Monarchy uprising, and the death of the princess Mary," said Luke. "Has the Venetian embassy given you leave?"

"My absence is short term. We head back to London tomorrow. I had a letter from Peter explaining to the steward here, that I was acting in his place to put in order the new routine following the death of the old baron."

"The Earl is convinced that Peter has removed his daughter for her own good and has not kidnapped her for his own selfish ends?" asked Luke.

"Which would be?" asked Henry.

"Similar I believe to your one time thought—marriage."

Henry gasped, and seemed to be extremely cross. "The scoundrel!" he muttered. Martha gasped, and grabbed his hand.

She turned to Luke, "Are you going to arrest us, and escort us back to London in chains?"

"I doubt that you have committed any crime. It is the Earl that I hold responsible for the removal of his daughter from the King's protection."

"He is currently on his estate in northern Lancashire. You would pass it on your way back to London," said Henry as he winked at Luke.

Luke thanked Henry and Martha and led his men away from the lake.

They headed for the Lancastrian coast.

Miles commented, "Why did they tell us where the Earl was presently located?"

"It was a clearly deliberate act, either to embarrass the Earl, or to delay our return to London."

Later the next day Luke and his troop approached the cliffside manor house of the Earl. Their arrival coincided with a major local event. Many coaches and horsemen were seen passing through the gates and heading up the long drive. On alighting the visitors all appeared to be wearing their most impressive habits. Luke surmised that the Earl was hosting a winter dinner and ball for his neighbors.

This created a problem. From recent experience Luke realized that many Royalist gentry and aristocrats detested the army—even though now they were acting in the King's name. The experience of the military dominated regimes of the Republic and Cromwell had left a lasting negative impression.

Luke turned to Miles, "Lead the troop to the nearest town for our overnight stop. I will catch you up. A large detachment of troops arriving at this Royalist festivity would not enhance the King's cause. I will go alone and talk privately to the Earl."

Half an hour later Luke was in the dressing room of the Earl as his valet assisted him into his most elaborate finery to host a dinner followed by a grand ball that would last through the night.

"Well, Colonel what brings you so far north for what my servant told me is only a few minutes chat?"

"Come, your grace. I am returning from a wild goose chase created by your substitution of Henry for Lord Peter and Lady Martha for your daughter.

The Earl looked generally puzzled. "I am surprised that that is how you have interpreted events. I had no idea that you would see me sending Henry to Coleridge Court as an attempt to mislead you, and thereby the King."

Luke backpedaled, "These are past events, and the King would not wish to come between a father and his daughter. His only concern is your daughter's safety, wherever she is. My only question is how you knew that Margaret would not be going to Craven Castle, and that Peter was delayed?"

"Two weeks ago, I received two letters within the same package sent from Bruges. One was from Margaret who said she was quite safe and had decided of her own freewill not to move to Craven Castle. She would stay where she was, until all the possible problems surrounding names on the list were resolved. The second was from Peter apologizing for not returning Margaret to England. He claimed she had made a very persuasive case, and he would stay with her until he was assured of her absolute safety. He asked that in return, would I or another family member travel to Coleridge Court and organize it in the way he would have done. There was a note attached to his letter setting out what he required. I was in London at the time and knew I would not have time to carry out Peter's wish, so I asked Henry to stand in for Peter."

"What about Lady Martha?"

"I made no request for Henry to take anybody with him. I only heard a few days ago that he had not arrived at Coleridge Court alone."

Luke's attention was suddenly diverted. He was amazed at the set of clothing that the valet had produced and was beginning to assist the Earl to dress. He had seen it before. It was the opulent gold and white silk combination he had viewed in the Lombroso workshop.

"My lord, what a magnificent set of clothes. I did not realize you dealt with the Lombroso family."

It was the Earl's turn to be astonished, "And I did not realize an army colonel in England was up to date with the latest Flemish fashion created by one of the finest houses in Europe. I was introduced to the Lombroso family when the King's court-in-exile was in Bruges. Just before I returned to England, I ordered these clothes to wear at the King's coronation. As that has been postponed, I decided to wear it tonight."

"How did you become acquainted with the Lombroso house?"

"They are a family of Spanish converted Jews who are tailors to most of the Spanish political elite in Flanders. Spanish officials recommended them to most of the English Court."

Luke thanked the Earl and departed, intrigued by the information he had received. There was no attempt on the Earl's part to deceive, Margaret failed to arrive in England of her own freewill, and the Lombroso House had close connections with the Spanish authorities in the Netherlands. In addition, why had Henry taken Martha with him, obviously without the Earl's approval?

Luke alerted his team to a possible three-pronged Spanish attack-sympathetic English politicians and officials, the Spanish embassy and now a group of agents acting on behalf of anti-Charles elements in the administration of the Spanish Netherlands. All three Luke argued were united on one issue. They were determined to stop an English Portuguese marriage alliance. Some hoped to recover the lost Spanish territories of Dunkirk and Jamaica.

Miles observed, "These rogue Spanish agents could have already acted by encouraging and financing the uprising of the Puritan fanatics. In attempting to seize the Tower and Whitehall, the intended victims may not have been the royal family, but the King's two leading ministers, the Lord Chancellor Edward Hyde and the commander of the army George Monk—both strong advocates of the Portuguese marriage."

Mark concurred, "Perhaps we have been looking at the predicted Spanish intervention from the wrong angle. Instead of an indirect attempt to belittle the Portuguese and advance their own position, they may have adopted a more direct and effective policy—assassinate as many Portuguese supporting English politicians and officials as they can."

"If you are right the list and three English aristocratic women named may have nothing to do with Spanish intrigue," Luke replied. "We must follow up this possible link between the Spaniards and the current uprising. To have English Protestants do their dirty work would be a brilliant ploy. Miles and I will return to Copper Lane and question again both Lombroso's employees and the Fifth Monarchy families in the area."

Luke and Miles without any armed escort were soon in discussion with Abraham Lombroso. "Sir, we have returned without an armed force to question your staff, and the fanatics upstairs about the recent uprising. We now believe that the man who ran away, whatever role he played in your organization, was also a Spanish agent. Has he returned? And can you tell us more about him?"

"Normally every consignment of goods from my family business in Bruges is accompanied by one of their workers. This was not the usual man. When I asked him, what had happened to Dominic who has successfully seen the transfer of our goods for the last three years, he said he did not know."

"Did he give you his name? Did he have authorization from your family for the role he was carrying out?"

"Yes, to both. My brother who prepared the paperwork in the letter of introduction the man gave me, said that Lorenzo Adamo was replacing Dominic on this one occasion."

"He didn't say why Lorenzo was sent on this particular mission?"

"Not directly, but one of his comments might be of particular interest to you, colonel. Lorenzo was not one of the family's long-term employees. The Spanish authorities in Brussels who provide most of the family business in Bruges, suggested that they would appreciate it, if this new man was given the opportunity to go to England."

"So, my assertion that Lorenzo is probably a Spanish agent does not surprise you?"

"No, but I can't see what he could have achieved to the detriment of your country in the short time he was here."

"Do you know which ship bought this latest consignment from Bruges?"

26

"Yes, it was the carrier we have used for five years—*The Lady Agatha*," was the reply.

"I know of *The Lady Agatha*, and its owner Viscount Craven," revealed a surprised Luke. "Was the Viscount aboard as captain or passenger on this last trip?" probed Luke.

"In neither capacity. I have never known the Viscount to captain the ship since we have been doing business with him."

"But you have met him?"

"Yes, he is one of our best customers. Often on its way from Ostend to London, *The Lady Agatha* stops at the Craven estate, and brings him up to London. It is much quicker for him than travelling by road. He did that some weeks ago when he was accompanied by a very attractive young woman."

"Would Adamo have ever met the Viscount?"

"Not to my knowledge, but he did reveal an interest in the Viscount. They may have met in Bruges."

Both officers were alarmed by the comment.

"In what way did Adamo express interest in the Viscount?" asked Miles. "He apparently expressed disappointment that the Viscount did not join the ship on its last visit, and according to one of my tailors Adamo had offered to accompany him to Craven Castle this week."

"Why would one of your men be travelling to Craven Castle?" probed Luke.

"The Viscount has an order for a range of outfits, some new, some that we renovated. Unfortunately, they were not ready to be sent to him on *The Lady Agatha* when it left London a few days ago. As he needs them for a spate of social occasions this winter, I offered to send them to him immediately they were completed."

"Did Adamo explain his interest?" continued Luke.

"I don't know, but my assistant John Cope spent more time with him than did I. I will call him over."

Abraham explained to his man what Luke and Miles were concerned about, and then sought permission to withdraw.

"Master Cope, how did Adamo explain his particular interest in Viscount Craven?"

"Simply! He had served under the Viscount when as Captain Guy Craven his lordship was a privateer working out of Dunkirk on behalf of Spain They met again when Craven was at the King's court in exile in Bruges. He said he jumped at the chance to oversee the Lombroso shipment in the hope of renewing his acquaintance with the Viscount."

"In that case why did he not return on *The Lady Agatha*, which was headed for Craven Castle, before it embarks on its next Channel crossing?"

"I asked him that, and he replied that he had other things to do in London and had arranged to return on *The Lady Agatha* on its subsequent trip in about ten days. When these plans fell through, he offered to accompany me to Craven Castle, where he hoped to board *The Lady Agatha* from its home base. I will spend most of the next month moving through the aristocratic houses of Suffolk and Essex repairing their expensive clothing and delivering their new purchases for the winter season. It was finally agreed that Adamo would accompany me just before he ran off during your last visit."

"And he has not returned?" queried Miles.

"No, but one of lads saw him lurking in the shadows watching this workshop."

"Maybe he will reappear, just before you set out for Craven Castle," suggested Luke.

"Was Lorenzo Adamo a Spaniard? asked Miles.

"He spoke Spanish, French and English fluently, but he was an ethnic Fleming of distant Spanish descent."

"He does not appear to be an ordinary worker for a textile company having such a range of languages. His experience as a privateer also raise other questions about his status," continued Miles.

"Why are you two officers so concerned about Adamo? Abraham mentioned he is a suspected spy."

"Yes, we obtained information that maybe the other things he had to do while in London was to sabotage English, French or Portuguese activities and facilities. Or even to assassinate leading English or Portuguese figures. Did he ever talk to the religious fanatics upstairs?"

"He was not here long enough, and nearly all the males there disappeared after their uprising, which was before Adamo arrived."

Luke and Miles were crest fallen.

Cope noticed their expression and smiled. "Gentlemen, Adamo had no connection with those fanatics, but his predecessor Dominic did. Every time he came, he visited upstairs. He delivered them goods from the continent on each occasion."

"Could these goods have been guns?" asked Luke.

"Possibly, I never saw whatever he had carried upstairs though I remember Abraham speculating on one occasion about the contents of a crate that he saw being carried past our door."

"When do you leave for Craven Castle, Master Cope?" added Miles. "Your presence has delayed my preparation, but we will still leave in the morning."

"Then prepare for an extra man. My assistant Captain Hatch will join you on the trip to Craven Castle. I would come myself, but in case Adamo joins you, he would recognize me. I will make my own way there in due course to question the Viscount and the crew of *The Lady Agatha* further on these matters," exclaimed Luke.

Luke had lied. He left London before dawn. Determined to reach Castle Craven before the Lombroso group, he took advantage of the government's network of stables that enabled couriers to ride their horses at full gallop for an hour, then change horses and repeat the process through a number of staging posts. Fortunately, the route between London and the naval base at Harwich passed close to the Craven estates.

Luke was at the gates of Craven Castle a full half day before the expected arrival of the tailor Cope and his assistants. As he dismounted Luke became aware that a group of soldiers had surrounded him, and as the gates opened, he was greeted by an infantry captain. These were part of a contingent of Royal troops sent by Charles to protect Elizabeth and Agatha.

Luke congratulated the officer on the effectiveness of their security. He recognized Luke and asked, "Do you bring us new orders, Colonel?"

"No, Lieutenant, I have come with an urgent message for the Viscount. Take me to him!"

A soldier who took his horse from him almost disapprovingly commented, "It must be urgent, you have ridden hard to get here. I have rarely seen a horse so distressed."

The lieutenant walked with Luke to the main door of the Castle and Luke informed the servant who opened it that Colonel Tremayne in the King's name needed to see the Viscount immediately. It was a matter of life and death.

Luke was asked to wait in the reception hall while the servant disappeared. He returned later with a wiry little man who was not the Viscount.

It was the Turk.

He confronted Luke, "Welcome Colonel, what is this rubbish about life and death? Whose death?"

"The Viscount's. Where is he?"

"An hour away on the edge of his estate, dealing with a tenant. What exactly do you fear?"

"A possible assassination attempts by a person that you both know—Lorenzo Adamo."

"That sniveling jackanape, an acquaintance, but no friend. I had the misfortune of carrying him from Bruges to London only a week or so ago."

"Why the negative assessment? He claimed he served under you in your privateering days, and renewed acquaintances with the Viscount during his stay at the royal-court-in-exile."

"All that is true, but from the beginning Guy and I distrusted him. I suspected he was an agent of the Spanish government on board to monitor our adherence to Spanish policy, given that our license was issued in the name of King of Spain. Why is he after Guy?"

"He tried to swallow a paper that suggested he assassinate someone. He showed an interest in the Viscount, and he may be heading this way. I have a man in the Lombroso group who will tell us in advance if he did in fact join them. His excuse will be that he missed the departure of *The Lady Agatha* from London and hoped to catch up with it here."

"I can confirm his interest in Guy. He was very disappointed that Guy was not aboard the ship. He even asked me if we were dropping in here to pick him up before we docked at London."

"Perhaps the original plan was to attack Guy at sea," suggested Luke. "Well, it would have been a lot easier there, than here. We have very tight security around the castle, strengthened by the detachment of troops sent by the King. When Adamo arrives with the Lombroso group, he will be treated as a servant, and none of them will come anywhere near the main part of the castle. I will ensure that Guy is never alone, if Adamo be among the visitors."

"I need to stay hidden as he knows me as a King's officer who is aware of his attempt to swallow incriminating evidence, which provoked his subsequent flight."

"Come to the most secure part of the castle where their ladyships are housed. They will probably enjoy your company after a long period of semi- isolation. I will ride out to meet Guy and inform him of the potential crisis."

Luke was most impressed by the security surrounding Agatha and Elizabeth. Both women were pleased to see him. "Any news about our fate, or any progress on determining why we were on that horrible list?" asked Agatha.

"Nothing proven, but there is some evidence that the list and Spanish intrusion into English affairs may not be linked after all. Their targets may not be the three women on that list at all. But we cannot be certain. It is a pity that Lady Margaret chose not to be protected here with you," observed Luke.

Agatha looked at Elizabeth who nodded approvingly, "We share your concern. Both of us have received letters from Margaret in the last week or so. The Turk brought them with him from Bruges. He said that just before they departed a well-dressed gentleman, who looked incredibly like the late King handed them to him and asked that they be given to us personally."

"So, what causes your concern?"

"The letter to Agatha was dated two days before mine in which she was looking forward to joining us. In the letter to me she had changed her mind. She felt very secure in the company of her cousin Peter Coleridge but was a bit anxious about her situation when he left. He had apparently been summoned home by his uncle, Margaret's father, the Earl of Greenham," said Elizabeth.

"As if anticipating our obvious question, why she was not returning with Peter, she made two outrageous claims against her own father," added Agatha.

"Which were?"

"That her father was a murderer, having had her long-term French sweetheart murdered, and that he was an agent not of the Spanish King, but of the Spanish Inquisition."

27

Luke was intrigued.

Agatha continued, "During the King's exile in Flanders, the Earl spent several months in Madrid, and returned to Bruges a special favourite of the local authorities."

"In addition to claims about her father, she had serious concerns about her cousin Henry. She became alarmed during their most recent time together, when you were tracking them in France that his initial amorous attempts were provoked by unsavoury motives, rather than genuine love for her. She felt that if she had not been protected throughout by French agents, he may have tried to take advantage of her. She fears that her father may use his privileged position with the Inquisition to coerce the Pope into allowing Henry to marry a first cousin," said Elizabeth.

"Why would the Earl risk his daughter's marriage with a first cousin?" asked a skeptical Luke.

"It keeps the title and wealth within the family. Henry as Margaret's husband would inherit the title and family wealth which would in turn descend to their eldest son. The current Earl's future grandson would be the ultimate beneficiary," she continued. "The aristocracy think ahead, that is why despite recent upheavals, they will continue to rule England," replied the arrogant Elizabeth.

Agatha changed the subject. "If you did not come down to Suffolk to talk to us, why is the King's most intimate special agent at Castle Craven?"

Luke did not want to alarm the women and lied, "His Majesty is very concerned about your welfare. He sent me here to check on your security, which I have to report is first class—unless you tell me otherwise."

Agatha came up Luke and pushed her face almost into his, "You are a professional liar, colonel. The King does not send the senior member of his special unit on such a menial task. A civilian clerk could make such an assessment. Is the expected Spanish attack, first revealed by Cardinal Mazarin, about to occur?"

Luke changed his mind and decided to reveal all to the women. After he had finished his explanation Agatha commented, "I remember that creature Adamo. He tried to ingratiate himself with me when I was a teenager aboard father's privateer. Later in Bruges he was always hanging about the English Court without any explicable reason. Father believed he was an agent of the Spanish administration in Brussels."

There was a knock on the door and the Lieutenant of the guard entered the room. "Forgive my intrusion, a Captain Hatch has arrived. He wishes to inform you that Lorenzo Adamo joined the tailor's party just after leaving London. The group should arrive in an hour. Is there anything I should know Colonel?"

"Yes, Lieutenant. Put everybody on high alert. I will contact you later after I have talked with the Viscount. Take Captain Hatch into your detachment. I will also speak to him later."

That evening a council of war was convened consisting of the Viscount, the Turk, Luke, Matthew Hatch, the commander of the guard and Master Cope.

Luke led the discussion, "If I were Adamo there are three things I need to achieve—how to get into the presence of the Viscount, how to be with him alone, and how to escape. Adamo is an experienced operator. He is not inclined to sacrifice his own life for any mission."

Cope volunteered, maybe a little too eagerly, "I can help him achieve the first two. He can assist me when I come up here in the morning to fit his grace, and I can find an excuse to leave them alone."

The Turk intervened, "That puts Guy in danger! We should prevent them meeting at all, and certainly make it impossible for Adamo to be alone with him."

"That is an option, but at the moment Adamo could be a complete innocent. All of our preparations and assumptions are based on circumstantial evidence, but any attempt on the Viscount would confirm these assumptions." Luke replied.

"And in the process achieve the enemy's aim of eliminating Guy," added the Turk.

"We can take precautions. In the circumstances Adamo can only attempt to shoot or stab the Viscount."

"The normal precautions of wearing a thick musket proof vest or concealing weapons on the Viscount so that he can defend himself are not possible. He will be down to his underwear for the fitting," contributed a pragmatic Cope.

Luke conceded the accuracy of this probable situation.

Matt suddenly exclaimed, "He won't attempt to stab or shoot his target. How would he escape? He will try a method that will not only kill the Viscount but prevent himself being followed."

"Which is? asked Luke.

"Grenades—the first to kill the target and the others to prevent him being followed," suggested the lieutenant of the guard.

"There is a major flaw in that scenario. Adamo will be under observation all the time he is with the Viscount. Even if he can prime the grenade without being seen, once it is thrown it takes some time to explode. In most cases in limited space, it can be picked up and returned to sender before it explodes," countered the experienced soldier, Miles.

"But there may not be anybody in a position to return the grenade. He may have shot everybody in the room, and used the grenades to assist with his escape," contributed the anxious Turk.

The Viscount raised his hand for silence, "I have listened with a combination of horror and amusement as you all discussed my fate. The simple question is whether I submit myself to possible assassination, or at the other extreme simply have Adamo eliminated during the night. I know Colonel Tremayne could justify the latter in the name of national security. I am surprised that over the years French agents have not removed Adamo. They certainly warned me of his role for what we might call Spanish intelligence a decade ago, when I was a privateer. Let's lead him into a trap!"

Next morning before the Viscount had dressed, Cope and Adamo arrived with several sets of clothes. Luke was hidden in a large wardrobe in the corner of the Viscount's dressing room, and the Turk was in an adjacent room ready to burst in. The Viscount's valet had been told not to enter the room until the Turk told him to do so.

The Viscount tried on a number of garments while Cope called out measurements which Adamo apparently noted down. After a quarter of an hour, Luke began to find his confinement in the wardrobe oppressive. He was breathing with difficulty and felt very hot.

He heard Cope play his part in the planned ambush of Adamo when he said, "Lorenzo, carry on here! I have left behind a pair of gloves. I will fetch them. Pack up the garments that are acceptable to his lordship, and we will leave them here."

Cope left the room, and Luke could hear the Viscount and Adamo chatting. Luke tensed, ready to spring out of the wardrobe should Adamo make any move against the Viscount. Another ten minutes expired, and a sweat soaked Luke heard Cope return.

A few minutes later Cope exclaimed, "Well that's it for today. I must get back to London tomorrow. We will leave just after dawn. Everybody except myself will leave before sunrise. I will delay my departure for an hour. Would it be convenient if I returned here with the garments that need adjusting so early?"

The Viscount replied, "I rise just after dawn. I will see you then." Cope and Adamo left.

Luke, the Turk and the Viscount later discussed the situation.

The Turk was direct, "You were completely wrong, Tremayne. Adamo was given every opportunity, and yet made no attempt on the Viscount."

A crestfallen Luke admitted his mistake but tried to regain some ground. "Adamo may not be the assassin, but he could still be a Spanish agent, whose reasons for being here remain a mystery. I would increase the protection of the women. They could be the target after all."

"Well, I can relax. Being a possible target is not the most comfortable position to be in. I will be glad when all of the Lombroso group have left the estate," announced the Viscount

As they were about to leave the Viscount's dressing room one of the Turk's men arrived and gave him some alarming news.

The Turk immediately informed the others. "A suspicious vessel is sailing slowly along our coast probably looking for the mouth of the network of waterways that cover the estate. It was one of those small sail and oared vessels that ply the Thames. My men from *The Lady Agatha* that is moored in the river estuary challenged it and were told that it was from the Lombroso factory carrying goods that were not ready when we departed London but needed to be in Bruges as soon as possible. I am to inform Cope that should he wish, it will stay in our estuary until tomorrow morning. It has room for two of his group and would have them back in London much more quickly than the road journey."

Luke asked, "Is the arrival of a Thames vessel unusual?"

"Unusual yes, but it has happened two or three time before, for the same reason," answered the Viscount.

The Turk went after Cope to inform him of the news, the Viscount called in his valet to complete his dressing, while Luke returned to his room to inform Matthew of the complete failure of the trap set for Lorenzo Adamo.

Luke and Matt rose early the next morning as they wished to reach London that night. As they trotted slowly up the long drive, they were overtaken by a galloping guard commander, "Stop Colonel, dreadful news!

"And what might that be?" asked Luke.

"The Viscount is dead—murdered. The Turk wants you to ride post haste to the river mouth. The murderer is trying to escape in that Thames vessel that came up the channels overnight, almost to the castle itself."

"What exactly happened?" asked Luke as all three galloped in the direction of the estuary.

They could see a horseman ahead of them that was presumably the Turk. It was touch and go whether he would reach his own ship before the Thames boat reached open sea.

Luke continued. "How did Adamo manage to get through your security and kill Guy?"

"It was not Adamo. All I know is that Cope arrived very early with the remaining garments. The Viscount sent his valet to the kitchen for some pre breakfast nibbles. When the valet returned the Viscount was back in bed and presumably asleep. Later the valet noticed marks around his lordship's throat and realised that he was dead, strangled—presumably by Cope. This delay in discovery allowed Cope and probably Adamo to board the Thames boat, and be well away before the alarm was raised. My men did not interfere with the boat, because we had been told that it had come to collect some of the tailor's party."

Luke thought to himself. It all fitted into place. Adamo was not the assassin, but the courier. The half-eaten note was meant for Cope, instructing him to remove Craven, but stay clear of the Spanish embassy.

The horsemen relaxed. The Turk had reached *The Lady Agatha* and it was slowly maneuvered into blocking the exit. A hidden gun deck emerged, and several cannon shots were fired at the approaching Thames boat.

28

Luke, Matthew and the guard commander reached the Thames boat. Its master seemed genuinely surprised.

"This is an outrage" he screamed. "We are engaged in collecting two members of the Lombroso firm who need to be back in London in a hurry. I have already delivered the goods from Mr. Abraham to *The Lady Agatha*, and now it is firing on us and blocking our passage to the open sea. I will inform the nearest magistrate of this impediment to free navigation. It is piracy."

"I am the nearest magistrate," replied Luke. "I have to inform you that at least one of your passengers is a suspected murderer. The Viscount Craven has just been killed, and we are arresting the people you have just taken aboard as prime suspects. Pull into this bank, or I will signal the ship to fire again to sink your boat. The soldiers, now taking up positions along the bank, will also open fire on my command."

As the boat pulled closer to the bank, a passenger jumped overboard and started swimming to the opposite shore. A volley of musket fire missed its mark, and it was Cope who was recognised as he clambered up the opposing bank and disappeared into the wilderness of the water lands.

Conveniently for this escaping murderer, a heavy fog suddenly descended. The Turk had joined the soldiers, and after he and Luke questioned the crew, it was decided that the offending boat could continue on its return trip to London.

Adamo, who was aboard made no attempt to escape. He pleaded complete ignorance of the attack on the Viscount, claiming he was aboard the boat a half hour before Cope arrived.

Luke ordered the guard commander to take Adamo back to the castle. He would be interrogated later. The immediate task was to catch Cope.

The fog disappeared as suddenly as it came, but Cope could not be seen.

The Turk and the soldiers raised the whole estate—sailors, workers and soldiers.

The boats of the estate patrolled the coastline. *The Lady Agatha* stood out to sea from where its lookout could see the coastline of the whole estate. A couple of the Turk's men manned the tower of the castle and directed the pursuers by the waving and pointing with a giant flag.

The Turk interpreted his flag waving men. "They have located the quarry. He is heading to the coast in a south easterly direction from here. He is heading for trouble. Years ago, peat was dug from that area so now it is made up of many deep pools. Our tailor assassin will not cope with that environment."

Cope's flight path was becoming much clearer—footprints in the mud, and broken reeds. Then all a sudden Luke and the Turk emerged onto higher reed- less ground, and there was Cope slowly wading through a pool whose depth appeared to be increasing. The water was now up to Cope's neck. He began to swim.

The Turk turned to Luke, "Leave this to me, colonel. It is personal." Luke acquiesced.

As they gained on the struggling Cope, it became obvious that the Turk did not intend to take prisoners. He was priming his pistol as he went.

Luke did the same. He would hand his to the Turk in case a second shot was required.

All of a sudden a rider appeared from nowhere and rode straight at Cope as he struggled out of the pool. There was no attempt to slow down. The horse trampled the struggling man into the mud. Only then did the rider halt, turn the horse around and encouraged it to rear, and smash its front hooves into the increasingly macerated, and now lifeless body.

The killer of John Cope, Spanish inspired assassin, was Agatha, now the Viscountess Craven.

Convinced that Cope was dead, she rode back towards the castle. Luke and the Turk reached the body. Cope was indeed deceased, but the Turk took his faithful scimitar, and decapitated the corpse. This was indeed personal.

Next day Luke and Matthew interrogated Adamo.

Luke was blunt. "Lorenzo, you have had the misfortune to fall into the hands of a secret agency of the English state. In essence you are a dead man. It is simply a question of how you want to die—a shot in the back of the head before we leave here or transfer to the Tower of London where expert torturers will probably gouge out your eyes for starters."

"Come, colonel. This is just a bluff. You have no evidence against me."

"Not true, you had on your person an incriminating note which you attempted to swallow. It was an instruction to do what has been carried out here—the murder of Viscount Craven."

"That note had nothing to do with me. I picked it up from the workshop floor, just before you arrived. I realised it was incriminating to someone there, so I tried to destroy it. John Cope alone is responsible for what happened."

"You are not arguing your case before a court of law, Adamo. Even if I have no evidence, I will have no hesitation in removing you as an enemy agent. I will not humiliate such an experienced spy by suggesting you could save your life, if you revealed to me details of the Spanish onslaught on English persons and institutions of which we have recently been made aware."

"You are correct colonel. I have nothing to reveal as your information concerning some Spanish intrusion into English affairs is overrated. Your faulty source is either French or Portuguese. The removal of Craven has nothing to do with English affairs. He was revealed to be a double agent who for decades while openly serving Spain was a secret agent of the diabolical French Cardinal Mazarin. He was probably betraying his English King twice over. You should thank Cope although I do not know why he acted. He was not one of our agents."

"Come on, Adamo, your people kidnapped Lady Elizabeth Rhodes whom you sent here, obviously before you discovered Craven's treachery. That suggests further interference in our affairs."

"I have not heard of any action to be taken against that lady. We only became interested because her name was found on a list emanating from the Portuguese. They are our enemy, not you colonel. We are now friends. Your King has just signed a peace treaty with us and sent his best friend off to negotiate for the hand in marriage of a princess suggested by the King of Spain."

Luke had second thoughts about any summary execution. He would have Adamo incarcerated in the Tower of London and formally hand him over to the Lord Chancellor for further interrogation. This fervently pro-Portuguese politician might enjoy the prospect.

Before Luke, Matt and their prisoner left for London, Luke paid his respects to the widowed Dowager Viscountess Arabella, and her now wealthy and powerful daughter the new Viscountess Agatha.

As he was about to leave Agatha followed him. "Colonel, what will happen to me?"

Luke smiled, having previously discussed the situation with the only other witness, the Turk.

"I don't know what you mean, your ladyship. You are not responsible, if a deranged man throws himself under your horse."

Agatha was visibly relieved. "I was so enraged when I heard what had happened to father. I followed Cope's trek from the advantage point of our tower for much of the time. My initial thought was not to kill him. I thought he might get away from you and the Turk. I knew I could cut him off before he reached the coast. I reached him as he was coming out of the pool. My horse did not stop in time."

Agatha smiled and continued, "Why did Cope do it? He was a close acquaintance. He has been coming here for years. Was the murder personal?"

"Probably not. The Spaniards discovered that your father was a double agent for the French. It was a political killing, perhaps as a warning to other openly pro-Spanish politicians, not to desert them in this time of crisis."

"But why Cope? He was a quiet English tailor who admittedly worked for a Jewish textile firm based in Bruges. I visited their shop there several times."

"I have no evidence regarding Cope. We all trusted him. Given the probable reason for your father's death, you also might be a target for the same reason. Your security here is excellent—if you continue to admit no outsiders," Luke advised.

Luke had noted that over the time he had been at Craven Castle, Agatha had not been herself. She seemed flushed and appeared tired and not as alert as normal.

He raised his concern with the Turk.

"Her ladyship is not herself, and the death of her father will not help, but in time all will be well," was the reply.

The Turk winked at Luke who was completely at a loss as how to interpret the gesture.

A week after Luke returned to London, two aspects of his Craven Castle adventure had become clearer. The Lord Chancellor's questioning of Adamo in the Tower of London had suffered a mishap. The prisoner had died while under interrogation.

The Spanish propaganda machine was very effective. Newsletters that flooded London, and rumors that swept through the lower orders were all presented with the same picture. Guy, Viscount Craven, one of England's leading Catholic peers, and a strong supporter of the Spanish peace treaty had been murdered by a Portuguese tailor. The Portuguese would stop at nothing to achieve their single aim—the marriage of Charles to their Infanta.

Luke discussed the matter with the King and was ready, as was the Lord Chancellor to counter this fake news. Charles was hesitant. He needed time. He would overtly accept the Spanish line, but Luke was to secretly inform the Portuguese ambassador of what really happened. Let the Portuguese counter these lies, the English did not want to be involved—a typical cautious reaction of the King.

Luke visited the Portuguese embassy and spoke to the ambassador who had just returned from Lisbon. "You are still fondly remembered by our Queen Regent, Tremayne. She hopes that if the King marries her daughter, you will lead an English contingent of troops to help keep the Spaniards at bay."

"I think my active army days are over. I have come to give you the truth about the murder of Viscount Craven. It was carried out by a Spanish agent but was not directly related to your campaign to achieve the marriage with the Infanta. The Spaniards took advantage of it. Craven was executed because for over a decade, while pretending to a Spanish agent, he was in fact working for the French. His Majesty is aware of the true situation, but for diplomatic reasons is pretending to accept the Spanish position."

"You are a true friend of Portugal, Tremayne," was the sole response.

Three weeks later the Turk arrived at Luke's Whitehall apartment.

"So, this is the seat of Royal power," he remarked flippantly.

Luke gave him a big hug and exclaimed, "What brings you here?"

"I bring a letter from my new mistress."

"And how is Agatha coping in her new role?"

"Brilliantly! Her father would be proud. Guy had tended to let things around the estate slide over recent years. Agatha has tightened everything up, and the place is running smoothly. But she brooks no opposition and has exiled her mother to a small property across the county border in Norfolk. She has already set in progress massive land works to create an effective port for *The Lady Agatha,* dredging many of the channels, and continues with enthusiasm the draining of the water lands around the Castle."

"Excellent news!"

"But there is a downside."

All of this activity may have all become a little too much. She has hidden herself away in a house in the middle of an island within the estate and is not to be disturbed for three weeks."

"I suppose the next thing she will do is emerge from her retreat and announce her betrothal to some fortunate gentleman," commented Luke somewhat prophetically.

29

"Not likely. Agatha as you remarked on your last visit had not been her lively optimistic self since her return to England from her holiday in Italy. I asked Guy just before his death whether there was a problem, and perhaps I should take her on our next voyage to Ostend to cheer her up. He said she had fallen in love with an English aristocrat in Italy, who had died fighting the Ottoman on behalf of Venice. He concluded that time alone and perhaps time to herself would heal her wounds."

Luke changed the topic. "Do you know the subject matter of this letter she has sent me?"

"Only that it is a request for your help, and that you might need my assistance, should you accept whatever she proposes."

The Turk handed Luke a large packet, which when opened contained two letters.

The first was from Agatha to him. Its key message was simple, "Margaret is beside herself. Peter left for England some time ago but may not have arrived. She has been unable to contact him, and she has received no letters from him since the first week of him leaving. I have enclosed her letter to me."

Luke turned to this second letter. It was clear that Peter had seen Margaret happily and securely settled near Bruges, and then headed home to take up his estates. He wrote to her every day after his departure, but this mail ceased after the first week. She asked Agatha could she try to find out if he had taken up his estates, and possibly convince Colonel Tremayne to try to find him, if he had not.

Luke turned to the Turk. "The King remains gravely concerned about the situation of Lady Margaret and would prefer her under his protection as is Lady Agatha and Lady Elizabeth."

"If you accept the assignment, I am to take you by *The Lady Agatha* back to Craven Castle and then on to Bruges as the next assignment of Flemish goods are ready for us to collect."

"Do you know if Lady Agatha has discovered whether Peter arrived in England?"

"No, she has not. Given recent events she has not been able to follow up on Lady Margaret's request. I was asked to find out from his uncle, the Earl of Greenham if he knew of his Peter's whereabouts, but as the House of Lords is not in session, he was not in his town house— and not expected back here for a month or more."

Luke replied, "I will help Lady Agatha as the King is determined that Lady Margaret Dash be protected at all costs. With her somewhere in the Bruges area, he currently has little say in that endeavor. But it would be unwise, if I left for Bruges with you on this trip. Although I regret the delay, I must first ascertain that Lord Peter is not in England."

"I fully appreciate your approach colonel, but Agatha will be disappointed. I fear she might order me to search for the missing lord. I'm a trader and a seaman. Just getting to Bruges is not straightforward. Bruges has not been a seaport for centuries. The canal that linked it with the sea has long silted up for ships even as small as *The Lady Agatha*. We dock in Ostend and then use a barge to get goods to and from Bruges. I have many contacts in Ostend that could help me, but very few in Bruges. I have usually stayed with the boat at that port and sent others to make the transactions and collect the goods in Bruges. Many of my former comrades who were based in Dunkirk during our privateering days moved their base to Ostend after Dunkirk fell to French and now the English. They may be able to help."

Luke bid the Turk farewell, and immediately wrote a summary of the discussion which he sent to the King. He received a response much quicker than he expected. He was summoned to the King's presence. Luke's reasonable approach was immediately vetoed by the King.

"I have already lost one of my senior aristocrats in Guy Craven, and now another has disappeared. As the second one has close connections with Margaret Dash, and she seeks help to find him, that is what you will do. Immediately Tremayne! *The Lady Agatha* is still in port and I have already sent a directive to its captain to expect you within the hour. While you search for Coleridge on the continent, Mark will make the necessary enquiries at this end. Should Coleridge be found in England, we shall get a message to you. Take Hatch or Oxenbridge with you. Whoever you leave behind can look into this tailor Cope's background. What drove him to kill Craven? If you can't find Coleridge, at least try and bring Margaret home. Tell her she can stay here at Whitehall, if reunion with her father remains so distasteful."

By noon the next day Luke and Miles were enjoying a meal with the Turk at Craven Castle. Luke had at least one vital question. "We cannot complete this mission that the King has endorsed without one vital piece of information—where do we find Lady Margaret?"

The Turk gave a teasing reply. "I don't know."

Luke was flabbergasted, until he saw the look on the Turk's face. He smiled, and added, "But I do know how to contact her. You will stay at De Drie Zwanen, and inform the owner there of who you are, and your desire to contact Lady Margaret Dash."

"Until the Anglo-French attack on Bruges some years ago it was Les Trois Cygnes. It still caters for the French speaking minority in the city," explained the Turk.

"Why do you think Margaret refuses to come home?" asked Luke unexpectedly.

"Her stated reason is that she does not trust her father. If she were in England, he would have absolute control over her. On the continent he cannot exercise the same authority, and none at all, if he does not know where she is located."

"Do you believe her?"

"Yes, but there may be another reason. She was always the wild one of the three named in the list. She took a French lover in the past, maybe she has done so again."

"Or even married him?" suggested Luke.

"That would traumatise the Earl, her father," commented Miles. "Not necessarily," replied the Turk. "It would depend on status of the gentleman. If she has married a French duke, he would be delighted."

"It would certainly devastate her two cousins. Both Peter and Henry had thoughts of marrying her. For a while when she absconded with Peter, I thought that that might have happened, but for Catholics marriage between cousins without papal approval is not possible," declaimed Luke.

The Turk continued, "Gentlemen I may not be able to conceal your military gait and general bearing, but at least a change of clothes would be advisable. You will be entering what until a few days ago when the peace treaty with Spain was signed, was enemy territory. The English are as unpopular with the populace as the French, and with the authorities, as the Dutch."

"And what change of clothing do you advise?" asked an apprehensive Miles.

"You will dress as one of my seamen. Such outfits have the added advantage of being purchased in Flanders—much cheaper than in England. At least if you are dressed in that way your clothes will not give you away as English spies."

Two days later Luke and Miles were seated in the De Drie Zwanen. Their trip across the Channel in *The Lady Agatha* and then up a waterway that could be called neither a stream nor a canal by barge, proved uneventful.

Luke who spoke fluent Dutch informed the innkeeper that they wished to see an English woman, Lady Margaret Dash. Contrary to the Turk's advice in this bi-lingual town, he was delighted that Luke had spoken Dutch. He whispered, "The Spanish authorities have spies everywhere seeking out French and English-speaking customers. Are you English?"

"Do we look or sound English?"

The innkeeper did not comment directly but noted, "Your Dutch is not quite Flemish, but clearly a variant of southern Dutch—but not spoken like a native."

"I learnt it as a soldier twenty-five years ago, just across the border to the north, fighting for the Dutch Republic against Spain."

"That will not endear you to the local authorities either. I will send a man to bring her ladyship's representative here. It will take half to one hour. Settle down and enjoy our beers and combination seafood stews and try not to draw attention to yourselves! The regular Spanish patrol is due here any minute."

Luke and Miles enjoyed the seafood combination with a range of spicy pickled vegetables. Out of the corner of his eye Luke saw a Spanish officer and two soldiers enter the inn. They surveyed the customers and Luke saw the officer point in their direction. He overheard the innkeeper reply in Flemish, "Two English sailors up from Ostend, regulars."

They were not troubled by the patrol.

Sometime after the Spaniards departed, a man approached their table. There was immediate mutual recognition between him and Luke. He put his finger to his lips signaling that his identity should not be broadcast across the room.

He whispered, "We are both deep in enemy territory. Neither French nor English officers are welcome here. It is only a couple of years ago that a combined Anglo-French force unsuccessfully tried to take the city from its Spanish overlords. I delayed my arrival until their regular patrol had passed, but this inn still has its quota of Spanish spies. There are even agents of the Inquisition in the city."

Luke asked very quietly, "What is Emile de Bussy, an officer in one of France's most elite units, the Household Guard of Cardinal Mazarin doing in Bruges dressed as a common labourer? You handed Lady Margaret over to us weeks ago. Why did you take her back under your protection without informing us?"

"She is not officially under our protection."

"Then why are you here?"

"We followed your party from Paris towards Ostend. When Lady Margaret and Lord Coleridge diverted from their designated route home, I became alarmed. Was the baron abducting Lady Margaret? She had left our protection, but also deserted yours. I was ordered to follow them even into enemy territory. I was to discard my military uniform and dress like a common Fleming. I was accompanied by two of my men who are with her ladyship as I speak."

"When did this general surveillance convert into closer monitoring, if not special protection?" asked Luke.

"After I approached Lord Coleridge, relaying a message from the Cardinal suggesting they would be safer staying in France. Lord Coleridge was known to the Cardinal. He had worked on joint Anglo-French activities in the Levant in the past."

"In what particular situation?"

"Within the Ottoman Empire. Coleridge worked for your Levant Company, and was attached to the English ambassador in Constantinople. He was there for almost twenty years. He was appointed by the former monarch Charles I, and only returned to England with the return of his son as Charles II. Most of the time there however he was a joint consul for France and England in Syria and Lebanon—and was very successful in pursuing Anglo-French interests at the expense of the Venetians and Spaniards. My master, the Cardinal, was very impressed with him."

"Why then did this shining example of successful diplomacy and trade negotiations, desert Lady Margaret?"

"He didn't. She rejected both his assistance, and our protection. She had found herself the perfect sanctuary, which Lord Coleridge reluctantly accepted, although the Cardinal refused to withdraw us completely. She gradually accepted our reduced role of maintaining her security from a distance. She was very pleased that she could conceal her whereabouts from everybody, by using me as a go-between. Finish your meal, and I will take you to her!"

The three walked for between half and three-quarters of an hour in a southerly direction, moving closer to the French border.

Eventually they came upon a large walled estate. On reaching the main gate Luke was intrigued. A large sign announced it as the Couvent de Sainte- Marie-Madeleine.

Margaret Dash had entered a nunnery!

"This is totally a French order, although located on the Spanish side of the current border," remarked De Bussy.

Luke remembered the three aristocratic friends as schoolgirls had made a pact to become nuns, if life did not go their way.

Such an act would force both the Earl of Greenham, her father, and Charles, her king, to vary the succession. Neither would allow such vast assets to be transferred from the Dash family and England, to the Church of Rome or to the French.

With Margaret removed from the succession to title and estates, these would now flow to the nearest male heir, who was none other than Peter, Lord Coleridge.

Luke was now greatly concerned. Was this religious sanctuary part of a very sophisticated plot by Coleridge to become the next Earl of Greenham?

After waiting in a cold reception room for twenty minutes a vibrant and bubbly Margaret finally entered the room. She addressed Luke very warmly. "I am pleased that Charles answered the plea I sent through Agatha by sending his top man. He must think I am right to be concerned."

Luke could not hold back his blunt question. "Did Peter persuade you to come here? In becoming a nun, you have virtually handed over the Earldom of Greenham to him."

"Do not be stupid, Colonel! We were both aware of that eventuality, but do not fret. I have not become a nun. I am simply a guest here, not a novice."

"Are you now in a position to return to England with me? His Majesty has offers you a place in Whitehall."

"And my Cardinal offers you a place at Versailles," countered De Bussy.

"I am very honored that the King of England and the Chief Minister of France seek to protect me. At the moment no one except you officers and Peter know where I am. If Peter had arrived safely in England, I would have been tempted to accept Charles's offer, but I fear his disappearance has something to do with me, and that frightful list, that started our problems in the first place. And that is why I want you here, Luke—to find Peter, not to take me home."

"Did he tell you which way he was returning to England?" asked Luke.

"Yes, as direct as possible. His uncle was furious that he had not presented himself on his estate in person."

"Ostend to the Thames estuary?"

"No, to the new English base at Dunkirk, and then direct to Dover."

"I can vouch for the fact that he entered Dunkirk the day after he left here. My men followed him," admitted De Bussy.

"Miles and I will head for Dunkirk immediately. Before I leave, can I ask your ladyship a simple, but basic question, why are you remaining here?"

"Colonel, in due course I will explain to the King, and ultimately to you. At the moment leaving here is a danger for me, and probably for several others. Time will solve all. Time will explain all."

The next evening Luke and Miles were having supper in the mess of the English garrison at Dunkirk. After showing the governor his letter of authority from the King, Luke was treated like royalty itself.

However, Luke and Miles did not feel comfortable among this group of soldiers. One of the King's first acts on arriving in England was to disband the pro-French Cromwellian troops manning the Dunkirk fortress, and replace them with Irish royalists who had spent the interregnum in the Spanish army. Perhaps another piece of evidence of a pro-Spanish element in the King's make up which was beginning to worry Luke.

Nevertheless, the presiding officer was both warm and friendly. "What brings an officer of the King's household to our outpost?"

Attempting to be humorous Luke replied, "The King has lost one of his peers, who was last seen entering this town. I must examine the port records to see if he ever left."

"That is not necessary. In the last month since we resigned from the Spanish army, and became the English garrison here, although we are all Irish, every subject of note of King Charles has been entertained within these walls. He would have stayed here. Who is he?"

"Peter, Baron Coleridge."

There was a gentle increase in talk around the long table and an officer jumped to feet, "Captain Patrick O'Brien, sir. We entertained him here. He is an old acquaintance of mine. He actually shared my room. He stayed two nights."

Luke replied, "Thank you Captain. I will talk to you after supper.

Luke and Miles later questioned O'Brien in his room.

"How do you know Lord Coleridge?"

"When I knew him, he was simply Peter Coleridge. During most of the King's exile I was in the Spanish army. Unlike most of the men here, I did not serve in the Netherlands. I was seconded to the Spanish embassy in Constantinople. Peter was Anglo-French consul in Syria. We clashed on many occasions as the interests of the countries we served, were in conflict. Despite this, on personal terms we got on well. It was a pleasant interlude, when he turned up here. Why is the King so interested in Peter? I am sure he doesn't send someone of your rank looking for every English landowner that goes missing."

"No, Peter had half completed a mission for the King involving one of His Majesty's special women."

"Typical! Peter had a roving eye, and was nearly sent home a couple of times, because his involvement with women was embarrassing to both the English and French ambassadors."

"I am surprised he survived. My brief sojourn in an Islamic country suggested Western involvement with the local women meant instant death to both parties," commented Luke, remembering his adventures in Bengali.

"It was not with the local women that Peter became involved, but with the wives and daughters of other European diplomats stationed in Constantinople, Cairo or Aleppo."

"Could this period of his life have had something to do with his disappearance?" asked Luke.

"Many of those diplomats who might hold a grudge against Peter have returned to their home countries or have been sent to places nearer to England. It is a possibility."

"I assumed his disappearance had more to do with his current half completed mission which involves women whose names were found on a list on the body of a murdered employee of the Portuguese embassy, and found by workers of the Venetian," confessed Luke. "Did he tell you anything about his recent past?"

"Yes, he told me he had been sent by his uncle and the King to transfer his uncle's daughter, his cousin, from French to English protection, but the woman refused to return to England and was now fortunately in a safe location. He was returning to England to take up his title and estates as the new Baron Coleridge."

"Why did he stay two nights? Was the weather poor and the packets cancelled?"

"He said he was waiting on a letter from another cousin to update him on the situation in England. He said it would determine whether he would take the packet to Dover, the Thames estuary or Harwich."

"That was probably information as to how urgently he was needed on his estate. Which one did he eventually board?"

"The Thames estuary—in reality London."

"You saw him board?"

"Yes, and watched the ship leave port and head across the Strait of Dover. It then took a northerly course which crosses the more dangerous southern edges of the North Sea before it enters the Thames estuary."

"The name of the boat he took?"

"One of the regular Dunkirk-London packets, The Maid of Richmond. It is currently in port and leaves for London at noon tomorrow."

"Then we will catch it home, and during the voyage question the captain and crew regarding Coleridge."

Having provided the captain with the date and particular voyage taken by Coleridge, Luke asked, "Did he disembark with the other passengers in London?"

"No, as soon as he was aboard, he informed me that when we entered the Thames estuary, he would like to disembark at the mouth of the Medway. This is not an uncommon destination for some passengers."

"Did you see what happened to him when he disembarked?"

"He immediately boarded a fast Thames wherry, on which I saw him welcomed by a man and woman. I was glad to be rid of him.

A high-ranking passenger complained that Coleridge was paying inappropriate attention to his wife, and another found his daughter in a compromising position with the lord. How he could create two such situations in such a short time amazed me."

Back in Whitehall, Luke mused on Peter's newly revealed womanizing behavior and commented to his unit, "He showed no signs of it when he with me. It does make you wonder whether he exerted his charms on Lady Margaret, which despite all denials may be influential in her refusal to come home."

"Given what you say French intelligence is sure there has been no marriage as special Papal exemption is required between first cousins," commented Miles.

"That may be the simple answer. Margaret is currently awaiting Papal approval. And who better to obtain it for a couple who have both served France than a Cardinal—Mazarin may be behind this after all," suggested Mark.

Luke turned to Matthew, "Anything about Cope that would explain his murder of Viscount Craven?"

"Everything, but it will not please you. I discovered from Abraham Lombroso that twenty years ago Cope lost his wife and daughter when the small boat they were in, was attacked by a Spanish privateer. Apparently, no attempt was made by the crew of the privateer to rescue the women and children who were drowning."

"Did Lombroso know the name of the ship?"

"Yes, La Ira de Dios."

"Not very helpful," commented Luke.

"But it is. Since England occupied Dunkirk the admiralty has its records regarding ships operating out of it. The privateer La Ira de Dios was owned and captained in the early forties on behalf of the Spanish king by Guy Craven. When he gave up privateering in the face of English naval dominance, he sold it, and bought a smaller vessel which he named *The Lady Agatha*. Sometime over the next twenty years Cope discovered that the owner of *The Lady Agatha* on which he travelled frequently, and a long-term customer of his firm, was previously the captain of the murderous *La Ira de Dios*."

"How would that have happened?" asked Miles.

"Easily, it is a wonder it did not happen sooner. Craven and the Turk had kept most of the same crew over the decades. Cope may have heard one of them discussing the days when they were jolly pirates aboard La Ira."

"I can see why you said I wouldn't be happy. Craven was murdered by a distraught man seeking revenge for the death of his wife and daughters. It had nothing to do with our general enquiries regarding Spanish intrusion, or the fate of the women on the list."

31

In the days before the King's coronation the resources of the Household troops, and the London and Westminster militias were stretched to breaking point. Although the new Parliament was not to meet for another week, most of its members had returned to London to participate in the coronation. The safety of his peers and ministers were of vital concern to the King. Luke's unit was to participate in this general protection of key people, while continuing their specific monitoring of potential Spanish disruption and anti-Portuguese activity.

Luke was therefore surprised that two days before the coronation one of the guards at Whitehall knocked on the door of his apartment. He informed Luke that they had arrested a tramp who was trying to enter the Palace. This destitute man claimed that he must urgently speak to Colonel Tremayne as it involved the safety of the King.

"Where is this man now?" asked Luke.

"In the guard house. Will we bring him to you?"

"No, I will come with you."

Luke immediately recognized the would-be informant as Austyn Bulstrode, a leader of a criminal gang known as the Chester Boys whom Luke had informally recruited to act for him if necessary.

Using his magisterial authority Luke released Bulstrode and commented,

"This must be important if you risked detention to get to see me. Let's find the nearest alehouse, and you can tell me what you have uncovered."

Settled in the Fallen Angel, Luke sipped his Irish whiskey, while Bulstrode downed in one attempt his first of many pints of local ale.

"What do you know?" Luke asked.

"With the King's coronation and the influx of celebrities into London our criminal opportunities have escalated. I made a deal with Jenny to limit our activities to Westminster and leave her men a free go within the city of London."

"The negotiations of criminal bosses is definitely not the concern of the King," remarked a smiling Luke.

"No, but in planning our activities several of our men have encountered the same problem—many of the lads that we were going to use as decoys and messengers have already something to do on coronation day. Someone had been around before us offering a ridiculous sum to young boys to throw lighted tapers into several coaches. The victims of these planned attacks may be the King's ministers or even the King himself. You may wish to question the boys and take steps to thwart their activities."

"This is valuable information. The authorities are stressed about such possible incidents and stretched in their ability to deal with them. To prevent them would be a great advantage. Where do I find these boys? I will interview them immediately."

"I have two of them safely confined in one of our houses on the edge of Westminster. Come armed—with several silver coins! They are a tough duo, who will milk you for every penny you have available."

"If they are such terrors, why have they remained in your safe house?"

"My men have recently created their own reign of terror. These boys know that if they step out of line with regard to me, it could be the last step they take. With me continuing to play that role, and you providing a glut of silver coins, the combination might elicit the maximum of information."

Half an hour later Luke confronted two boys. Austyn was short on introductions. "Colonel Tremayne, meet Jimmy and Bob!"

Luke was direct, "Tell me about coronation day which you will spend tossing lighted tapers into coaches."

"I'll tell you nothing. You will try and stop it, and we will lose half of the money promised," said Jimmy.

"If you do not complete the task, how much money you would lose? I will double it."

Bob answered, "We were paid sixpence, and will get another sixpence on coronation night."

Luke guessed Bob had inflated their payments, but went along with their claim, "If you answer my questions, I will give you each a shilling now."

"But then you will have your troops lie in wait and arrest us, or shoot us down when we attack the coaches," claimed the unconvinced Jimmy.

"If you take my shilling, I will not expect you to risk your life. To be blunt, I am less concerned with the damage you might cause to coaches and their inhabitants, than in capturing the man who employed you. Did he give you a name?"

"No," replied the more compliant Bob. "He referred to himself as the Captain. He was a foreigner."

"Had you seen him around the area before?"

"No," continued Bob, but my friend Ratty said he had seen him talking to one of those religious fanatics that rose in revolt a month or so ago, some of whom are still being hanged."

Luke was delighted. Maybe his earlier thought linking the agents associated with the Lombroso factory and the Fifth Monarchy rebels may have been true. He continued, "What exactly are you to do on coronation day?"

"We will collect tapers from a wooden box that will be on the grave of Alderman Ferdinando Fox in the north west corner of the parish cemetery of St. Swithins on Copper street. Details of the coat of arms of the coaches to be attacked will be attached to the tapers."

"How will he convey these details to you. You cannot read."

"I asked that, and he said there would be a simple drawing of the coat of arms the coach would have emblazoned on it, and in any case, he would be around to help up locate the right vehicles.

"Did he tell you who your victims were?"

"He said they were corrupt officials who had sold themselves to foreign powers. That did not concern us. What the superior classes do has nothing to do with us," said the largely disinterested Jimmy.

"So, at what time will you to collect the tapers?"

"When the bells tell us, it is eight in the morning," answered Bob. "But the captain did not say he would be there at that time?" probed Luke.

"No, he would be a fool to be seen in the area," continued Bob.

"However, you might be able to catch him earlier, even today," offered Jimmy. "My friend Ratty said he knows where the captain is living—just along from the church in Copper street."

Luke could not conceal a smile—the captain lived near or even in the edifice that had included the Lombroso factory and Fifth Monarchy rebels. It could not be a co-incidence.

Luke handed over a shilling each, and another sixpence for their friend Ratty, although he did not expect Ratty to receive it.

Austyn told the boys they could leave.

Luke thanked Austyn for his help and arranged to have the Chester Boys in the vicinity of the church on coronation morning to assist in this preventative operation. A large sum would be forthcoming from the Royal coffers for their assistance.

Luke went to Copper Street and climbed the stairs to the Fifth Monarchy inhabitants on the second floor who were women and young children.

He was appalled by the abject poverty he saw around him.

This might make his task a little easier.

He lied.

"Ladies, I come to repay a debt. Master Adamo from downstairs has asked me to pay to one of your number the money he owed. He unfortunately left for Flanders before he could do this. To which of you do I owe the money?"

Luke's request was met by complete silence. The godly would not communicate with the heathen. Luke even jingled a handful of coins that he made obvious to the stressed gathering.

It was to no avail.

Luke headed down the stairs to the Lombroso factory. He had almost reached the ground floor when he felt a tug on his coat.

A young child about nine or ten had obviously followed him downstairs and was tugging at his coat tails.

"Sir, I should have Master Adamo's money."

"That I cannot believe. You are too young to have helped Master Adamo."

"That is true sir. It was my brother Billie who did a lot of things for Master Lorenzo and his friend Dominic who preceded him."

"What sort of things did your brother and Dominic and Lorenzo do together?"

"Dominic helped us to rise against the ungodly and create the Kingdom of Christ."

"How did he help?"

"He told our leaders where they should attack, and with our money provided arms and weapons. Lorenzo subsequently came to see how we had fared."

"Why doesn't Billie claim what Lorenzo owed him?"

Tears welled up in the boy's eyes. "Billie was hanged last week."

Luke quickly changed the subject.

"With Dominic on the continent, did Lorenzo have any other local friends that Billie helped?"

"Sometimes, there was someone else from downstairs who came along with Lorenzo."

Luke could have jumped for joy.

"Would you recognize him?"

"Yes."

"Then come with me. He may still be in the factory."

Luke and the boy entered the Lombroso establishment. He explained to Abraham that he wished to speak to some of his employees, and the boy was with him to help identify the person.

They spent over half an hour wandering around the factory floor chatting casually to the employees. Eventually Luke asked, "Is he here?"

"No, sir, "was the deflating answer.

"Are you sure?"

"Yes, Lorenzo's friend was red haired."

Luke first impulse was to strike the boy. He overcame this gross inclination, gave the boy sixpence, and approached Abraham.

"Sir, do you have a worker with red hair, who is not here today?"

"Paul Chubb."

"Was he a particular friend of Lorenzo Adamo?"

"He was certainly a friend of Dominic's. I believe they drank together."

"Where will I find Chubb?"

Abraham gave Luke the address but warned him that Paul had been absent for a few days. He had not been well for a week or so previously.

Luke was delighted. Adamo and Dominic had an accomplice. Paul Chubb was absent from work because he was busy organizing an extensive attack on the coaches of English notables. This widespread attack was probably a cover for specific targets. To capture Chubb and interrogate him seemed the immediate priority.

He would pretend he had money from Adamo to pay the religious fanatics, but Adamo had not given Luke any of their names. Could Chubb tell him? Luke whistled to himself as he approached the Chubb residence. He knocked on the door of their small hovel. No one answered.

He tried the neighboring house.

Eventually a large obese man emerged with a butcher's knife and demanded menacingly, "What's up?"

"I have a message for Paul Chubb, but I cannot raise anybody next door. Could you pass it on to him?"

"Not likely, friend. If I did, he could do nothing about it. He died of smallpox two days ago. He is in the cemetery of St Nicholas. His family have already moved to his wife's mother in Hampshire."

Luke could have smashed everything in sight. A simple explanation and solution to the threatened coach disaster, which seemed obvious ten minutes earlier, was totally destroyed. The active agent could not be Paul Chubb.

O n the morning of 23 April 1661 Luke, Miles, Austyn and two of his men met in the nave of St. Swithins. A number of parishioners had already gathered for a service to celebrate the coronation. The streets were lined with pedestrians, and movement along the King's proposed route from the Tower to Whitehall and then to Westminster Abbey was almost at a standstill, even at this early hour. Impeding the pedestrians heading towards the Abbey were hundreds of horsemen, and dozens of elaborately ornamented coaches and carriages.

All the troops in the London area had been seconded to line the route to prevent any demonstration or attempts at disruption. Luke had informed the relevant authorities that young boys running along any coach may be about to throw a lighted taper through the window.

The previous evening, at the final briefing of the key officers involved in the coronation, the King had initially suggested that if Luke knew where the cache of tapers were, he should confiscate them all and put an end to this attempt at multiple arson.

Luke countered by arguing that if that was done 'the captain' would know his plot had been revealed, and certainly not appear. Luke strengthened his argument by suggesting that it would be a rather fruitless attack on the coaches in any case. Little harm would be done. Little boys throwing a single lighted taper may miss its target, the taper could be extinguished in the act of throwing, or easily picked up and thrown out of the coach by one of its occupants.

The need to catch 'the captain' far outweighed any potential damage to one or more of the coaches. The King eventually acquiesced when the Duke of Albemarle supported Luke's plan.

Luke went on to explain its details. When the boys collected their tapers, they would be followed. No attempt would be made to apprehend them, until they began to run alongside a coach. It was hoped that 'the captain' might emerge to confirm their target.

Luke's group left the church and spread themselves around the cemetery, already crowded by over imbibing citizens. The first few boys arrived, and they were followed by Austyn's men. Whatever happened Luke ordered that everybody reassemble in the nave of the church at 11 .30, just before the official procession began.

Luke recognized two of the next group of three boys to arrive. Luke indicated he would shadow them. Miles was surprised when Luke actually accosted the three before they left the cemetery. Then all of them disappeared behind a large bush.

Luke had recognized Jimmy and Bob and had quickly indicated they move behind the briar. "I'm not surprised you are double dipping. Have you seen 'the captain' this morning?"

"No, we may not see him at all," said Bob.

"Where and when will he deliver the remainder of your payment?"

"In the church before evening prayer tonight, but I don't expect him to turn up," added Jimmy.

'You have your tapers. Can I see the coat of arms of the coaches you are to attack?"

"Yes, but it is strange," continued Jimmy.

"What is?"

"The drawing for Bob and our friend Ratty here are the same as mine."

Luke looked at the paper attached to Bob's taper. He recognized the markings immediately. This was not a coat of arms of any aristocratic family—it was the official coach of the country's top official, the Lord Chancellor, who had been created the Earl of Clarendon only the previous day.

Luke thanked the boys and let them disappear unfollowed.

Miles was further concerned when he saw Luke head for the corner of the cemetery where the box of the tapers was located.

Luke quickly opened the box, did a brief survey of its contents and returned to where a confused Miles was waiting.

"Why did you let those boys go without following them, and then risk being seen by 'the captain' going to the box of tapers?"

"This is far more serious than we thought. The planned attack is not on a number of coaches. All of the attacks, at least a dozen in number are aimed at the same coach, that of the newly created Earl of Clarendon, the Lord Chancellor of England who will leave the Tower just ahead of the King, a little before noon."

"What are we going to do?" asked a surprised Miles.

"You inform Austyn what has happened and update the military commanders along the route to forget attacks on coaches, except that of the Lord Chancellor. I will ride immediately to the Tower to inform the new Earl and seek further instructions."

After a slow journey against the flow of traffic, Luke was ushered into the Tower, and found the Chancellor being dressed for the first time in the garb of an Earl of the realm.

He paled as Luke explained the reason for the visit.

"It will be a Spanish interest behind this outrage. They are probably aware that I have been asked by the King to formally begin negotiations tomorrow with Portugal for the hand of their Infanta. Unfortunately, he told some of our Spanish loving nobles, for what was for them, very bad news."

"Is the King genuine? He often changes his mind or pursues contradictory paths at the same time," asked a surprisingly blunt Luke.

"No, this is his final decision. I have seen two of his personal letters. One to the Earl of Bristol telling him to cease negotiations with Padua and return home immediately, and another to our ambassador in Madrid who is about to return to England to gently inform the Spanish government. I will tell the Spanish ambassador here tomorrow. What should I do regarding the planned attack? Forewarned is forearmed, and a few lighted tapers will do little harm. A couple of men on board to hurl the tapers out will be all I need."

"True, but I have a nagging concern this whole taper throwing exercise is to conceal the real nature of the attack. While the authorities concentrate on young boys throwing tapers, an enemy agent dressed as one of the thousands of loyal citizens will toss a grenade or two which for inhabitants in a coach could be fatal."

"What do you suggest?"

"Your coach will process in its rightful position according to protocol, but you will not be aboard. My men and I will be in the coach with windows curtained and with weapons primed to shoot any suspect who comes close to the coach and tosses anything other than a lighted taper at us. You will take part in the procession in an unmarked coach and get to Westminster Abbey in time. Your coach will also have armed troops on board in case something unexpected happens."

Luke next sent a message to Miles and to the Chester Boys to reorganize their plans. They should all hasten to the Tower. Miles would join Luke in the Lord Chancellor's coach, and the Chester boys would walk beside it ready to grab anybody who tossed anything offensive at it.

The authorities had badly miscalculated the congestion on the roads. From time-to-time movement stopped entirely while troops cleared the way for the official cavalcade.

Then it happened. The cavalcade stopped for longer than usual and bursts of gunfire erupted not far ahead of the Lord Chancellor's official coach. Luke peeked a look through the window and was seriously alarmed. The troops lining the road were all running in the direction of the gunfire, leaving the coaches in the procession without their protection.

Austyn came up to the window and whispered, "I have sent a man ahead to find out what has happened. Since the soldiers converged on the scene, the shooting appears to have stopped."

Luke and Miles primed their pistols in case an assassin took advantage of this delay to attack the coach.

Sometime later the soldiers returned to their positions and Austyn reported back, "Not our concern. A dispute over precedence by the ambassadors of two minor German states. One tried to push his coach in ahead of the other, and their retainers resorted to firearms to enforce or defend their positions. Our troops have disarmed both parties and removed them from the procession."

As they approached Whitehall the crowd beside and, on the road, became denser. A young boy seemed to be pushed against the almost stationary coach, and a lighted taper was lobbed through the window. It went out on hitting the floor of the coach. Luke smiled. The lobber was Bob.

Within minutes from the other side of the road another boy took advantage of a gap in the crowd and ran at full speed and hurled his well alight taper into the coach. This one did not go out, and the fabric of the coach burst into flame.

Miles extinguished it with a rug.

A few hundred yards on Luke froze.

As he looked out from the coach he exclaimed, "My God, a ghost!"

And with those words he fired at a person in the crowd who was about to throw something.

The shot hit the man, and his projectile went astray. Luke heard an explosion, and according to Miles several people in the following crowd were injured, if not killed.

The wounded man fell to the ground but was almost immediately back on his feet—and running.

Austyn and his men witnessed the incident and correctly assumed that the shot man was the attempted assassin and gave chase. Luke stopped the coach and followed Austyn. Miles was to continue on, pretending to be the Lord Chancellor. There may be another attack. Before Luke left, he shouted back an explanation, "The grenadier was Lorenzo Adamo the man who died in the Tower weeks ago."

The crowds were so thick Adamo had trouble escaping out of the sight of his pursuers, but equally they found it difficult to close the gap. Luke shouted to Austyn, "He is headed to the Lombroso factory or his fanatical friends, upstairs. Keep with him! I will take a short cut and use the deserted minor roads and try to get there before him."

Luke's assumption proved to be correct. As he waited in the doorway of the factory, he saw Adamo heading toward him.

Then without warning he fell to the road.

Luke saw Austyn and his men fast gaining on the inert body.

Luke reached the body at the same time as the Chester Boys.

"What happened?" asked Luke.

"He bled to death. He left a massive trail of blood, which was obvious once we left the heavily populated area," answered Austyn.

The corpse then surprisingly sat up, "I am not dead yet."

He drew his dagger which Luke kicked out of his hand as one of Austyn's men quickly tied Lorenzo's hands together.

"How did a dead man live to fight another day?" asked Luke almost cordially.

"Through the typical corruption of English officials. It took very little money to buy my freedom. Another prisoner died, and the officials recorded that it was me. The body was buried somewhere within the Tower, and I walked free with one of the guards, who was also bought for a pittance."

Luke was silent and then announced, "Then we can't let that happen again. Gentlemen, Adamo is so badly injured that Christian charity demands that he is put out of his misery."

Without further comment, Luke primed his pistol and shot Adamo behind the left ear. The body was rolled into a free-flowing drain that would eventually dump the corpse in the Thames. Rats were already gathering around the body in the drain.

But from a local doorway, a shadowy figure had witnessed the execution.

Celebrations for the coronation continued for two days. Luke drank twice as much as his comrades but vomited a lot less. His unit had an additional reason to celebrate. Sir Mark Cowper his deputy had been elevated to the peerage by Charles. He was now Mark, Baron Cowper.

This was only the first step in his rapid rise in status. Mark had already set out to visit William, Earl of Maldon to ask for the hand of his daughter Elizabeth in marriage.

Luke thought Maldon would not be entirely happy. A newly created baron was a hardly match for the daughter of the Earl. Mark later mentioned to Luke that was in fact the earl's initial reaction, almost immediately countered by the pragmatic view that as Baron Cowper was a close friend of the King, such a marriage could only be in the best interests of the house of Maldon.

Luke was now the most relaxed he had been since coming to London.

With the King's intention of marrying the Portuguese Infanta now general knowledge, any link between the names on the list, and the diplomatic conflict between Spain and Portugal involving the King's marriage was no longer relevant. The women were no longer pawns, if they had ever been, in this diplomatic battle. Spain had lost, and Portugal had emerged victorious.

Luke would withdraw troops from Castle Craven, and Lady Elizabeth Rhodes could return to her father, pending her marriage. There were still a few loose ends to follow up—to find Lord Coleridge, to bring Lady Margaret home—and the need to understand the significance, if any, of the dead man's list.

There were two immediate developments closer to home. Mark who was to take his place in the House of Lords within the week resigned from the unit. The King suggested that given the importance of women at his court and their overwhelming role in the intrigue and politics of that place, that Mark should be replaced by a woman.

A compromise was reached between the King and Luke. Finally, two women were to be associated with his unit, but not formally part of it—Lady Matilda Tremayne his wife, and Jane, Dowager Marchioness of Nith, his friend and former associate on an earlier mission. Both were already at Whitehall.

Matilda was living with her husband and children, and the Marchioness was in the process of transferring from being lady-in-waiting to the Queen Mother who was returning to Paris without her English ladies, to that of senior companion to the new Portuguese born Queen. Luke decided not to separate his two assistants—Matt and Miles would be his joint deputies.

 Mark's last mission for the unit was to go to Craven Castle and bring his future wife home to her father.

Three days later Luke was in his private apartment at Whitehall when there was a loud knock on the door. Luke opened it and was surprised to find Lady Elizabeth Rhodes.

"My lady, I thought Mark would have taken you to your father's by now. Let me congratulate you on your betrothal. What brings you here?"

"I seek your help urgently Luke. Mark has disappeared."

"How can that be?" asked a concerned Matilda.

"Mark and I arrived back from Craven Castle last night and stayed in his old apartment here. He was to be measured for his wedding habit this morning at nine and be back by ten. It is now twelve, and he has not returned."

"I wouldn't worry too much my lady. Tailors often take hundreds of unnecessary measurements, and then double or triple check them. He may simply be delayed," commented Luke.

"No, it was very important for Mark, as my future husband and as a new member of the House of Lords to back here by ten. We were due at father's town house at half past ten for him to introduce Mark to a number of fellow peers, both as my husband to be, and as one of their new members. You would know as you worked with him for a while that he is very ambitious. He would never have missed this opportunity."

"Who is his tailor?"

"Father recommended his own tailor and supplier of fabrics and clothes. You are very familiar with them, given the murder of Guy Craven. It is the Lombroso Brothers."

Luke felt uneasy, "They are just a few blocks away. I'll gather some of my men and go there immediately. You stay here with Matilda."

Within fifteen minutes Luke and Miles were at the Copper Street factory and were about to question Abraham whose clothing was a good advertisement for his trade. He wore the most exquisite emerald green silk doublet. He commented, "More trouble with the fanatics upstairs. I hope it is not the young lad to whom I have given a job?"

"No, sir. We have lost a peer of the realm. Lord Cowper had an appointment to see you at nine. He has not returned home, and we are concerned for his wellbeing."

"His lordship kept his appointment, but left here well before ten," Abraham replied, perhaps a little too quickly.

"Did he have an appointment elsewhere after he left here?" asked Miles.

"Yes, he joked that he must hurry as he had a meeting with his future father-in-law and must not be late. As I know the Earl of Maldon, an excellent customer, I agreed with him. Punctuality and status are the twin gods for that peer."

Luke thanked Abraham. "We will ask questions along the streets between here and Whitehall. Someone would have seen him."

Luke and Miles left the building.

Unfortunately, Copper Street was largely deserted. They had just turned out of that street, when a breathless lad caught up with them. It was boy from the Fifth Monarchy group that Luke had paid earlier for information.

He did waste words. "My new master lied. That nine o'clock customer never left our building."

"Where is he then?" "In the cellar!"

"By choice?" asked Miles.

"Why would anyone want to be locked in a cellar by choice?" asked the boy, somewhat surprised at what he thought an idiotic question.

"He was forced into the cellar by Master Lombroso?" asked an incredulous Luke. "That could not be possible, Abraham is a small man, Lord Cowper was strong, and more than a match for the little tailor."

"He was drugged, and carried there by a couple of men," answered the boy. Miles.

"How was he drugged? And how do you know all this?" asked a skeptical "Master Abraham always offers his customers a glass of mulled wine, while they are being fitted. It must have been drugged. As I went upstairs to check on my mother, I looked back down the stairwell and saw two men carrying a body to the cellar."

"And you did nothing about it!" commented Miles.

"A new worker does not raise such concerns with the all-powerful master. To be quite honest, I was not concerned. I assumed it was a fellow worker, who had turned up drunk and who was being locked in the cellar to sober up—not an unusual occurrence. It was only when you arrived concerning a missing client, that I had any doubts. As you were so kind to me and my family, I decided to follow you, and tell you what I just have."

"So, you risked your job on the off chance that the man you saw taken to the cellar was our missing peer?" asked a suspicious Miles.

"No, I have not risked my job. The master has sent me out to collect some thread from a spinner down this lane. You should hurry back and enter the cellar. Whoever they put there, is in great danger."

"How?"

"He could drown. When I was little boy my brother took me down there, when Master Lombroso and his workers were absent. Parts of it are dry, but if you go deeper into what is a man-made cave, it is under water. My brother told me that the water level rises and falls depending on the tides in the Thames. If the missing man was unconscious, he may have been thrown into an area that could be under water when the tide comes in."

The boy went on his way. Luke instructed Miles to hurry to Whitehall and return with a platoon of soldiers to search the Lombroso premises.

Luke ran back to the factory where he lied to Abraham. "Sir, we have an elderly witness who is confined to her chair, and her only activity is to look down on your entrance from the upper story of the house opposite. She says no one has left your premises this morning other than us, and a small boy. I have sent for a platoon of soldiers to search upstairs, but I notice there is a cellar. Can I look into it?"

"Why?"

"Those religious fanatics upstairs may have kidnapped Lord Cowper and locked him in the cellar," continued Luke.

"No, it is my cellar, and I keep it locked."

"That devious group may have created their own keys."

Abraham appeared anxious, but all of a sudden relaxed. "Come with me then, colonel."

"Do you have a taper or candle?" asked a cautious Luke.

Abraham called out to one of his men to bring a lighted candle to the cellar. He unlocked the cellar trapdoor and raised it. Luke took the lit candle and descended the stone stairs that led down into its depths.

He had just reached the bottom and turned to see if Abraham was following him when the trapdoor fell shut, and Luke heard the locks being re- engaged.

Luke was lucky. Despite the rush of air created by the shutting trapdoor, the candle remained alight.

He advanced further into the cave cellar, and saw a body lying face upwards in water. It was Mark. He had been lucky. If he had been thrown face downwards, he would probably have already drowned, or been asphyxiated.

The water level was clearly rising. Luke dragged Mark's body to the higher reaches of the cellar. Luke was happy. Mark was breathing normally. Luke wondered what Abraham hoped to achieve. He had been told that a platoon of soldiers were on their way. Unless the whole cellar filled with water, all Luke had to do was to wait for their arrival in relative safety.

The wait seemed unending.

Mark regained consciousness, and within a few minutes had fully regained his senses. His first comment was an attempt at humor. "I am glad you have joined me here. I was a second choice as victim. Ideally the target of Lombroso's obsession was you, so he would have been delighted in confining you here."

"But to no avail. Help is on its way. Did he explain his antagonism?"

"Vividly. Whatever drug was in the mulled wine, I lost the use of my limbs before I passed out. My death was to be a revenge killing for what he saw as your murder of Lorenzo Adamo."

"Why would the death of a distant business associate lead him to such an extreme reaction?"

"Lorenzo Adamo was his illegitimate son." Luke sighed.

Then both of them headed for the stairs.

There was a sudden rush of water, as if someone had suddenly opened a sluice gate and diverted water into the cellar. This was not a simple tidal increase.

Miles had better hurry.

They were now crouched on the third top step and the water was only a foot below their heads and rising fast.

"It looks as if locking us in here was not a futile gesture after all. The successful revenge of a bereaved father is imminent," commented Mark.

"Let's start making a noise. Someone out there might hear us. Maybe if both of us pushed against the door it might spring open," suggested Luke, somewhat belatedly.

34

The door did not budge. Luke thought of Matilda and the twins as he struggled to keep his head above water. Mark slipped below the water level, as Luke struggled to hold him up.

Then Luke heard a noise above them. The trapdoor opened. Luke did not even thank his new deputy but demanded. "Miles, have you arrested Abraham?"

"No, he has disappeared," replied Miles.

A bedraggled and dripping Luke called the Lombroso workforce together and asked, "Where is Mr. Abraham?"

An older man replied, "He is delivering an order to a newly created peer at Whitehall."

Mark gasped.

Luke did not hesitate, "Yes, it looks that having disposed of us he is moving to deal with our wives. Vengeance is indeed a powerful motive. Mark, take a horse from one of the men, and get to my private apartment as quickly as possible. Elizabeth is with Matilda."

Luke then asked the gathered workforce, "Why did the cellar suddenly fill with water?"

Two of the older employees appeared in serious discussion and one of them said, "An underground river passes close to here. It can be reached by entering the house two doors down. Master Abraham when he first came here discovered that water entered his cellar from two tributaries of that river. The first, closer to the Thames, simply reflected the movements in the tide of that river. There was one further upstream which carried water from inland. The master had this blocked off. I have never seen it, but there is probably a gate that can be lifted to allow the flow from that tributary into our cellars. I have heard that you can follow the river underground until it enters the Thames, somewhere near the House of Lords."

Miles expressed alarm. "If Abraham lifted the gate to drown you and Mark, he may be heading to the House of Lords to get rid of other peers. He may be headed for the Lords, rather than Whitehall and your wives."

"No, not necessarily. Parts of Whitehall can be reached by moving upstream beyond the sluice gate, and other parts by heading towards the Thames. I saw him head for the house two doors down where he can join the underground river and move either up or down," said the informant.

"Lead us to that house!" demanded an anxious Luke.

"Do you think he is trying to emulate Guy Fawkes and blow up the Lords? On second thoughts a tailor is not likely to have weapons and ammunition," Miles concluded.

"Don't be so sure. Dominic from the Lombroso firm supplied the Fifth Monarchy group upstairs with arms and ammunition. Abraham could have kept some for himself. Lorenzo did."

The arrival of a troop of horse and several musketeers traumatized the inhabitants of the house two doors from the corner, until it was explained that they were following a fugitive along the underground river.

"No fugitive has passed here today," the owner of house protested.

A disheartened Luke asked, "Are you sure nobody has entered the river course today?"

"I didn't say that. No fugitives, but Mr. Lombroso on his regular visit came an hour ago, and I have not seen him come back."

"Why does Lombroso enter the underground river course?" asked Luke.

"Pure water. He regularly heads upstream with a couple of buckets to obtain the purest of water for his dyers. The Thames is too polluted."

"Surely Lombroso sends an underling for such a task?"

"Yes, each day he sends one or more of his workers to collect more water, but at least once a month he comes himself to check on its quality and whether it will be necessary to obtain it further upstream than he does at present."

The houseowner continued, "By the way sir, there will not be room for horses in the stream, and given recent rain, if you head downstream to the Thames, you will be wading through water at least up to your knees and perhaps a lot higher."

Luke ordered most of the dragoons back to Whitehall. Two of them without their horses but armed with muskets remained. Luke ordered one of them to accompany Miles upstream to find the gate that Abraham had lifted, which led to the flooding of his cellar and then move back towards Whitehall. Luke and another soldier would head downstream to the Thames. Before entering the river course, Luke had sent his would-be companion back to the Lombroso factory to obtain a number of tapers, and a tinder box to light them.

Luke still sodden from his cellar experience took to the water without comment. Miles found his initial confrontation with the flowing river a very chilling experience.

The soldiers parted company. The water where Luke and his companion had entered the stream was about a foot deep.

What was unexpected was the large number of drains and tributaries than entered the stream as they came closer to the Thames. The pristine nature of the upper reaches of this underground watercourse had quickly been converted into a polluted soup of sewage and household waste that had been washed down the street drains. And the few parts that were not underwater, and provided an excuse for a bank, were covered with a heaving mass of large rats.

Luke could only hope that the rubbish accumulating in the stream provided sufficient food to satiate the appetite of these rodents. A few rats could be repelled but given the number they had passed any general attack would be unstoppable.

A further worry troubled Luke. He hoped that Abraham had headed for the Thames. If not, would Miles catch him before he emerged within Whitehall? Abraham's desire to murder Matilda and Elizabeth could be reconciled with his adventure in the underground stream, but he could have exited along one of several large drains and emerged anywhere between the City and Westminster. He hoped Mark had reached the Tremayne apartment within Whitehall and alerted the guards to the possibility of a murderous intrusion well before Abraham could reach the area.

To add to his concerns was the rising water level. In the first place he had noticed for some time that it was now up to his waist, rather than his knees, and secondly, the tide had not turned. Water was still flowing in from the Thames. How much deeper would the route ahead become? And would the inevitable flooding of some of pitiful riverbanks send the rats into the water in pursuit of human flesh?

Luke's anxiety increased further. He noticed that his taper had burnt down, and would soon be extinguished, and the spare that his companion carried had become very wet. Would it catch alight from Luke's dying flame? To be left in pitch darkness in a rapidly rising polluted stream harboring hundreds of potentially ravenous rats was a nightmare not worth contemplating.

Luke was in luck. The spare taper had been well soaked in a flammable liquid, no doubt from the dyers' repertoire, and burst into flame immediately. It continued to burn vigorously. At least one fear had been eliminated.

The water level ceased rising, but the smell of the polluted water was so horrendous as to become vomit-inducing. Luke now began to feel quite nauseous, and at the same time lightheaded.

The two soldiers reached a drain entering the stream that was larger than usual. "Let's escape possible drowning or poisoning by the sewage, and see where this drain leads us," suggested an unwell Luke.

They were fortunate. The drain was a continuation of an open surface ditch flowing with fresh rainwater. They emerged beyond Whitehall and on seeking entry to the Palace they were immediately confronted by armed guards, who refused to believe the smelly, water-soaked men before them were fellow soldiers.

They sent for their commander, the head of the King's personal security Lord Ashcroft—Luke's one time enemy, now friend.

On seeing Luke, he laughed, "Why are you celebrating the King's coronation in the sewer?"

Luke explained the situation. Ashcroft immediately put all the Whitehall detachments on alert that a would-be assassin may have entered the area.

"Luke hastened to his own apartment to find Mark with several troopers effectively guarding Elizabeth and Matilda."

"Then Lombroso must have continued on to the Thames."

"That would have done him no good. There is a massive iron grate that only the river authorities can open. They do it regularly to remove the rubbish that would block the exit in no time. If Lombroso got to the gate, he has to wait at least a week. It was only opened yesterday," explained Mark.

"He may realize that, and is making his way back, or at least trying out other drains to escape. I must go back down. Is there a drain almost at the exit gate? If I can use that I can start at the grate and work my way back upstream."

Luke re-entered the underground stream alone.

He had no plan. Abraham could have exited through the very drain he had just come down which would have brought him very close to the House of Lords. All he could hope for was that he could ascertain that Abraham was still not within the network of drains and tributaries of the stream.

He began to wonder whether this new enterprise was a fruitless exercise. On entering the complex near the Lombroso factory, he had caught no sight of a burning taper ahead of him, nor had he smelt any such fumes at any time. The lack of light might have forced Abraham out of the river complex much earlier than Luke had assumed. Luke had no element of surprise. His own burning taper would alert anybody else in the area, long before he became aware of them.

Three hours later Luke was back in his apartment. Mark and Elizabeth had left for her father's town house, and Miles had just arrived to report on his mission upstream.

They concluded that while their mission to rescue Mark had been a success, their failure to capture Abraham Lombroso was a dangerous failure. It had to be assumed that if he had escaped the underground network of streams and drains the potential murderer may still be determined to wreak his revenge on anyone associated with Luke and his unit.

Those located at Whitehall were well protected. Lady Elizabeth was no longer a concern for the unit, as she was now under the direct protection of her father and her husband-to-be. The King no longer felt personally responsible for her fate.

To find Abraham Lombroso was of immediate concern.

The major remaining issue for the King was for Luke to find Peter Coleridge—and ultimately to get Lady Margaret Dash home.

Whatever plans Luke had been put aside when he received a courier from the Venetian embassy requesting his presence as soon as possible. Within the hour he was in conversation with the ambassador.

"Tremayne, I have called you in regarding the behavior of Sir Henry Hunt. He was sacked some months ago and restored reluctantly by me under pressure from both the French and English governments—an action in which you played some part."

"Henry creating further problems?"

"Absent from his position during the very time he was needed most. With your King's coronation, I had to negotiate with the English government almost daily, without the man appointed for that very aspect of our diplomacy."

"I am not a diplomat, ambassador, so I do not see why you have called me in."

"Correct, Tremayne! I have already sent a letter to the Lord Chancellor informing him that Henry is no longer an official attached to our embassy. I am personally informing you because his behavior in the last month or so has been unusual, and his disappearance completely for the last ten days concerns me. Hunt has disappeared."

"Henry has disappeared?"

"He is not in his apartment, and we asked at the home of his friend Lady Martha. She was not at home, but her servant said they had not seen Henry for over a week."

"When was the last time you saw him?"

"About a fortnight ago. His erratic behavior stemmed from his trip down the Thames about that time."

"A trip down the Thames? Did he explain its purpose?"

"Vaguely, he informed us that he would be absent for the day as he had family business in the Medway."

"What happened after that trip?"

"He came into the embassy very irregularly, then his attendance stopped entirely ten days ago."

"Thank you, ambassador, I must find Henry. His disappearance could be related to several issues with which I am involved."

35

Luke reported this conversation to Matthew and Miles.

"The timing fits. Henry went down the Thames to pick up his cousin—our other missing gentleman, Peter Coleridge. Our first step is to question the London watermen."

"I will come with you. Under the previous regime most of those watermen were on the government payroll and were an excellent source of information. I know most of them personally," announced Matt.

Luke and Matt made their way to the banks of the Thames where the watermen waited for a fare. Matt made clear that they were after information about a trip to the Medway two weeks earlier, which included Sir Henry Hunt which some of them would know, and a woman. If any information was forthcoming, he would be in The White Swan at dusk the following night.

One of the watermen was direct, "Are you paying for information at the same price as you paid under the old Protector?"

His comrades laughed. One added, "The King hasn't enough money to pay for a trip across the river."

Luke intervened, "Here is a shilling for each of you to spread the message that we seek information on this particular trip. If the watermen involved come forward, they will receive double that."

Suddenly a coach sped down the ramp to unload a couple of clients obviously late for an appointment that required them to cross the Thames Matt was forced to jump clear. A couple of watermen ran to assist the latecomers to board their wherry.

One of the remaining watermen commented, "You were lucky sir with that coach. A day or so ago some poor soul emerged right in front of a similar speeding coach. He was cut to pieces by a combination of horse's hooves and carriage wheels. The lads say he surprisingly emerged from the drain a second before he was hit. His eyes had probably not adjusted to the sunlight."

Luke could not believe his fortune.

"Did this man have any distinguishing features?"

"There was not much left of him intact that would help identify him. For a man who by the smell of the scattered remains had just emerged from a sewer, there were the remnants of a most expensive silk doublet."

"What color were these remnants?" "A very bright emerald green."

Luke could have given the waterman a hug. He turned to Matt, "Abraham Lombroso is no longer a threat to anybody."

Luke and Matthew sat at a bench in The White Swan—the drinking house of the watermen. It was a rough establishment but clearly the presence of Matt who appeared to be known to many of the drinkers, protected Luke from verbal or indeed physical assault. A few drunken customers rolled up to Matt and offered him information on several murders, an arson and a major smuggling ring. He explained that these were matters for other authorities. He was only concerned with a particular trip down to the Medway and back.

Eventually two small but wiry men approached the soldiers.

"Master Hatch, we rowed Sir Henry and that woman down river on the day mentioned."

"You recognized Sir Henry?"

"Yes, the Venetian embassy regularly uses us when it has business on the river."

"Do you know the woman?"

The second man commented, "I don't know her name, but the lads call her the ugly duckling."

"That's a bit cruel," commented Luke.

"Not really. We used to carry her and her sister across the river on many occasions. The sister was the most beautiful woman I have ever seen. She was murdered months ago. We did not see the other sister again until this trip. I still don't know her name."

"We do," announced Luke.

"Your ugly duckling is Lady Martha Langley, a friend of Sir Henry."

"What did you do at the Medway?"

"Sir Henry and the lady collected a gentleman who came off a packet from Dunkirk. We were both staggered at the appearance of this gentleman—I thought it was a ghost of the late King."

Luke was delighted with the information. Henry and Martha had gone down river to collect Peter Coleridge. The two male passengers in that wherry had now disappeared. The events must be related.

Next day Luke found only servants at home in Henry's apartment. They had alerted the Venetian embassy to his unexpected absence. Luke asked whether Henry had indicated his future plans to them before he disappeared.

"Yes, sir. He was very clear. He and Lady Martha were to travel north to the estates of his cousin. That cousin, Lord Coleridge stayed here a couple of nights, and then moved in with Lady Martha. When the master did not return home, I went to Lady Martha's but was told that she was not at home, and that Lord Coleridge had also left."

"Doesn't that suggest all three have headed north?"

"No."

"Why not?

"You do not travel halfway across England without any possessions. All of the master's clothes and personal items are still here. We were not asked to pack anything, nor was the groom asked to ready his horse. That is why we expressed concern to the embassy. We thought he might have gone off suddenly on embassy business with the Venetians providing all the master's needs. They were as mystified as us."

Luke next visited the Langley town house. Luke was informed by a valet that her ladyship was absent, but that her personal maids might know something of her whereabouts.

Luke found that the maids were the two he had visited at the Langley estate, Leah and Rose, who had revealed considerable antagonism towards Martha, and had remained immensely loyal to her deceased sister.

Luke hoped that their antagonism had remained, and that they would be very free with their information. He was not disappointed.

Luke asked how life differed under the reign of the contrasting sisters. Leah replied, "Lady Dinah treated us almost as equals, but to Lady Martha we are hardly above the animals."

"Where is she?"

"We don't know where, but we do know with whom," said Rose.

The girls giggled.

"Sir Henry Hunt?" suggested Luke.

The two women now laughed loudly. "Perhaps that's the story she wants to be made known. For months her ladyship and Sir Henry allowed their long-term friendship to develop into a passionate love affair. He was always here, and very intent on planning their future, which I assumed was to be together. Her ladyship once confessed that she was not Sir Henry's first choice, but as he could not marry his cousin Margaret, she might be his ultimate choice."

"She has not run off with her lover?"

"Yes, but it is no longer Sir Henry," revealed Leah.

"This is very confusing. Who is her new lover?"

"Their mutual cousin, the Baron Coleridge," said Rose.

Luke was impressed with this vital piece of information. "Did this develop during his stay here?"

"Yes, Sir Henry and her ladyship went down the Thames to collect him. After a few days staying at Sir Henry's apartment the baron moved in here. That Lord Peter is a beautiful man. He swept her ladyship off her feet—literally," Leah confessed.

The girls giggled again.

"He was in her bed after just two days," added Rose.

"Did they leave here together?

"Yes," said both girls in unison.

"To travel to Lord Peter's estate?"

"Yes, we spent days packing for her. We are to stay here until summoned. She made asides about needing our help to prepare for her wedding, although she also commented that seeing how useless we were, she might send us back to the Langley estate," Leah announced.

"You have been very helpful. If Lord Peter and Lady Martha have travelled north. It still leaves the whereabouts of Sir Henry a mystery. When was he last here?"

"Not for a while. A week after Lord Peter moved in the staff were instructed not to admit Henry," continued Leah.

"Did he realize that Peter had replaced him in Martha's affections?"

"He would be an idiot if he didn't, but I do not know," admitted Rose.

"You have no idea where he could be?"

"No, for years, if he was not at the embassy or on embassy business, he would be here. At present it is clear he is at neither," concluded Leah

Given this information Luke returned to Henry's apartment to ask some further questions of the servants.

"Did Sir Henry express to you any indication that his long-term friendship with Lady Martha Langley had come to an end?"

"Not in as many words, but on one occasion after informing us he would be staying with her ladyship for a few days he returned within the hour and began throwing things around his bedchamber. He then took to heavy drinking for two days. This was never his approach to problems in the past, but he did not divulge any reasons for this unusual behavior to us mere servants."

Luke brought Miles and Matt up to date and indicated that their new priority was to find Henry. The men considered the possibilities that he had been murdered by a rival lover, his cousin Peter; was a victim of random foul play; or given his possible emotional state, had taken his own life.

Luke sent messages to the two local crime bosses—Jenny and Austyn asking if any bodies that might have been Sir Henry's had been found in the last ten days. Henry had worked in the area for over a decade and was well known among the locals.

An answer was received within two days and fitted none of the possibilities discussed. Then he was asked to visit Jenny Longlegs.

Luke arrived just in time for the midday meal and was showered with a variety of delicious sweet and savory nibbles and the best French wine available. Jenny revealed nothing until both were satiated and relaxed.

"Have you found Sir Henry for me?" Luke finally asked.

"Most likely, but I can't be sure, because I did not see the unfortunate creature myself."

"Tell me more!"

"According to one of my men there was a destitute man wandering around the area. He had originally been well dressed—a gentleman who had fallen on hard times. His clothes were dirty, and he had grown a beard that had never been trimmed. He appeared vaguely familiar to my man. When your query came through and I passed it on, this man came to see me and suggested the wandering homeless man could have been Henry."

"Why didn't your man ask him who he was?"

"He did but was told by the derelict that he could not remember. My man noticed he had a nasty wound to the back of his head and possibly other damage to his legs, as he walked in great pain. To me he was probably the victim of a vicious attack and left for dead. He survived but wandered around for days not knowing who or where he was."

"What happened to him?"

The watch finally came upon him and given the strange answers he must have given to their questions they transported him to St Mary Bethlehem near Bishop's Gate just outside the city walls."

"Bedlam—the hospital for the insane?"

"Yes. It may not be Henry, but it is worth following up."

Some hours later Luke left Jenny's house, but wisely decided to delay his visit to the mental asylum until the following morning.

36

Next morning Luke and Miles made their way through Bishop's Gate to St Mary's Hospital for the insane.

Luke entered it claiming to be a magistrate given the task of identifying a recent arrival. He and Miles were taken to a large ward with a dozen or more beds, occupied by men at various levels of madness. They were met by a doctor who by accent and name was a Scot.

Dr. Callum Thom took them to the bed of a man who had arrived at the behest of the local watch a few days earlier. The man looked confused and disoriented. He stared vacantly at an uneaten bowl of what at the best could be labelled gruel.

There was no mistake. It was Henry.

Luke asked the doctor, "What has your examination of this man revealed?"

"His clothing indicated he was a gentleman. His injuries revealed that he had either suffered a tremendous blow on the head, or more likely had fallen from a great height onto a hard surface. He also had a broken leg and shattered wrist."

"Could a fall from an upper story onto the cobbled street below account for both his head injury and the broken bones?"

"Certainly. He should be removed from here immediately. He is not mad. He has simply lost his memory due to the blow on the head."

"I will have him moved to his own apartment where his servants and family doctor can look after him. Can I question him?"

"Yes, but remember you are dealing with a mind that is in a sense only a few weeks old."

The questioning proved futile. Henry only remembered waking up amongst rubbish in a street whose location he could not recall and moving around London finding food amongst the garbage. An almshouse had given him sustenance and shelter for a few nights.

Luke's unit discussed the implications of what they had been told. Both Henry and Martha's apartments were multiple storeyed. He could have jumped or been pushed from the upper levels of either.

The Earl of Greenham, Henry's uncle insisted he be moved to the Earl's country estate where he would benefit from the care of dozens of servants, two physicians and the happy surroundings of his boyhood. This might provoke the return of his memory. The Earl once more asked Luke if he could make yet another attempt to persuade his daughter Margaret to return home.

Luke was non-committal but decided to probe possible developments within the Dash family.

"Has your other nephew approached you regarding his possible marriage?"

"What, Peter to marry! That is sudden."

"Yes, and it could explain Henry's condition."

"In what way?"

"The possible bride is Henry's long-term friend, Lady Martha Langley. It is possible that a distraught and rejected Henry jumped from an upper floor balcony," suggested Luke.

"What you suggest would be a physical mismatch. Peter is the most handsome of men, and Martha was considered ugly, compared to her beautiful sister, Dinah. No, he has not mentioned it to me. Is he still in London? Or has he finally gone north?"

"My information is that he has gone north. As a member of the Lords, I thought he would have to stay in London, especially over this coronation period," Luke commented.

"Not at all. Westminster could hardly hold half the peers of England. You attend the Lords at the invitation of the King or Lord

Chancellor. Peter as a recently elevated Levant merchant was obviously not invited. Any peer can claim their right to attend, but who would be foolish enough to irritate the King over such an issue, and arrive without an invitation? Peter has never been in a position to have political views, so I don't expect him to develop a taste for such activity now."

"Even when he becomes Earl of Greenham?"

"That's hardly likely."

"Is it? If you were run over and killed by a London coach tomorrow, Peter, as your nearest male heir succeeds to the title. Your daughter needs to marry before your death to prevent this happening."

"Yes, being a peer of the realm has its problems. Without any sons, I am in a personal quandary. The law is clear, so who would make the better inheritor to my titles and estates, my nephew Peter, or some as yet unknown husband of my daughter. Her marriage needs to be settled as soon as possible. That is why it is essential that you bring her home— and I marry her off before the year is out."

"So, your lordship is not necessarily committed to your successor being your daughter's husband?" asked a surprised Luke.

"It will depend on relative rank. My sister's son Peter is a baron. If Margaret's husband is an earl, I would be delighted. If he is a common gentleman, a baron would be preferable," replied the status driven aristocrat.

Luke could understand why Margaret was in no hurry to return to England—but he would seek instruction on this matter from the King. Surely with the King's decision to marry the Portuguese Infanta, the names on the notorious list were no longer relevant to the security of the state, and the personal protection of Elizabeth Rhodes, Margaret Dash and Agatha Craven should now fall on their families.

But the nagging question remained. Why were those names on that list in the first place?

Luke's report to the King at their first formal meeting since the coronation and its subsequent week of celebration, was simple.

"Sire, given your decision to marry the Portuguese Infanta and the return and impending marriage of Elizabeth Rhodes, the secure isolation of Agatha Craven and the absence of Margaret Dash in an obscure French run convent with continued surveillance by French agents, our need to monitor their safety as potential victims of foreign spies out to prevent your marriage, is no longer necessary. We can conclude that the list, whatever its origins and intent, proved to be no threat to the security of the state."

"Are you suggesting that all this should no longer be of concern to your unit?"

"Yes, I can see no further threat to Your Majesty in these matters that have consumed my unit for the last few months. Any unfinished aspects of our investigation can be handed over to the regular law enforcement authorities."

"In general, I accept your recommendations, as I intend to send you to Portugal. My cousin King Louis had been reminded of your joint service there on behalf of both France and England some years ago. Apparently you made a lasting favorable impression on the mother of my bride to-be, the Queen Regent."

"I thought your marriage negotiations were being well handled by your ministers."

"They are. Your mission would have nothing to do with that. Essentially the Portuguese are worried about Spanish infiltration, and the potential treachery of some Portuguese leaders. Part of my marriage negotiations involve me sending English troops there within two years. Would that be a reliable use of our now very limited military resources?"

"A repeat of my mission of three years ago?"

"Yes, but I am still concerned about two unresolved aspects of your long investigations—Margaret Dash's sojourn in a French convent, and a base feeling that Sir Henry Hunt's latest misadventure is somehow related to his recovery of the yet unexplained list."

"I still think the continued investigation of Sir Henry's misfortune, and the possible role of Baron Coleridge and Lady Martha Langley in it, should be pursued by the relevant magistrates."

The King chuckled. "You forget Tremayne that you are, in addition to leading my special intelligence unit, a relevant magistrate. Until my need to send you to Portugal becomes paramount, I want you to continue your investigation into both the Henry Hunt situation, and Margaret Dash's reluctance to return home. Why has the French government shown a continuing interest in her? The French government's interest might still impinge on our national security, and therefore this remains a subject for your unit's continued investigation. The cardinal is dead, so the French situation may rapidly change."

"Lady Margaret does not trust her father whom she has accused of having had a previous lover killed. The French may have retained in interest in her because for years she spied on her father, and his pro-Spanish allies on their behalf."

"No, I do not accept your explanation of French interest. Margaret is no longer of any use to them. You cannot be an effective agent locked up in a convent. There must be another overwhelming reason for their continued concern."

"So, what are my instructions?"

"Yesterday I received a note from the Lord Chancellor indicating that he had received a deputation from the Venetian embassy, not only to discuss Hunt's replacement but suggesting he had been murdered. Follow that up!"

"It must be new information. When I spoke to them last there was no suggestion of murder. Do they think it involves the interests of the Venetian Republic?"

"Find out! Then revisit Lady Margaret Dash and your friends within the French state, to find an answer. I asked my cousin Louis directly why they still concerned themselves with Margaret and have as yet received no reply. It makes me suspicious."

Later that day Luke met the Venetian ambassador's deputy.

"Your ambassador, in discussing the replacement of Sir Henry Hunt suggested that there was some evidence that he had been murdered. What is that evidence?"

"I am surprised that your many paid informers among the underclasses that inhabit this area have not alerted you to a piece of gossip one of our servants picked up at a local drinking house."

"Despite my connections with a lot of such people, London is a large city with thousands of drinking houses and my sources do not have access to hundreds of them. What did your man have to say?"

"He was leaving here late at night, and as he was passing Sir Henry's adjacent apartment, he heard what could have been a scuffle on the balcony above him, followed by a crash of railings and a body fell onto the cobbled street. He immediately recognized it as Sir Henry's. He ascertained that Henry was still alive and went to the nearest tavern to get assistance. When a group of men and a wise woman returned with our man to help, the body had gone. They searched for a while, but never found him."

"All this happened some time ago, why have we only just heard?"

"Our man only returned to the embassy yesterday. He had to leave for the country to be with his dying mother, so when you questioned us previously, we were ignorant of this incident."

"Could he be certain that there was a scuffle on the balcony?"

"No, it could have been an excessively drunk Henry stumbling around and swearing who crashed into a balcony that gave way. On the other hand, there is a possibility that he was pushed. Was it by someone who wishes to replace him here at the embassy? If so, it is in the interests of the Republic to clear the matter up."

"Well, it does add one key item of fact to my investigation. He fell or was pushed from his own apartment. I will go back there immediately."

Luke's visit to Henry's apartment solved nothing. His servants took Luke to the balcony, but suggested he not step onto it. It was much in need of repair, and one could fall through the rotting floor quite easily. Only half of the railing remained, and this provided no safety barrier at all.

One servant suggested that Henry in his right mind would never have gone onto the balcony as bits of the railing fell into the street below on a regular basis.

A drunken Henry could have plunged to the street below, but if he was pushed then the assailant took a great risk, and the weight of two people on the balcony should have sent the whole structure to the ground.

Both servants were unaware of any visitors at the time the accident occurred.

37

A week later Luke once more embarked for France overtly as a courier between the Royal cousins. Charles was asking Louis yet again, why his government maintained an interest in Margaret Dash?

In addition, Luke was asked to seek answers to the same question from the late cardinal's Household Guards which was the unit that still provided Margaret with protection.

Having delivered Charles's letter to the appropriate officer of King Louis he was told that an answer would be sent in due course, and that there was no need for him to stay on at Versailles.

Luke was astonished at the changes which had occurred at the French Court in a few months since his last visit. The Cardinal was dead, and King Louis was now his own chief minister. The Cardinal's Guard had been absorbed into the King's Household troops. It had become the second regiment of the King's musketeers.

Luke had no contacts within the reorganized political and military setup. He was forced to seek past contacts. Before embarking for the French-Spanish Netherlands border to visit Lady Margaret Dash, he went to see the late cardinal's long-time deputy.

The Count of Vargeau was now retired, but warmly greeted his English visitor.

"If you have been to Versailles you will have noticed some changes. Although the Cardinal has gone, our King will not greatly alter our foreign policy. He will continue to seek an English alliance against both Spain and the Dutch Republic, and in that context continue to support Portugal, which I gather by the announcement of your King's marriage, will become your major ally.

"Sir, I have not come to discuss foreign policy, but the singular case of the English aristocrat, Lady Margaret Dash. Why does the French state continue to provide protection for a one-time minor agent, who is no longer in a position to help you in any way? I had hoped to ask the officers which I know in the Cardinal's Guard, but they have been absorbed into the King's musketeers."

"Their internal organization has not been altered. The old guard maintains its structure and personnel. It is completely separate from the original King's musketeers who comprise the first regiment of household troops. The Cardinal's soldiers now comprise the second regiment. Officers in the field such as those seconded to watch Lady Margaret are still there."

"My King has raised this issue with King Louis, who so far has not responded. Why this veil of secrecy and continued protection?"

"My dear Tremayne I would like to help you, but I am under orders from the King himself not to reveal any details. Set your mind at rest, our interest is personal, and in no way political. It does not concern the security of France or England."

On arriving at the main gate of the convent, Luke was greeted by his old acquaintance, Captain Emile de Bussy. "I imagine our English colonel wishes to see Lady Margaret?"

"Yes, I hope she is still Lady Margaret, and not Sister Margaret," replied a relaxed Luke. I see you still wear the red uniform of the late Cardinal."

"For the time being the first regiment of Royal musketeers will wear their traditional blue, and we, now the second regiment retain our red, but I doubt if the difference will last long."

Luke was led by a nun along the corridors of the convent. It was in the opposite direction to what he remembered of his first visit. He quickly realized that Lady Margaret appeared to have a suite of rooms—not the single simple cell of the nuns.

On entering what amounted to her reception hall, he was overwhelmed by the obvious opulence of the fittings, and what appeared to be a large number of servants.

Margaret appeared, and her clothing reflected the affluence of her aristocratic origins, rather than the simple dress of her religious co-inhabitants.

"And what brings you back to my convent, colonel?"

"To bring you up to date with developments in England that may affect you, and to ask you a question which your French protectors refuse to answer."

"Which is?"

"Why does the French state continue to provide you with protection?"

"Whether I can answer that question depends on what you tell me."

"Your one-time companion Lady Elizabeth Rhodes has announced her betrothal to my former deputy who has been created a baron in the coronation honors, which seems to satisfy the Earl of Maldon regarding status."

"Agatha did not mention that in her last letter."

"I doubt if she knows. Elizabeth and her husband faced a new challenge of an enemy agent seeking revenge. Luckily this would-be assassin was killed by rampaging horses. Their situation and location had to be kept a secret until a few days ago."

"Those two managed to keep their feelings for each other hidden for such a long time."

"My second piece of relevant news is that the King's announcement that he will marry the Portuguese Infanta, removes any suggestion that the Portuguese-Spanish antagonism over this potential marriage may have involved the capture or killing of one or more of three aristocratic women on the list. It ceases to be an issue."

"My father must be devastated by the news."

"He is more devastated by what has happened to your cousin Henry."

"Which is?"

"He fell or was pushed from a great height and landed on his head, which resulted in a continuing loss of memory and several broken limbs. Your father is monitoring his recovery at your family home."

"The fact that you are still involved suggests that you suspect it was an attempted murder."

"Yes, a possibility. The Venetian embassy certainly thinks so."

"Do you have any suspects?"

"Yes, but no evidence at the moment."

"Who?"

"Your other cousin Peter Coleridge."

"What would be his motive?"

"A lover's triangle."

"Involving which woman?"

"Henry's long-term friend and person well known to you—Lady Martha Langley."

"The Ugly Duckling!"

"Yes."

"Well, I can see why that sex starved old maid would fall for the charming handsome Peter. Poor Henry, but I cannot see any reason why a man that would have dozens of beautiful women of the right status available to him would even encourage Martha. In addition to not being beautiful, she was always a bit weird."

"I have reservations about any explanation that involves issues of the heart. Apart from Peter, none of those involved appears to me to be of a romantic nature. I have a different explanation of the conflict between the cousins which involves you."

"In what way?"

"The succession to your father's titles and estates. There is one of three people who might fill that role—your husband or your two cousins depending on when you marry and when your father dies. I understand that both cousins played with the idea of marrying you, but that you rejected both."

"Father rejected Henry because of his lowly status, and I made clear to Peter that I was not interested, and that my then protector Cardinal Mazarin would ensure that the Pope would never grant an exemption to allow first cousins to marry in my case. But I just can't believe my rejection threw him into the arms of that dried up hag Martha."

Luke was silent for a time. "Good God! A horrendous possible explanation has just come to me. Maybe Henry had a long-term plan. He would prevent your marriage, murder his cousin Peter and then kill your father. He would then immediately become Earl of Greenham."

"Are you suggesting that his attempt to kill Peter backfired, and he nearly lost his own life?" asked Margaret.

"A possibility, but if I am right, I must return to England and send troops to guard your father."

"From whom? Henry has lost his memory."

"True, but what if Peter has taken over his cousin's plot? And where does Martha fit into this? Is she an innocent victim or a conniving accomplice?"

"Lady Margaret, given all this information and speculation, are you now in a position to explain to me the continued interest of the French state in your well- being?"

"I am sorry Luke, but I need to consult with others, but some of the issues just discussed indicate that I should treat your request with some urgency. I can give you some information that might fit your picture of a long- term Henry plot."

"Which is?"

"I have known since Henry took me to the Venetian embassy in Paris and then on to the chateau of the Count of Vargeau that the fateful list on which much of your activity revolved is a fake."

"What do you mean fake? uttered an astounded Luke.

"It never originated in the Portuguese embassy. Henry created it himself."

"Did he say why?" continued an amazed colonel.

"Yes, his courtship of Elizabeth and myself. He thought that if our fathers believed their daughters were under threat, and a man associated now with the King's attempt to uncover what was happening, offered to save them through marriage, his chances would be greatly improved. I must admit when he offered to take me to Paris, I was initially inclined to look favourably on his intentions."

"What you have just said fits more readily to my succession conspiracy than to an international marriage plot. To raise questions of international intrigue would allow him to better conceal the murder of yourself or your father as the work of foreign agents. It would make us think that it was in some way part of the Spanish, Portuguese and French conflict."

"But all the time we were alone together, Henry surprisingly made no advances towards me, or in any way attempted to seduce or harm me."

"No, this brings us back to the obvious, which I completely missed. The essential link, if any conspiracy exists is not your fate, but the possible murder of your father."

Back in England Luke consulted his unit. The issue was not straightforward. The protection of the Earl from outside attack was easily achieved, but what if Henry regained his memory, and had intended to murder his uncle. He was ideally placed. How could one now diplomatically separate nephew and uncle without revealing their suspicions?

Matthew came up with the answer.

"Inform the Earl, that we have grave fears for Henry's safety as evidence that his accident may have been an attempt to murder him emerged. The would-be murderer might strike again. It would be better if Henry was transferred to Whitehall, where not only would he have excellent medical treatment, but be well protected."

"An excellent idea Matt. He would be very well protected in one of our small cells, which would provide excellent confinement, should he regain his memory, and confess to his possible crimes," was Luke's response.

The King was unhappy with Luke's latest report. "Cousin Louis has not replied to my letter and Margaret won't answer a simple question, and still refuses to come home, and you have been told that the list which has consumed us for months was a hoax designed to advance the love life of a minor official whom you now want moved into Whitehall. The issue never involved national security, although deliberately framed in a way to exploit Spanish-Portuguese tensions, and my concern for the three women named. In addition, you suggest that I send Royal troops to protect the Earl of Greenham."

"Yes," was Luke's limp reply.

"I now agree that these matters should be handed over to the normal authorities. I am not in a position to send any of my decreasing number of troops to guard any of my nobles. The Lord Lieutenants in the relevant county can raise the new militias to provide any such protection when a threat can clearly be seen. You can end your role in these matters and prepare for Portugal with one last trip to the Greenham estate. Since I announced my intended bride, the group of strongly pro-Spanish peers have been very cross with me. I have taken steps to give them positions at court that increase their status, while dulling their influence. You will take my offer of a high position to the Earl of Greenham, whom you can warn of your suspicions that he may be the object of an attack, and that his own convalescing nephew ought to be watched in this regard."

38

Luke set out from Whitehall later that day carrying a highly ornate document appointing the Earl as a Gentleman of some newly created gathering of sinecure and status-hungry peers. Luke as a messenger from the King was immediately shown into the reception hall. Within minutes a man appeared, but it was not Greenham.

"Colonel Tremayne, I am Francis Redman, physician to the Earl. I regret to inform you that his grace is dying, and I have been asked by the household to inform his daughter. She may be able to come home before he passes away, but nobody here seems to know where she is."

"I do and will get a message to her as fast as possible."

"The household has also sent a message to Lord Peter Coleridge whom I understand is the heir to the title and estate."

"What is wrong with the Earl? He seemed well enough when I saw him in London last week."

"He is finding it increasingly difficult to breathe. It is clearly not the plague nor smallpox. Smallpox has been rife in London, and especially at court having taken off both the King's brother and sister. My best guess is that it is a virulent form of influenza."

"Can I speak to him?"

"Yes, but don't expect him to reply verbally."

Luke was taken into an opulent bedchamber, and found the Earl propped up by a lot of pillows and clearly finding it difficult to breathe.

Luke was direct and handed the Earl the King's appointment. The Earl read the details and nodded approvingly at Luke. Luke felt it was inappropriate to raise the question of a possible murderer lurking in the background, or to cast suspicion onto Henry. He simply informed the Earl that he would ensure that Margaret arrived home as soon as possible. The Earl smiled and Luke left the room with the physician.

Luke turned to the doctor and asked, "Do you also examine Henry Hunt?"

"Every second day."

"Is his memory recovering?"

"Little sign of it at the moment. Life began for him when he awoke amongst rubbish on the street beneath his London apartment. Someone from the embassy was here a few days ago. I thought that might jog his memory, but he did not respond to their presence."

"I suffered a similar problem in France about seven years ago. My memory only returned when I suffered another hard blow to the head, similar to the one I received which in the first place."

"You were lucky colonel. Such a positive result is uncommon, but not unknown. To deliver a similar blow to Henry would probably kill him."

"Can I see him?"

"No point, take my word for it."

"May I suggest something, which I hope you can justify on medical grounds—can Henry be placed in a locked room?"

"As if he was a madman?"

"Yes, you could suggest that with his memory loss, his sense of right and wrong may have been impaired, and for his own and other's safety he should be isolated and locked away."

"You have evidence that he could be a danger to someone?" "I do, but I cannot go into detail."

"Easily done. He is in an upstairs room, so he cannot escape through the window. I only need to have a lock installed on his bedroom door."

Luke thanked the doctor and left.

Luke informed the King of the Earl's imminent demise, and the need to bring Margaret home. The King used his fast couriers to get a message to her. The same couriers delivered messages to the French government explaining that their help would be appreciated in getting Margaret back to England before her father died.

A week later Luke was summoned by the King. "Good news Luke. I have just received a message from the French embassy. Lady Margaret Dash is there, and I want you to immediately escort her with a troop of my horse and the use of one of my coaches, to her father's bedside."

Luke carried out the King's orders but was surprised to find Margaret was accompanied by her French protector Captain Emile de Bussy.

The household came out in force to welcome home the long absent daughter. She, still accompanied by de Bussy, was immediately shown into the Earl's bedchamber. They were alone with him for over an hour.

The doctor spoke to Luke. "How much changes in a week or so. Lord Coleridge arrived three days ago, and immediately made it clear as heir, the changes he would implement the moment Randolph died. He is certainly about to apply the mercantile rules he learnt in London and the Levant to the running of the estate. He has already told the current steward that his services will no longer be required. Fortunately for the household his succession may be delayed for some time. The Earl had an intense fever for a few days and now that it has subsided, his breathing has improved. Nevertheless, the baron has called a meeting of all senior household staff, and relatives of the Earl who are here, for eleven this morning."

Luke attended and sat with the physician, while Peter with Lady Martha by his side outlined the changes that would be made immediately. It was clear that the staff would be more than halved, and the tenants would be required to pay much more for their leases.

Margaret sat in the front row of three or four rows of chairs. Most of the audience stood in the overcrowded room.

At the end of Peter's address, she rose and spoke quietly, "Cousin Peter, thank you for outlining the future of this estate, but there has been an unfortunate misunderstanding. My father will eventually be succeeded here, not by you, but by the man who sits beside me."

There was a divided reception to this unexpected news. Those who had been affected most by Peter's reform agenda cheered and clapped their hands, but the majority of the assembly were stunned by the revelation.

Margaret continued, "Captain Emile de Bussy is my husband, and I am carrying his child. I have here letters from the King of France and from the late Cardinal Mazarin certifying to my marriage over six months ago. By the laws of England on the death of my father, my husband succeeds to the title and estates. He is also heir to the Duchy of Bussy. One day I will be a duchess of France. Father has just been informed and has given our marriage his blessing."

Pandemonium broke out. Much of the household continued to applaud Margaret.

Peter and Martha were incandescent with rage.

Luke gathered his troopers and pushed through the crowd to protect Margaret and her husband from the crush of well-wishers. The general atmosphere was one of relief that Peter was not to succeed.

Luke was delighted. The reluctance of Margaret to come home and the continued protection offered to her by the French government was now explained. Luke recalled that the Duke of Bussy was a leading French courtier. Some had suggested that if the French King had taken a first minister to replace Mazarin, it would have been De Bussy. King Louis had obviously been aware of the situation for months but thought it unwise to inform his cousin.

Luke expressed his congratulations to the couple. Margaret apologized, "You can see why I could not tell you earlier. While my cousins and father planned and plotted outcomes to suit them, I remained confident in the ability of the French state to protect me. Emile and I do not need father's estates and titles. The Duchy of Bussy is one of the richest in France. At one stage we had decided to pass this inheritance to the next in line, but given Peter's performance today, that will not occur. When we return to France, Emile will join his father at the Court in Versailles. He refused to resign from the army earlier and become a courtier until his protection duties involving his wife came to an end."

"You could pass the Greenham title and estates back to the Crown who could reallocate at least the lands it possesses to some of those hundreds of returning Royalists who are landless," suggested Luke.

"We'll think about it," replied Margaret.

Luke took his leave and was about to exit the room when the physician ran past him with the words, "Stop!"

He approached Lady Margaret who uttered a scream and began crying.

The doctor adopted a formal tone, but had to shout to be heard, "His Grace Randolph, Earl of Greenham is dead, long live Emile, Earl of Greenham."

Emile led Margaret away, and the doctor approached Luke, "Come with me Colonel!"

Luke was led back to the Earl's bedchamber. He commented, "What happened? You told me an hour ago that Randolph was on the mend."

"He was."

"So, what happened?"

"I can't be sure, but I think he was smothered with one of these many pillows. Randolph was murdered."

"Who could have done it?"

"To me it's obvious. While most of the household were absent from their normal duties listening to Peter, one of his lackeys entered this chamber and smothered Randolph. I imagine this would have become known immediately after Peter's speech, and he would be by now, implementing his reformist regime. Margaret's announcement must have shattered him."

"And where have that couple gone? I must apprehend them."

Luke quickly ascertained that Peter and Martha had left the estate and were seen heading north, presumably to his own estate.

Luke was just about to mount his horse when the doctor reappeared.

"I am glad you have not left. We have a second death."

Luke was led to small, locked room. There on the bed was the body of Henry Hunt. "Cause?" he asked the doctor.

"From the coloration around the mouth, he was poisoned. And the source was obvious—a plate of half-eaten snacks which have been heavily laced with poison."

"If it was so heavily laced with toxic material why did Henry not notice the unusual taste?"

"The knock to the head may have affected his taste buds. He was recently claiming his food lacked salt, which the kitchen staff denied."

"When did the kitchen staff bring Henry the fatal food?"

"They didn't. I checked immediately I found it."

"He would not have accepted food from a stranger. If it was not the kitchen staff here, it must have been one of the guests which he knew and trusted, but why was he killed? Henry was out of the succession race."

"Maybe if he recovered his memory. He might have remembered who had had pushed him from the London balcony."

"A distinct possibility. When do you think this second murder occurred?" asked Luke.

"Probably around the same time as that of the Earl. Their rooms are close together."

"But Henry's room was locked?"

"When Peter claimed he was the imminent new Earl, the steward handed over many of the estate's keys to him, but I have to admit that the keys to Henry's room were often left in the lock. The aim was to keep Henry in, not to prevent him having visitors. The servant who found him dead claims the key was in the lock. So, anybody could have done the deed."

"Anything about the room that might help identify the killer?"

"No, but there was a basket with an unusual weave in which the killer may have brought the food. The servants claim they have not seen it before."

"This has been a very dramatic visit. The old Earl is murdered, his daughter's previously unknown husband succeeds, the expected heir leaves rapidly suspected of a double murder— and the mystery of her ladyship's long absence in France and her reluctance to return is explained. I must return immediately to Whitehall to inform the King."

39

The drama of the visit was not yet over. Luke was riding down the long drive of the Greenham estate when three riders galloped through the gate towards him. It was Peter, Martha and a servant.

Peter pulled up in front of Luke, "Colonel, we must talk, please return to the house with me!"

Luke, Peter and Martha were soon in a small alcove off one of the large reception halls.

Luke did not waste words, "Why have you come back?"

"I left in a rage. I was led to believe that I was the heir. I thought Margaret was my friend. Now I discover she was married all the time I was in France. I thought I was protecting her. I was furious and embarrassed following her announcement. I had made a fool of myself. I fled. We were overtaken by one of my servants, who was still here when the death of the Earl was announced. He told me of uncle's demise—in fact murder. Having calmed down, I would have returned simply to tender my condolences to Margaret, but the decision was also motivated by the thought that you and others might have interpreted my rapid departure as the action of a fleeing murderer."

"Absolutely correct. You are my prime suspects."

"When did uncle die?"

"Somewhere between his daughter's visit, and the time of his discovery which was about the same time as you left the manor."

256

"When did Margaret leave her father?"

"Ten to fifteen minutes before you began your address to the Greenham household."

"Thank God! I have an alibi for an hour or more before I began my address. Many members of my own party, and the Earl's household can vouch for my presence, well away from the Earl's bedchamber."

"You don't have to convince me. The investigation into the Earl's murder will be undertaken by the local authorities, but I am happy that you can clear yourself. But can you do the same regarding Henry?"

"What do you mean regarding Henry?"

"He was also murdered. Poisoned."

There was a gasp of surprise from Martha.

"Henry is dead?"

"Yes, my lady, and Peter and yourself are seen as suspects."

"Why would that be?" she asked.

"Rumor has it that Henry and yourself were long term lovers, but Peter on his return to England won your affections, and to remove a discarded lover, Peter pushed Henry off his balcony."

Martha was about to speak, but Peter put up his finger to silence her. "Colonel, if you are not the investigating magistrate into the two deaths here, we have no more to say, except to deny any involvement."

Luke was relaxed. He was happy that the deaths of Randolph and Henry would be followed up by the local authorities. He was delighted to spend weeks at home with Matilda and children before embarking for Portugal.

However, his departure south was delayed as negotiations between England and Portugal over the marriage treaty still had a few details to overcome. Luke's immediate departure would indicate to all that England intended to send troops to combat any Spanish intrusion, and the King did not want this aspect of the treaty publicized at this stage.

Charles wanted more concessions before he would officially agree to such military involvement.

Luke's domestic happiness was interrupted on an early summer's afternoon when one of Charles's personal valets knocked on the door and announced, "Colonel, the King wishes to see you immediately."

Charles took him into a small alcove. "Tremayne, I have just received a letter from Agatha, Viscountess Craven. She has startling revelations regarding the Randolph and Henry murders. She refuses to put the details in writing and will only speak to you. Get yourself to Castle Craven immediately!"

Two days later Luke arrived at the castle. He was welcomed by a female servant who said that her ladyship was in the nursery and he should follow her.

It now became clear. Agatha's indisposition on his last visit, her retirement into isolation for three weeks or more was because she had been pregnant.

Entering the nursery Luke was welcomed by a radiant Agatha who pointing to the crib announced, "Let me introduce Geoffrey, Earl of Hastings and Viscount Craven."

Luke expressed his congratulations and observed," So it was you who married the Earl just before his death."

"Yes, much to the disappointment of my friend Dinah Langley who was besotted by him."

"I never expected to see you again, my lady. The King has withdrawn my unit from what became known as the case of a dead man's list— three beautiful aristocratic women known to the King during his exile threatened by an unknown enemy. For him to send me here now, suggests your information must be vital."

"Perhaps, but it may also be nothing. Over the last few weeks, it has preyed on my mind. I have not been able to sleep. Even the Turk has claimed that I have not been my efficient self."

"Who does it concern?"

"My long term friend. Margaret now Countess of Greenham. We were together at the King' s court in exile, we were linked in that nasty list, and while she remained on the continent as you know, I was her only contact with England."

"What has got you so agitated about your friend?"

"The murder of her father and cousin."

"How is Countess Margaret involved?"

"It is possible that she and her husband killed them both."

"Not possible, I was there. More likely suspects were her cousin Peter and his unpopular partner, Martha Langley, although they did appear also to have an alibi."

"Not according to the local authorities. That is why I wrote to the King. I understand that the magistrates in Cumbria and Lancashire have sent Peter and Martha to the Tower of London. They may get a fair trial, but as you know so many prisoners there seem to die before their cases comes to court. I would not like to see innocent people killed."

"What has put into your mind that Margaret was guilty of patricide?"

"She pledged to do so with me as her witness. Her first French lover whom she was ready to marry was murdered. She was absolutely convinced that her father was responsible. She took an oath in my presence that her lover's death would be avenged. At the time she vowed that one of her best friends was also involved. He too would suffer for what she considered his betrayal. That could have been Henry Hunt."

"But surely her subsequent marriage to Emile de Bussy obliterated such thoughts of revenge from her mind?"

"Quite the opposite. Her murdered initial lover was Pierre de Bussy, Emile's older, and only brother. She would not have needed to use her charms to convince her new husband to assist her."

Luke was silent for some time.

He eventually spoke, "It is all circumstantial. What you say certainly raises another explanation of the two murders, but I need to clarify your own motives. I don't believe an abstract love of justice would force you to betray your long-time friend in this way. After all, if her father was responsible for the death of her lover, his death by the hands of the victim's brother is indeed a form of justice. The law and justice are not necessarily the same thing. For much of my life I have had to justify placing justice above the law."

"That may indeed be justice, but the legal or more likely illicit death of Peter in the Tower is not. I have a personal, if convoluted relationship with Peter Coleridge."

This was indeed another surprise announcement.

"Secret lovers?" muttered Luke in an unguarded response.

Agatha laughed, "Not likely. You could say that Peter and the Cravens were business associates. When father was a privateer on behalf of Spain he often ventured into the Mediterranean, where to attack Ottoman merchantmen was both in the political interests of Spain, and the profits of the privateer. Father was able to attack the most valuable or less defended ships because he had advice from a person within the Levant Company stationed in Constantinople. Father would meet Peter in Aleppo and receive a fairly accurate account of the richly laden, but poorly defended ships about to head west. However, given time delays, weather and general changes of circumstance the advice was incorrect more often than not, and father eventually found richer pickings in the Bay of Biscay and in the Channel."

"Was that the end of Peter's involvement?"

"No, he subsequently sent messages detailing western ships which had taken on expensive cargo in Ottoman territories which would eventually pass up the Bay and through the Channel. This was also grossly unreliable because the ship carrying the message from Peter to father was often slower than the merchant ship that was to be the target. Father viewed Peter as the son he never had, and now would be proud of me trying to save Peter's life."

"Even if I believe you concerning Peter's innocence regarding the murder of his uncle, he remains as the most likely attacker of Henry in his apartment, and his subsequent murder."

"Why do you continue to believe that?" asked Agatha.

Luke outlined his interpretation of the lovers' triangle and the need to remove an obviously distraught and depressed loser.

It was Agatha's turn to become silent.

"Luke, you have it all wrong. There may have been a menage trois developing but not in the way you describe. I have hesitated to tell you this because you will immediately jump to another scenario blaming Peter."

"In what way should I alter my picture?"

"Peter did not win over Martha's affection leading to the discarding of Henry. Peter has no interest in women. He is a homosexual. He obtained all that valuable commercial information for father by sleeping with the relevant Turkish male official. That is why I knew Margaret would be safe when Peter became her protector in France."

"But I have received reports of Peter's successful womanizing past," a surprised Luke replied.

"He did it to conceal his real inclinations."

"You suggest that Peter and Henry had a lover's tiff, and in a resultant scuffle on Henry's balcony he fell to the street below, making it manslaughter instead of murder?"

"For an investigator you are very narrow-minded Luke Tremayne," said Agatha. "Who would lose most from a Henry Peter affair—that nasty witch Martha Langley. She attached herself to Henry, solely in the hope of becoming the Countess of Greenham."

"That is far-fetched. To achieve the title for Henry, both the Earl and Peter had to die before Margaret married," exclaimed Luke.

"Exactly, and therefore it was one step easier to later attach herself to Peter. Then she only had to remove the Earl before Margaret married. Henry's survival was a constant threat to her relations with Peter. If their homosexual relationship intensified, Peter would discard her."

"So, you have modified your earlier view that Emile and Margaret were the murderers. It may have been Martha?"

"Only so far as Henry's death is concerned. Martha may have pushed Henry off his balcony and brought him that plate of poisoned food at Greenham."

"With that I agree."

"I don't think you are greatly concerned if I were proved right concerning Margaret and Emile's role in the death of her father. You would probably not take any action."

"Possibly, I see a major difference between a daughter and husband seeking revenge against a man who had the daughter's lover and husband's brother killed, as opposed to a claimant to title and estates removing rivals to the succession."

Luke would not articulate even to himself the negative effect that Agatha's revelation that Peter was a quean had on his views. It certainly increased his bias against Peter Coleridge and Martha Langley. They deserved their fate.

40

Several days later Luke arrived at his pre-breakfast meeting with the King expecting an update on his planned Portuguese trip. The King began the meeting, "After your recent meeting with Agatha I had expected to receive an urgent plea from you to become re-involved in the murders at Greenham. Were you not intrigued by what she had to say?"

"To accuse a foreign noble who also happens to be the son of one of the French king's favorite courtiers, of murder is a matter for Your Majesty to deal with. I shall gather further evidence on this matter, if you desire it."

"I have already acted on the matter. Randolph's murder is officially a closed case. After discussions with Emile and Margaret who deny any involvement in this Louis and I decided to impose a diplomatic solution. As suspects in a horrendous case of patricide, it was deemed in their own interests that they be exiled from England, and that their estates revert to the Crown. I have already designated Greenham to be part of my bride price. The Earl of Greenham's estates will become the property of my future wife, Queen Catherine and the title reserved for any male child we may have."

Luke smiled to himself. Charles would not have acted in this way unless evidence of the couple's guilt had not been stronger than Luke was aware of. Maybe the couple had confessed, and the two monarchs saw it as an act of rough justice rather than a vengeance murder, which was his own inclination.

"Will you now order the release of Peter and Martha from the Tower?" asked Luke.

"The case of Randolph's demise is closed, but not that of Henry's. The local magistrates have provided some evidence to suggest that they were guilty of that murder."

"Agatha's information has led me to wonder whether only one of that couple were guilty. I assumed it was Peter, but the murderer of Henry may have been Lady Martha. I would like to question her once more."

The King reluctantly agreed.

Luke decided to create a false sense of security for Martha. His lies and false emphases flowed quickly from his mouth, but Martha remained suspicious and cautious.

"Why are you here colonel? To gloat on our fall from grace?"

"Not at all your ladyship. I do not believe an innocent should die because of the actions of their partner. You seem to have been very badly treated by both Henry and Peter. Even if you participated in some of their dastardly behavior, I am sure that you would have been coerced or tricked into it into it."

"Such as?"

"That stupid list that wasted time and resources and caused unnecessary angst to so many people. We now know that Henry compiled it himself to advance his marriage prospects and his status."

Martha sensed an opportunity. She owed neither Peter nor Henry anything. If she helped the colonel, she could possibly leave the Tower.

"True, I was fooled at the beginning, but Henry told me his creation of that list which was essentially to put himself in a better position to successfully court Elizabeth Rhodes, had improved his status, and his contacts with people close to the King such as yourself."

"Why did he include his cousin Margaret and Agatha Craven as well. Were they a random choice, or was there a specific motive?"

"I think the list had a second purpose. It was also to enhance his standing within the Venetian embassy. He chose the other two women because they had four things in common with Elizabeth. They were wealthy sole heiresses, they were Roman Catholic, their fathers were the most powerful aristocrats who supported the Spaniards against attempts of the French and Portuguese to influence events, and at one time they had been close to the King. He hoped that this would cause sufficient a stir within the government to be obsessed by what the list meant to national security. And that is precisely what happened. You, colonel were immediately put on the case. As a result of his closeness to your investigation, Henry could give the Venetian ambassador information they would not otherwise have which was very useful in the Republic positioning itself in regard to the Portuguese Spanish conflict."

"Did Peter kill his cousin?" Luke suddenly asked.

Martha would co-operate with Luke, but she would proceed carefully. "I do not know. I was not with Peter before his meeting with the household. I joined him just before the meeting began."

"Did he push Henry from his balcony?"

"Yes, but it was in self-defense," she openly admitted.

"Tell me more!"

"After Henry failed to impress the Earl of Maldon for the hand of Elizabeth, and was rejected by his cousin Margaret, he changed. He became obsessed with getting his revenge on people who he believed had humiliated him. He would have the ultimate triumph. He would show them. He would emerge eventually as the next Earl of Greenham."

"By murdering his uncle and his cousin Peter, before Margaret married?"

"He never said as much. He simply invited Peter to stay with him when he returned from France. Henry and I went to the Medway to collect him from the packet."

"Did Henry plan to kill his cousin during that stay?"

"I knew nothing of any such a plan, but as matters turned out that might have been his intention, but the unexpected occurred. I am not a beautiful woman and have not been shown much interest by men.

Peter and I fell in love. He left Henry's apartment, and came to stay with me. Henry was furious. He threatened me. I was to return to him and tell Peter to leave London immediately. I could not understand Henry's reaction. We were close friends, but never lovers. Peter went to his apartment to tell him to cease his threats. He informed Henry we were leaving together for the north the following day, and that he intended to marry me."

"And did he marry you?" probed Luke.

"No, the banns were issued in the local church, but we had to head south to Greenham before the marriage service. It was rescheduled on our return, but that service had to be curtailed as we were arrested before the due date and brought to London."

Luke almost felt sorry for the equivalent of a twice jilted bride. "What happened when Peter went to warn Henry off?"

"Henry attacked him. The ensuing struggle spilt out onto the balcony where the railing gave way suddenly and Henry fell to the street below. Peter's first thought was to rescue Henry but was delayed leaving the house because he did not want to alert the servants that he had been there. He hid in an alcove for some minutes. By the time he reached the street Henry was gone."

"After that you convinced Peter to adopt Henry's plan. It would be much easier now. Kill the Earl before Margaret married, and you would become Countess of Greenham."

"Not true! I never discussed Henry's plan with Peter, other than confess that I thought Henry was out to kill him, and given the unfortunate accident that had just occurred, it might be wise to deny having visited Henry."

"It has been suggested that when you knew that Henry had survived the fall, you killed him in case he revealed that Peter had pushed him over the balcony."

"Not at all, Peter was quite happy that the truth should come out. No law authority, not even secret agencies of state such as your own, could prove one way or another whether the fall was an accident, suicide or murder."

"Thank you, Lady Martha for your frank discussion. It is quite possible that you and your husband will be freed by order of the King. As you suggest the evidence against you may not be strong enough to convict, and without wanting to humiliate you, your alleged crimes are not sufficient to call on extra-legal means. I am not going to shoot you in the back of head."

Luke next visited the cell of Peter Coleridge.

"My lord, I have just been talking to Lady Martha. I told her that the evidence against you for the murder of the Earl is non-existent, and that for the murder of Henry somewhat flimsy. The worse that you could be convicted of is the attempted murder of Henry, when you threw him from his balcony."

"I am even innocent of that—it was an accident."

"So, I have been told, but I do not believe it."

"It was an accident."

"That I believe, but not that you were present when it occurred. An old acquaintance of yours sent a message to the King, suggesting that you had nothing to do with Earl's murder. Someone else had a much stronger motive. It was not you that pushed Henry over the balcony, it was Martha. Then she dealt with the unsuspecting Henry at Greenham by providing him with what she knew were his favorite nibbles, laced with poison."

"And why would she do all this?"

"You were the first man to have shown a romantic interest in this aging spinster. Then she discovers you prefer men to women, and that Henry is her rival for your affections. In a cold fury, she visits him and pushes him through the decayed railing."

"You may speculate, but I have nothing further to add. Thank my old acquaintance whoever he or she is for their help, and I look forward to our immediate release."

"The matter will not be pursued. Will you marry Martha when you are freed?"

"Yes, but as you imply it will not be a love match. She has talked to her parents. Neither of us enjoy the north so when we marry Martha and I will move to the Caribbean and manage her father's plantation. Her parents will return to England and look after their own, and my estates. On her father's death, we will have considerable property both in England and overseas."

"Did Martha push Henry through the railings of his apartment?"

"No comment!"

Finally, Luke closed the case that began as an inquiry into a list of three women, a list that may have had security implications for a monarchy in the process of establishing itself. The list was a fake aimed at advancing the status and marriage prospects of a low-ranking diplomat. Most subsequent deaths have been explained but the most significant murderers had escaped the law.

Luke's conscience was not troubled by Margaret and Emile's escape due to a diplomatic agreement between the monarchs of France and England. In a strange way it began the improvement in the strained relationship between the two countries and their leaders.

Peter and Martha would escape simply because of the lack of conclusive evidence. Nevertheless, the King was in no hurry to release them.

This was fortuitous as he received a piece of staggering news that freed one couple from all suspicion, and finally helped convict another suspect.

The new steward appointed by the King to prepare the Greenham estate for Queen Catherine picked up on gossip amongst the servants that the investigating magistrates had missed. A servant who on the day of the murders had been dismissed, and not subsequently interviewed by the authorities, was returned to his position under the new regime.

He claimed that he had seen a bandaged man limp into the bedchamber of the late Earl, just after Lady Margaret and her husband had left. Someone had failed to lock the door of Henry's room either by accident or as the result of bribery.

It was Henry who had smothered his uncle. Emile and Margaret were innocent of the death of Randolph.

The same servant had seen a gentlewoman whom he identified as his potential mistress Lady Martha enter Henry's room with a basket, a basket that he recognized as of Cumbrian weave.

The King decided that Martha would not be brought to trial, nor would she be eliminated by members of his special unit. She would stay in the Tower of London indefinitely at his pleasure probably for life.

Martha however was fortified during these long years of imprisonment by the thought that in one sense she had outwitted the authorities. She had poisoned Henry but she rather than Henry was responsible for the death of Randolph. She had visited Henry and convinced the confused man that an opportunity to murder his uncle had arisen. He must act immediately. She led him down the corridor to his uncle's bedchamber. After he had smothered Randolph Henry returned to his room where Martha presented him with a plate of nibbles and then left, locking the door after her.